I0691487

Airship 27 Productions

Published by Airship 27 Productions
www.airship27.com
www.airship27hangar.com

Interior and cover illustrations © 2024 Ron Hill

Editor: Ron Fortier
Associate Editor:
Marketing and Promotions Manager: Michael Vance
Production Designer: Rob Davis

ISBN: 978-1-953589-70-5

Printed in the United States of America

10 9 8 7 6 5 4 3 2 1

I, Barbarian!

Heroic Fantasy and Sword & Sorcery Tales
Inspired by Robert E. Howard
By
Gary Lovisi

CONTENTS

INTRODUCTION: HOWARD, CONAN & ME!.............................5

THE GEM FROM THE STARS..9

THE BLACK HAND OF SET...50

THE SNOW MAID...83

THE LION OF THE NORTH..95

THE MUMMY OF QUELANG..127

THE LAST CITY...134

TOWER AT THE EDGE OF THE WORLD..............................146

THE JUSTICE OF RED VENUS..154

THE OASIS..176

THE TREASURE OF SHEOR KHOT......................................185

THE INTERVIEW WITH CROM...197

INTRODUCTION –
HOWARD, CONAN & ME!

There once was an age of men before the dawn of pre-history, when magic ruled and heroic warriors fought with blood-drenched swords in vicious battles for treasure, power and honor. It was a time undreamed of, faraway in lost eons of time, where lived the most heroic men and women who had ever trod the earth under their momentous bold and brave hearts. In *I, Barbarian*, I try to recreate those adventures.

One such hero was Conan The Barbarian, created by Robert E. Howard. These incredible stories touched my heart and soul as a young man. They sang their songs boldly and honestly. Those stories, and others like them, by Howard, and other writers, made up my youth and are imbedded in my consciousness today—even so many decades later.

The stories that make up this book were written early on in my writing career, in unabashed imitation and homage to the Heroic Fantasy and Sword & Sorcery works of Robert E. Howard, and other pulp writers, mostly from the pages of *Weird Tales*. Howard was the founder of this sub-genre of Sword & Sorcery and Heroic Fantasy fiction, and he wrote exceptional stories with exceptional heroes. There were also other authors who influenced the stories in this book. They include masters of the genre such as Clark Ashton Smith, Jack Vance, Henry Kuttner and C.L. Moore, with a sprinkling of H.P. Lovecraft— but mostly Robert E. Howard—and especially his incredible Conan stories.

Conan was my introduction to, and therefore my ideal of, what a barbarian was. The barbarian stood against the rot and corruption of civilization. Conan had always been a barbarian and he was proud of it. That was the heritage, tribe, clan and family. The cold grim gods of the northern lands were an unfeeling lot. However, 'The People', as they called themselves, were sure they were the chosen ones of the grim grey gods of the northlands. To be a victorious barbarian warrior was the highest calling one could ever attain in the eyes of these moody gods, and my own barbarian hero, Zarum of the harsh Calgar Wastes, was one of the most victorious of them all—I hope in the Conan tradition. Zarum always bested his enemy, he championed his own causes, as well as lost causes, and his deeds were legendary. He proudly proclaimed himself, *I, Barbarian!* These are his, and others, heroic tales.

The first story in this collection is "The Gem From The Stars". It was written in 1974, almost 50 years ago, when I was just 22 years old. I wrote it with my brother, Kenneth, who was then just 19 years old. We were rabid Howard and Conan fans at the time, and gorged ourselves on the original Conan stories, back then published in paperback by Lancer Books with those amazing Frank Frazetta covers. So it was just natural that we decided to write this one together. It was great fun. This story was originally written as a Conan story—as were all four Zarum stories in this volume—but I changed the hero's name to Zarum. So Zarum was meant to be Conan in everything but name. Of course, he is no Conan, and I am no Howard, but I tried my best to make these stories as close to the original as possible.

That first story was originally published in my early ditto fanzine *The Galaxy Times* #1 and 2 in two parts, in 1976. (Yes, a ditto machine? Any of you remember them? Way back in the day, a ditto machine was an inexpensive way to print multiple copies, pre-Xerox, usually with that sweet smelling purple ink. Some of you might recall ditto machines used by teachers for school work a long time ago.) Back then, in the old days, I had no money for a printer, but I did have access to an old, ditto machine, so I used that to print my first fanzine. I even sent the story to Conan editor and fantasy author legend, L. Sprague de Camp some years later in 1982, but he was not accepting stories by unknown tyros. So it languished in my files for over 40 years—since I could not use the Conan name, if it was ever published. However, I never forgot that story, or my other three Conan/Zarum stories—nor lost my love for the sword & sorcery fiction of Howard and his Conan tales.

"The Black Hand of Set" and "The Lion of The North" were originally Conan stories, where I again changed the name of the hero to Zarum. I think they fit well with the flavor of Howard's Conan tales—certainly not as well done as the master—but I hope they offer you some enjoyment. I certainly enjoyed writing them. They appear here for the first-time ever. The Zarum story, "The Snow Maid" was heavily influenced by the Conan story, "The Frost Giant's Daughter"—at least in mood and feeling—though it is a different kind of story. "The Justice of Red Venus" stars my female S&S hero, Red Venus—obviously a rank imitation of Howard's swordswoman, Red Sonja—a spunky gal and very dangerous with a weapon in her hand and revenge in her heart. In "The Treasure of Sheor Khot" I offer my version of one of Howard's Asian pulp adventure tales set in long-ago Afghanistan. The last story here, "An Interview with Crom" is where I actually put Howard himself into a story. Some of the other tales here show the influences of Clark Ashton Smith, Henry Kuttner, C.L. Moore and Jack Vance to various degrees—with an overall shadow and mood of H.P. Lovecraft in the background. How successful I have been in re-creating the action and flavor of these writers and their classic work, I leave to you.

Some of the stories that make up this book were originally published in small fanzines with print runs of just a hundred copies or less in the 1980s and 1990s that are scarce today—and never reprinted. They have all been edited, expanded and re-written for this special edition. Some of the stories in this book have never appeared in print before, being original to this volume.

My roots in Sword & Sorcery are also long and deep. They go back to 1984, with the first book published under my Gryphon Books imprint, *Elak of Atlantis* by Henry Kuttner. Kuttner was a classic pulp author, whose Elak tales were also an unabashed homage to his friend, Howard, and his Conan stories. That book was a collection of all four classic Elak pulp stories from the 1930s published for the first time ever in book form. *Gargoyle Nights* (Borgo Press, Wildside Double #16, TPB, 2011) is a collection of inter-connected heroic fantasy/horror stories by myself, heavily influenced by Clark Ashton Smith, H.P. Lovecraft and Jack Vance. So my roots run deep in this sub-genre as a writer and a publisher—but it all began as a fan and reader.

The stories in this book are not contemporary tales—or what is sometimes termed 'grimdark' in modern fantasy—in fact they are what could be looked at as time-capsules, originally written back in the 1970s and 1980s. They are all based on the classic pulp fiction that appeared in *Weird Tales* magazine from the Golden Era of pulp fiction in the 1930s. They were meant to have that flavor and feel.

Here we have pulse-pounding tales burning with the traditions of fire and steel, wizards and magic, fantasy and horror. These are some of my earliest efforts at fiction, and hence they do show some of the faults of a young and new writer—but they also burn with the passion and enthusiasm of a writer who loved what he was writing. In a sense, each one of these stories is a love letter to my writing gods of the classic 1930s *Weird Tales*—Clark Ashton Smith, Henry Kuttner, C.L. Moore, H.P. Lovecraft and especially Robert E. Howard. I hope you enjoy the stories in *I, Barbarian*, as much as I enjoyed writing them.

Gary Lovisi
Brooklyn, New York
March 1, 2022

ACKNOWLEDGEMENTS:

Introduction: "Howard, Conan and Me!" is original to this edition, copyright ©2022 by Gary Lovisi.

"The Gem From The Stars" was originally published in *The Galaxy Times* #1 & 2, in 1976, and is copyright ©1976 & 2022 by Gary Lovisi.

"The Black Hand of Set" is published here for the first time, and is copyright ©2022 by Gary Lovisi.

The Snow Maid" was originally published in *Classic Pulp Fiction Stories* #45 in 1999, and is copyright ©1999 & 2022 by Gary Lovisi.

"The Lion of The North" is published here for the first time and is copyright ©2022 by Gary Lovisi.

"The Mummy of Quelang" originally appeared in *Classic Pulp Fiction Stories* #19, 1996, and is copyright ©1996 & 2022 by Gary Lovisi.

"The Last City" is published here for the first time and is copyright ©2022 by Gary Lovisi.

"The Tower At The Edge of The World" originally appeared in *Zine* #2 in 1983, and in *Weird Stories* #18 in 1998, and is copyright ©1998 & 2022 by Gary Lovisi.

"The Justice of Red Venus" was originally accepted for publication in *Barbarian Scrolls* in 1989 but I am not sure if it ever appeared. I believe it is published here for the first time and is copyright ©2022 by Gary Lovisi.

"The Oasis" was originally titled "Midnight Oasis" and appeared in *Eldritch Tales* issue #20, Summer 1989 issue, and is copyright ©1989 & 2022 by Gary Lovisi.

"The Treasure of Sheor Khot" originally appeared in *Classic Pulp Fiction Stories* #79 in 2001 and is copyright 2001 & 2022 by Gary Lovisi.

"An Interview With Crom" originally appeared in *Nightwind* #1, 1979 and in *Timewarp* #2, 1985 in a substantially different version, and is copyright ©1979 & 2022 by Gary Lovisi

All the above stories have been edited, rewritten and expanded for this new edition and are copyright ©2022 by Gary Lovisi. All Rights Reserved.

THE GEM FROM THE STARS

It was a hot, dry, desert morning as Zarum awoke. He could not believe the staggering heat of this eastern desert, so different from the cold northern climes he was used to. He stood up and stretched his mighty limbs. He was a large barbarian from the northern Calgar Wastes, who had come south to seek his fame and fortune. So far both had eluded him, but by sheer brain and brawn he had risen to command a troop of the King's soldiers. The others in his command, 140 Turan regulars, were still asleep, except for those who stood watch. This was dangerous country and Zarum knew it. At any given moment a massive band of desert rats, known as the Hizards, could fall upon a band of travelers and in moments, level their campsite as well as tear every living thing in sight apart, and then cook it and eat it! They were a fierce band of nomadic cannibals—the eaters of human flesh. And if the Hizards did not get you, the Zueds probably would. The Zueds were an equally deadly tribe of vicious desert dwellers who raided and looted all travelers passing through this land; whether they be traders or even the Imperial Guard of the great king of Turan himself. They killed all in their wake, and were known as fierce slavers. With this on his mind, Zarum thought it best to once again inspect the campsite and see to it that the guards he had posted were alert and awake.

—

Two figures stood leaning over a dimly lit table in a huge hall well beneath the king's palace at Agraphur in Turan. It was a dark, damp, but well-structured room, probably once used as a combination dungeon and torture chamber.

One of the figures wore military robes and armor. He was a tall, powerful man, captain of the King's personal bodyguard, and second in command of the Turanian army. The other was a small, strange-looking fellow wearing the dark cloak and hood of a Stygian priest. Stygia was a feared land of dark magic and black-hearted people, mysterious towers and blood-drenched pyramids. Its priests were known and feared world-wide for their brutal power and vile practices of the black arts. Human sacrifices were not unknown to them. This priest held a candle in one hand and pointed to a map with his other hand. He turned and looked intently at the captain and then spoke.

"This is the last spot my spies saw Koraj. He was heading south past the oasis of Rathol in the Great Desert. Have you done what I asked?"

9

The captain, after looking at the map once more answered the mysterious priest. "I talked the King into sending a company of soldiers out to track down Koraj and bring him back. I let it be known to his majesty that Koraj stole certain military and state documents. He believed everything."

"Good, Captain Toj. Once we have Koraj, we can make him tell us where he hid the Star Stone. And he will tell me for I shall tear it out of his mind!"

A cold shudder ran down the captain's spine as the priest spoke of the use of his dark powers. This Stygian priest, known by the name of Tijh Kih, had once been a wizard warlord in far off Kihati, but had been banished by the Supreme Council of Wizards because his increasing power threatened their very existence. Now, he was a priest in the service of the Stygian priest-king, Amon Thoth and a worshiper of the god, dark-evil Set.

Toj feared Tijh Kih, for he suspected that once he had done his part of the plan there would be no more need for his services, and he knew what this Stygian priest did with unnecessary servants who knew too much.

"Here," spoke Tijh Kih, as he tossed a bag of gold coins into the captain's eager hands. "I will send for you again when you have Koraj."

With that the priest slowly walked away towards the other end of the chamber—a moment later he was gone—seemingly having disappeared into thin air.

Captain Toj quickly left the chamber.

⸺

Zarum walked through the campsite, past tents and smoldering campfires to a small rocky peak which he began to climb. When he reached the top of the rocky defile he looked south, and then in all directions. He saw nothing but more sand in this sandy desert. Zarum wondered why he had been ordered out with a company of soldiers to track down one man, a thief named Koraj. He must have stolen something of great value from the palace, or the King himself, to warrant such a strong pursuit. He did not know the man Koraj personally, however he had seen him at times around the palace. He was one of the King's many foreign advisors. It was a gentle name for men who were renegades or traitors in their own lands, who for a sum of gold betrayed their homes and friends to the imperialism of the ever expanding Empire of Turan. None of these men were in high respect in Turan, but they were useful in the ambitious plans of the King and so tolerated.

Zarum looked out, his sharp eyes scanning the desert, but still nothing was visible. Koraj could not be too far ahead of him, for he had been following clear tracks for three days. The sun was beginning to rise over the distant sand dunes and Zarum began the walk back to camp to awaken his command and continue the pursuit.

⸗

Koraj had been riding hard for three days straight, with very little rest for he knew that Tijh Kih would have him quickly pursued and brought back to pay for his daring theft. Koraj had learned of Tijh Kih's plot to steal the Star Stone that had been secreted in the Royal Library of Agraphur. How Tijh Kih knew the gem was there, he could not say. All Koraj knew was that he must take the Star Stone and flee, for if it fell into the wrong hands, its power could be used to destroy the world, or even worse, enslave it in a loathsome horror of demonic terror beyond imagination.

Koraj was in essence a spy, a secret priest of Mithra from the now leveled city of Makalet. His aim was to gain the confidence of the Turanians and accompany the Star Stone to Agraphur and remain there, making sure the gem stayed safe from all enemies who knew its true power. However, that was all done now. Koraj had safely hidden this stone and was now attempting to hide himself. The stone was secreted on a caravan on its way to far off Nemedia. It was in a package he had given to a friend to deliver, and while he hoped the man did not know the true contents of his package, he had been paid handsomely to see that it was delivered safely.

Koraj had given the stone to his agent on the caravan eight days ago back in Agraphur, and by now the caravan was many days ahead of him. It must be very far away by now, and the stolen gem must be safe. Or so he hoped.

Koraj continued riding west. He had ridden for hours when he noticed something becoming visible over the horizon. It was uncanny. Then he heard the sound of giant wings flapping in the wind, he heard it clearly now, as two black flying figures came towards him. A look of sheer terror overcame his face as he saw the approaching creatures, and he kicked his shrieking horse into a headlong gallop. When he looked back over his shoulder, he could see the black winged creature's hideous faces. They were coming on quickly and soon they would overtake his weary steed. Their talons were extended, ready and eager to tear flesh and bone. Koraj rode onward as fast as his tired mount would go, then he just closed his eyes and muttered a silent prayer to Mithra…

⸗

Zarum was on the move again. He had found a fresh set of tracks and with his troop had been following the thief for the better part of the morning.

His men were short on water and the horses were growing tired in the hot desert heat. Zarum looked forward to finding this Koraj and then returning to Agraphur after this mission, to find himself a nice quiet tavern where he could quench his mighty thirsts in the proper manner. This desert heat was not too his liking at all.

It wasn't long before one of Zarum's scouts returned with some news. The man walked towards his barbarian commander with horror shown in his eyes.

"Captain Zarum, we have found Koraj—at least I think that we have found him."

"What are you talking about, man! Either you found him—or you didn't! Why didn't you bring him back here to me?" Zarum asked impatiently, but he could not help notice the fear that had grown and now covered the scout's face.

"Balthus?" Zarum asked carefully. "What is it?"

"There was not much to bring back, Captain. He was not in one piece."

One piece wasn't the word. As Zarum and his command approached the area, the smell of decayed human flesh assailed their nostrils. The big barbarian noticed human and horse remains shredded and scattered all over the sand. The sight was disgusting enough to even make the barbarian's stomach turn in sickness and disgust.

Zarum let out a gruff curse as he fought back the urge to vomit. He looked about the area and then called out to the scout who had first found the remains of Koraj.

"Did you find anything lying around? Anything of value—or not?" Zarum asked the man forcefully.

"No, sir," was the only reply.

"Get the men, search the area for anything which looks important, " Zarum ordered. "And you two, dig a grave."

"You fool, you let it slip between your fingers!"

"No, the men I sent found his body, but there was no trace of the Star Stone," Captain Toj told the Stygian priest nervously. He had failed his master, and nervous sweat dripped down his face now.

"Then where is it? Where can it be?" Tijh Kih demanded in frustration. "I grow weary of these games."

"I swear to you, I do not know. The Captain of the search, a lout of a barbarian, sent a messenger back to the King with the news."

"Who is this man who led the search? A barbarian, you say? If he is holding out, he and you shall both pay for it!"

"His name is Zarum. He is a captain in the King's cavalry, but he is just a stupid barbarian lout. He knows nothing of the gem or even why he was sent to track down Koraj."

"Bring this man to me. I will open his mind and peel the truth from him. Be gone, I need some time to meditate under the powers of the *Rose of Exhumanities*. Remember this; I will have that stone, if not by mortal means, then by others!"

Captain Toj left the chamber nervously. He knew that if Tijh Kih did not have the stone and quickly, he might not see many more days. Toj now left the secret chamber and headed into the royal palace to see what he could find out.

Zarum had no reason to wait around in the desert any longer now that they had found Koraj, except that his troops were tired and thirsty and would not make the long ride back to Agraphur without fresh water. He had ordered most of the remaining water given to the messenger he had sent out so that news of what had happened could reach the king quickly. He now had second thoughts about his duties as a soldier and the sacrifices he must make. However, he knew there was a water hole a half day's ride to the south. His men could find fresh water there, and maybe some food, and then continue home. Zarum so ordered his men.

Towards the end of the half day ride, Zarum and his troops came upon the remains of an attacked caravan. As they approached, he ordered his men to fan out and scout the area. There were burned wagons and dead merchants and slaves spread over the sands of a large area. Zarum knew it for the work of the Zueds. It must have been a large party of the nomad bandits because the caravan itself had been large and would not have been easy prey for any small force. As Zarum eyed the desolation he did not see a single living thing. His scouts quickly reported back with news of the attackers.

"What have you to report, Sergeant?" Zarum growled, annoyed at this unexpected turn of events.

"Sir, we found some tracks leading south towards the ruins of Zarf."

"How many raiders did you make it out to be?"

"About three hundred, maybe more. A large group, for sure."

"I figured as much. More than twice our number," Zarum mused.

"It would seem so," the sergeant agreed.

The large barbarian commander nodded, then gruffly said, "Gather up the men, Sergeant. We ride south towards Zarf."

Zarum could tell from the remains that the caravan carried little of value, mostly food stuffs and slaves. Not much in rare silks or spices, either. No women, perhaps, though that was yet to be seen. However, there were no signs of any women and the Zueds were not known for their kindness towards their female prisoners. Zarum knew that the Zueds were excellent desert fighters and he was outnumbered at least by two to one, but he was a hunter, and as long as he kept it that way, the advantage would be his…

═

Tijh Kih and Captain Toj were again in discussion far below the royal palace. Only this time, a look of confidence covered the face of the Stygian priest.

"Well, Toj, have you any news?"

"No, My Lord priest. However, I have sent spies out to find the stone and am hopeful that we will have it before long."

"You are sure, Toj?" the priest said mockingly.

"Yes, My Lord," the captain replied earnestly.

"It seems that my stay here is useless. I will return to my home in Stygia and employ other methods in the search for the stone. Through the use of the *Rose of Exhumanities* I was able to discover that the stone is no longer in Turan. It was also able to discover that other—shall we say magical forces— from what agency I do not know as yet—were used in Koraj's death. It seems that someone else wants the Star Stone. Someone who also knows its great value and how to use it. I will enjoy doing battle against this one, and I will enjoy feeding his mind to the dwellers of the pit. But let us not think of good things to come just yet. It would also seem that this barbarian, by the name of Zarum, is in some way associated with the stone—or at least he is within a short distance of it. Nevertheless, I am off for Stygia. But first a drink to cement our partnership. There shall be much added gold in payment for your good work, Toj. That should warm your greedy heart," and the wizard-priest suddenly pulled a small container from underneath his robe and poured the contents into two small cups which just seemed to mysteriously appear in his hand. He handed one of the cups to Toj.

"Drink up, Captain," Tijh Kih said with a sly grin. "It is a rare Stygian brew."

Toj stepped back, his eyes full of suspicion. He did not drink yet.

"No, please, I, I…no…I do not want to drink anything right now…" and the Turan captain fell to his knees pleading, his face drenched in fear.

"Drink…" Tijh Kih ordered in a mesmerizing tone, his eyes bright as fire. It was a voice with a power that could not be denied.

The Captain could not look away from those powerful eyes, those terrible eyes! He could not disobey the order from that mesmerizing voice.

"Drink!" Tijh Kih whispered again, more forcefully.

Almost automatically Captain Toj lifted his arm and put the tiny cup to his mouth and then drank.

"Good," the wizard said with a evil smile as he watched the captain take his first—and last—swallow from what was in that cup.

Then a scream filled the chamber for a moment or two, and soon all was silence…

—

Zarum and his troop rode quickly towards the ruins of Zarf. The water hole he was heading towards was a few miles from that ancient ruined city. That night he and his men set up camp there, away from the ruins. He dispatched twenty of his troopers with hide bags to go to the water hole and fill them with fresh water, while he took ten men and scouted out the ruins of the dead city of Zarf.

It seemed that the Zueds had reached Zarf hours before and had already made their camp. Many fires burned and Zarum could see that the Zueds were celebrating their looting of the caravan. He estimated those in the ruins to number about two hundred men. About twenty men stood watch on the city walls—or what remained of them. Zarum shook his head, earlier his scouts that day had said that the Zueds numbered about three hundred or more men. Where were the others? Had they found out that Zarum and his men were following them? Were they lying in ambush at that very moment? A cold river of sweat trickled down the barbarian's back. He had brought his men here to hunt the hated Zueds. Had things reversed—so that now Zarum had become the hunted? He had no more time to think about it. A distance away he heard the sound of horses and the fierce war cry of the Zueds. He could also hear the screams of his men as they were set upon and being cut down. It had been a trap! His camp had been attacked in a surprise raid, during the few crucial moments when the men's weapons and mounts were not at their sides as they built up the camp. The men had also grown lax and over confident.

But Zarum had troubles of his own now. Those Zueds who were in the city had now mounted up and were charging out from the ruins towards the main body of his troops. They would soon pass by his position. He found that he was in the center of the trap. Over a hundred bloodthirsty enemy riders had just swept his camp and were now heading for him, as well as the ones coming from the city. What should he do? The question ran quickly through his mind. To fight would be suicide, for he could see now that the main body of his command had been slaughtered, there were only a few troopers left alive.

He quickly gave his men the order. He knew they had no choice now but to run for it.

Zarum's men quickly mounted and were heading out of the sides of the trap, only to be cut down by a flurry of arrows. He turned his horse to escape but it was suddenly struck by an arrow in the neck and the mount crashed to the ground dead. Zarum struck the ground hitting his head upon a rock, instantaneously consciousness left him.

—

It was later on that Zarum sat up slowly, his head throbbing. On his wrists and ankles he found heavy iron chains which ran through links attached to a large brick wall. The chains, although centuries old, were still strong enough to hold him firmly bound, at least for a while. Zarum found himself in a dark, damp chamber, probably beneath the ruins of Zarf. He was chained to a wall opposite a large iron door. The other walls of his prison were made of large stone set into ancient mortar. He noticed that also chained to the wall on his right were three of his soldiers, two of them not yet conscious, and one badly wounded. Zarum could see no way out—but he was not one to ever give up!

—

A tall man dressed in an all obscuring long black shroud slowly turned and faced a group of five who were similarly dressed. They were known as The Secret Six. They were seated around a large wooden table. Carved in the legs and sides of that table were terrifying images of dragons and serpent figures. Most people would have found the images severely disturbing, perhaps even evil incarnate. The tall man spoke to the others in a deep sonorous voice.

"Fellow warlords, we have been searching for the Star Stone for many centuries but were always unable to locate it—obscured from our vision by strong enemy sorcery. For centuries it has been secreted in a deep vault in the palace of once great Makelet, protected by a spell put on it by the head of the priests of Mithra. This spell made locating it by mind scanning under the power of the *Rose of Exhumanities* quite impossible. Then it was moved to Agraphur after Turan's conquest of Makelet. But now that gem has left the vault of Agraphur. Our spies in Turan made us aware when it was taken from its protected place of hiding, and it is now in the desert heading towards Nemedia. The priest of Mithra who took the stone met with an untimely accident. However, the stone is still somewhere in the desert."

"Then all we have to do is send someone out to retrieve it," spoke one of The Secret Six.

"It is not quite that simple, Mir Uj, my friend. It seems we have a rival who wishes the stone for his own purposes."

"Who is this who would oppose the Supreme Council of The Secret Six!" shouted Mir Uj in anger and surprise. "Who would be foolish enough!"

"I am sure you all remember the wizard priest Tijh Kih?" As he spoke this name the other five wizards began muttering among each other. Then one of the Six, by the name of Tor Leh, stood up and addressed the Council.

"He should not be too great a threat. He opposed us once and we were able to banish him. This time we shall…"

"Yes, banished him, but did not destroy him," answered Mir Uj showing his anger and frustration. "His power is as great as any three of us."

"But that is not the worst of it," spoke up the tall leader of The Six. "It seems he has joined forces with a quite formidable opponent of ours, one Amon Thoth of Stygia."

At this news a low whisper hissed through the chamber as the other wizard-priests became uneasy at the mention of the joining of two of the world's most powerful sorcerers.

"Our goal is clear then. We must get the Star Stone before our rivals, or be destroyed."

"How do we go about accomplishing this?" asked Mir Uj.

"We must join our minds and dispatch the winged beasts into the desert to recover the stone for us immediately."

The Secret Six nodded and took their places seated at the table, lowering their heads in deep thought and communion. There was no more movement in that chamber but a great growing source of energy seemed to have suddenly appeared.

—

Zarum glanced around the chamber once more. Looking for any opportunity of weakness he could exploit to escape. As far as he could see, the only way out was through the iron door across the room from him. He began to study the chains which bound him more carefully, but his concentration on them was soon broken by footsteps that he heard from without his cell. They were heavy steps like those of men at arms. The jingle of keys was also heard followed by the creaking of a slowly opening door. Six tall warriors of the southern Zued tribe entered the cell and approached their prisoners.

"Well, dogs of Turan, welcome to our fine city. Here we rule. Now we want to know what brought you here?" spoke the leader with a mocking smile on his face.

Zarum looked at the nomads with fire in his eyes, but said nothing.

"No answer, huh? Well, fear not, Kamos Ka, our chieftain has ways of loosening the tongues of even the most obstinate of men. It is said he can even make the voiceless speak! Take them down," the leader ordered his men with a nasty laugh.

Zarum and his three troops were quickly unchained.

"Sha Nor," one of the guards said to their leader, "this one is dead."

"Take him out and feed him to the desert rats. They may have three more to whet their appetites in a short time."

The guards started laughing again as they collected their three remaining prisoners.

Two guards carried the dead body out of the chamber, while the other four took Zarum and his two men at sword point down long dark corridors, up many flights of stairways, until they came to a large hall.

The city of Zarf had once been a wealthy trading center but had been ruled by two kings, each serving a different group of wizard-priests. These priests were ruled by sorcerers who soon became very powerful and wanted complete rule over the city. This led to a civil war which resulted in the destruction of Zarf. In time its lands were annexed by the Empire of Turan. This hall, like all the other buildings was just a skeleton of the once great marble structure which had been the kingly palace of ancient Zarf.

Zarum and his men were brought before a huge ornate throne where sat a large, powerfully built warrior with a bright stone on a gold chain hanging from his neck. The stone was bright yellow, glowing with the color of the sun itself, and shone directly in Zarum's eyes forcing him to turn his head away.

Kamos Ka, the chief of the Zueds stood up, looked at the prisoners curiously and spoke in a deep voice.

"So you are the Captain of the soldiers of Turan we killed last night. What was your purpose in following us? Was it this, perhaps?" and Kamos Ka held out the stone around his neck in front of Zarum's face. The barbarian captain did not know why he was sent to track down Koraj, but it was obvious that if Koraj had stolen this stone, its value well warranted a search and recovery by the King of Turan.

Zarum growled in anger but said nothing.

"You had better answer me, barbarian. Have you ever been thrown into a pit full of desert rats? They are always hungry. They are large and ferocious and not very pretty to watch as they rip a man to bloody shreds."

Zarum made no answer. His two men whimpered beside him in terror.

...bright stone on a gold chain hanging from his neck...

"Ah, still no reply? No matter. Take them away to the pit," Kamos Ka ordered his men returning to his throne.

As Zarum and his men were being driven back through the hall, a sudden screeching and flapping of giant wings was heard. Then there was the sound of men screaming and cursing, followed by the terrified screams of two Zued warriors running into the great hall to fall upon the stone floor before their chief.

"What is it?" Kamos Ka demanded angry at the intrusion.

"My Lord Ka," spoke one warrior frantically, "we are under attack!"

"Attack!" shouted Ka. "By who? Turan? Why did not the sentry's warn us?"

"We are under attack by creatures from Hell itself! They tear our men apart!"

A few seconds later one of the incredible beasts entered the chamber from one of the openings in the ruined walls. What Zarum saw was a large birdlike creature with a long, sharp beak and incredible razor talons—and it stood about sixteen feet tall.

At the sight of the creature, the hall was instantly full of fear and confusion. Most men ran for their lives, while some who were the bravest—or the most foolhardy—stayed behind to do battle with the creature, only to be ripped apart by massive sharp red-stained talons. It was disaster.

In all the confusion, Zarum and his two troopers saw their chance for escape. He was able to make a grab for his sword from the scabbard where it rested at the foot of Ka's throne, who stood frozen in abject panic at the attack of the bird-like creature.

The barbarian kicked the Zued chief aside, then turned with sword in hand to witness one of his men suddenly beheaded by the swift swing of a blade by another Zued warrior. Zarum was on this attacker quickly; his voice shouting in rage and revenge, ducking the Zued's sword swing, the barbarian returned one of his own which bit deep into the man's vitals. Kamos Ka, now regaining his shocked senses, and seeing it useless to fight this terrible flying creature, was now on his way fleeing to safety. However, he was seen trying to escape by the big barbarian. Whether it was revenge for his massacred men which spurred him on, or the sheer lust of battle, no one could truly say, but Zarum chased after the man and was close behind the Zued chieftain.

Kamos Ka ran into an adjoining room with Zarum quickly upon his heels. Seeing the big barbarian right behind him, Kamos Ka had no choice but to turn and fight. With a swing of his blade—a sudden and wild reckless swing which he hoped would kill his pursuer quickly—he almost took the on-rushing barbarian by surprise. Lurching out of the way just in time, Zarum returned a sword swipe which came down hard upon the Zued chief's shoulder plate of his armor, knocking him down to the floor, and knocking the sword out and away from his hands. The Zued's armor saving him from what would certainly have been a mortal blow. Kamos Ka now reached for his dagger and hurled it toward Zarum, where it imbedded itself into the hard leather of his harness, preventing the blade from sinking deep into his flesh. Zarum then lowered his blade in a whirling windmill swing that smashed into the Zued chieftain's head and crushed it into a pulpy mass. On the floor next to the dead Zued leader was the stone gem he had worn on a gold chain around his neck. It had become dislodged in the fight. Zarum picked it up and put it away in a small pouch in his belt. He then left the hall as he heard the continued sounds of battle growing ever louder.

Outside the great hall there were dozens of Zued warriors being ripped and shredded apart. It was horrendous butchery. The flying beasts still remained as if they were looking for something or someone. Zarum knew that he must hide himself until these beasts left. To battle them alone—as it appeared that soon he might be the only one here left alive—would be foolish and useless. The flying beasts had not seen him yet. Zarum entered the ruins of the palace and made his way to the underground chamber where he and his men had first been held prisoners. The beasts could not get to him down there...

A great distance away two men were conversing in a dimly lit hall decorated with all manner of grotesque statues depicting the worse of hell-spawned beasts. Seated upon a large throne, facing a misty round ball set upon a alabaster table, sat the leader. Across from him sat another form that was a man. Both wore long dark shrouds and black hoods to conceal them from the light and sun, and all that was good and pure.

"Well, my friend?" asked the man on the throne in a powerful voice. "Have you obtained the Star Stone?"

"No, My Lord," answered Tijh Kih with some reluctance and trepidation. "It seems there are others who would have the yellow gem."

"Who are these who would cross me and my aims?"

"I am not sure, My Lord Amon Thoth, but there is only one person powerful enough to oppose our combined power, and that is Ujthol, leader of the Supreme Council of Wizards of Kahiti."

"The Secret Six?"

"Yes, they are known by that name as well," Tijh Kih replied.

"And where is the stone now?"

"I think..."

Amon Thoth interrupted, "Never mind, I shall find out for certain." Then reaching for the object on the table, the master wizard of Stygia mumbled strange terse words never meant to be uttered by a human throat.

"Look closely, my friend," Amon Thoth spoke up softly.

All at once the mist cleared and a deadly scene took shape. Among the ruins of an ancient city men were being torn apart by huge birdlike beasts. The flying creatures were all over the city, tearing human flesh and crushing bodies into bloody pulp.

"Do you recognize the city, Tijh?"

"Yes, My Lord, it is Zarf in the Great Desert."

"And the winged creatures?" spoke Amon Thoth.

"The Harpies of Kihati, Ujthol's calling card, My Lord."

"Yes. Well, I can handle the flying creatures," spoke Amon Thoth. With a mysterious gesture of his hand and the whisper of his voice, the cloudy magic ball upon the table before the two wizards slowly cleared up. Soon the flying beasts quickly turned a bright red and then were gone; leaving only deserted Zarf, once more empty and silent.

"They are gone now. Go, and bring back the stone, and remember, should you attempt to keep it, or hide it from me, I shall have *Ghiht* hunt you down and bring me your soul. He will hunt you down and take you in your sleep, so there is no escape."

Turning Amon Thoth looked across the chamber at a grotesque statue of a multi-tentacle creature whose alien ferocity can not fully be conceived by the human mind. It was a nightmare of the darkest dreams. For a moment the statue seemed to come to life, but then returned to complete stillness.

"Have no doubts about my loyalty, My Lord," answered Tijh Kih nervously. He could not even look at the statue, for it terrified him to his very being.

⸺

Ujthol, leader of the Supreme Council of Kihati, walked slowly across the hall of his palace. The massive hall was empty except for him and Mir Uj.

"I do not understand, Mir Uj. We summoned my pets to Zarf. After a complete massacre of its occupants, they were unable to find the stone among any of the bodies. There is something we are missing. As I was watching the events through the viewing crystal, some force entered into Zarf destroying my flying creatures."

"Do you think it was Tijh Kih?"

"Along with his Stygian wizard master, Amon Thoth," answered Ujthol, completing the thought.

"I see."

"Well, then we must take stronger measures," spoke Ujthol firmly. "Go to Zarf, we of the Council will aid you through mind projection. You will be the center of our combined powers. You must obtain that stone!"

"I understand, My Lord. I leave now," answered Mir Uj.

⚊

Zarum woke up from his sleep and left the cell to explore. How long he had been sleeping he did not know, nor did he really care for now he was well rested and wanted to leave this thrice-damned dead city. He assumed the flying monster birds were gone, but he remained ever watchful and alert as he explored his surroundings. The long corridor that led outside his cell was pitch black for the torches had all burned out and there appeared no one left alive to replace them. Zarum was ready to climb the stairs when a strange cry caught his ears. He quickly turned, drawing his sword, and listened, trying to make out what the wild sound might be. He heard the sound once again. It came down the corridor from a cell he had just passed. Most carefully with sword ready, Zarum stepped down the corridor making no more sound than would a stalking tiger. He came to a bolted wooden door and stopped there. The sound certainly came from within that cell.

Zarum looked through the slit in the door at what was within, but he could see nothing. Again Zarum heard the sound. He could make it out plainly now. It was a terrible low wailing, the sound of a weak man in pain. Zarum unlocked and opened the cell door carefully. He had heard of beasts who drew their prey by imitating human cries, then sprung upon them unawares to feast upon their souls. Zarum was no fool. He held his sword tightly, ready for anything, but he was also a man who had a massive curiosity. He would be the last to admit that he was affected by the man's cries of pain, for such was life, but if possible he would make an attempt to find out what was going on here, and maybe even help him.

As Zarum entered the cell, he looked around the small chamber. There was very little light to see by, but once his eyes became adjusted to the light he could make out a small form huddled in the far corner of the room.

"Who is there?" asked a man's strained voice.

"I am Zarum. Who are you?" the barbarian asked, taking a torch from the wall and using his flint to set it aflame. There was some light now from the torch.

"I am Ja Nan, a priest of Mithra," spoke the other. With the torch now lit Zarum was able to make out the man more clearly. He was a small man dressed in the white and gray robes of a Mithran priest. He looked to be Nemedian, or maybe from Aqualonia. His arms were chained to the wall and his feet were chained to the floor. Zarum looked at the priest with some surprise and some sadness. Whatever was a priest of Mithra doing here? He was surely not any type of danger to be bound so securely.

"What has happened? Where are the guards?" Ja Nan asked curious.

"The guards, and everyone else in this city, except you and I, are dead. The city was attacked by some type of giant birdlike devils. It is just you and I now. We have to get out of here fast, before they return."

"Mother of mercy!" the man cried with joy.

Zarum shrugged at that, but then bent down to sever the man's chains with his mighty sword. Cutting the man's arms free, Zarum turned to the chains on Ja Nan's legs. In doing so, the gem in Zarmm's belt pouch, which he had won in his fight with the Zued chief the day earlier, fell to the floor. In the torchlight the gem shone brightly, a fierce striking yellow, like a miniature sun. Its rays of golden light filled the chamber as it lay there on the floor of the jail cell between the two men.

"The Star Stone!" blurted Ja Nan eagerly, noticing the gem with awe and surprise. "How? You found it, thank Mithra! Where did you get it?"

As Ja Nan reached for the gem, Zarum grabbed his arm and pulled it away.

"No! It is mine now!" Zarum told the priest in no uncertain terms. "I took this from Kamos Ka the chief of the Zueds after ending his life. Where he obtained it, I do not know, but if you try to take it from me, I will…"

"No, Zarum! You do not understand. This sacred gem was entrusted to me by my friend, Koraj."

"The thief?" spoke Zarum with scorn.

"He was no thief, but a priest of sacred Mithra. His mission was to make sure that the Star Stone remained safe from evil sorcerers. When Koraj found out that foreign wizards knew of the stone's location he took it to keep it from falling into the wrong hands. He gave it to me and I boarded a caravan to Nemedia, but we were attacked by the Zueds and the stone was taken from me. But now it is here. You have it and it is safe. Praise be! The stone has great powers and there are many who seek it to do their dark bidding."

"This whole thing stinks of sorcery!"

"Indeed it does," answered Ja Nan plainly. "But if this stone falls into the wrong hands the fate of the world will be doomed."

"What do I care about the fate of the world?" Zarum asked the priest.

"Millions will die and millions will be enslaved, and you and your people of the north will not be safe from it this time," Ja Nan told the barbarian sincerely.

"What do we do with the stone then?" asked Zarum thinking it through, for the fact that this all stank of sorcery did not make him over fond of keeping such a bauble for long.

"We must deliver it to Famar Khand in Nemedia where the priests of Mithra will be able to protect it."

Zarum thought about that for a moment, then shrugged. He knew the priest was right, and while he would have liked to keep the stone to sell, he did not want to keep it too long. He would be glad to be rid of it, but wondered if he might gain by it in some way.

"Will you buy it from me?" he asked the priest.

"No, you must give it to me."

"Hah! It must be worth a fortune!"

"It is, but its power will corrupt your very soul if you keep it."

"Then buy if from me, I am glad to be rid of it."

Ja Nan nodded, "Very well, when we are safe in Nemedia, I will have you amply rewarded."

"In gold?"

"Yes, in gold," and the priest's words brought a smile to the barbarian's face.

"Then we had better get going," answered Zarum, cutting the priests legs free. "It is a long way to the Kingdom of Nemedia."

The two men left the chamber and went up the steps to the surface above. Zarum looked around carefully, but he could not see any of the flying creatures - they appeared to be gone—and all the Zueds seemed to be dead. He knew they would need horses to cross the Great Desert, but it did not appear as though there were any left alive in the ruins of the city. All horses had likely been killed by the flying beasts as well.

"We will have to walk," Zarum told the priest. "We will make our way towards the Black Lake. Then through the Great Plains instead of going through the desert."

After filling their backpacks with as much food and water as they could hold, the two men left the ruins of Zarf.

—

Zarum and the Mithran priest Ja Nan had been walking for perhaps an hour when the barbarian noticed a strange sight far in front of them.

"What devil's brew is this before us, priest?"

"I know not Zarum, but whatever it be, it can bode only ill."

Zarum just grunted angrily at that response, for he had already assumed as much.

Ever so slowly a bright unnatural glow appeared in the distance. Then it quickly changed into a weird unholy fire with bright flames reaching twenty feet into height.

Zarum drew his sword, and slowly the fire shape changed again and came closer. The barbarian drew back a step, for sorcery always put fear and rage into him, even while the priest muttered some strange prayer to his god, Mithra.

Now they could make out the image and it put the holy terrors into both of them. Both men now looked upon the giant visage of the eye of the Stygian god of evil, monstrous malignant Set, the vile snake from the deep depths of Hell itself.

It stood there horribly, fully twenty feet in height, hissing with its horrid poisonous tongue as it swayed hypnotically before them. For a moment the fatty folds upon the back of the hell-spawn cobra neck expanded and then the shape changed once more.

Now before Zarum and the priest of Mithra stood a man in a long dark hooded robe. He was human size now, but he had that about him that seemed… evil, and extremely dangerous.

"Warrior, I am Tijh Kih of Stygia, and I have come a long way for the Star Stone."

Zarum spit upon the ground. He hated sorcery!

"You, nor any like you, shall have it!" the Mithran priest spoke up boldly.

Burning eyes of fire looked into Zarum and Ja Nan until both realized that somehow the wizard had frozen their will, as well as their bodies. They could not move. Zarum helpless now could not even move his sword arm.

"Give me the Star Stone now, or prepare to die!" the wizard demanded contemptuously.

Neither Zarum nor Ja Nan could move, both stood frozen as if dead men, which it appeared that they would soon be. A vicious smile crossed the Stygian's lips as he slowly lifted his shrouded arms aloft.

Almost as if in answer to this gesture, they saw a fearsome demon fly overhead, one out of the legends of Eastern nightmares. As it neared the three men, Tijh Kih nervously looked upwards at it and quickly brought down his arms to conjure some new magic to kill the two men before him.

Zarum and the priest, frozen by the Stygian's magical power, wondered at the seemingly delay in their deaths. They could not move, nor see what had produced the fear in the wizard's countenance, now evident to see.

Once again, the wizard before them who called himself Tijh Kih, changed shape. Now he had re-appeared as the horrid giant snake form of Set to sway before them, waiting. Poisonous venom dripping from hissing fangs, red eyes of hate burning fire—but not for Zarum or Ja Nan—but for something else.

That something else, turned out to be a terrible flying beast, all great horns and teeth and scales that dove down at the giant snake in front of Zarum. The look in the barbarian's eyes showed the terror that his still frozen body could not express. Sweat dripped from Ja Nan's face, but he could not utter one word. Neither of the men could move at all, they could only watch what was going to happen.

Zarum had heard tales of these horned flying beasts from far off Khaiti. Dragon was what the yellow-skinned inhabitants there called them. It was some kind of huge flying reptile, looking similar to the reptilian crocodiles of the River Styx, except in size. The size was enormous. What made this apparition even more terrifying was that a man in a dark robe sat upon the back of the beast as one might ride a horse. It was uncanny. Incredible and terrifying. The dragon, now with flames of fire shooting from its jaws, dove down upon the giant snake again, while the man upon its back let out a blood curdling chant.

The snake suddenly sprang upwards and caught a wing of the dragon in its spike like teeth. The man laughed while the reptile's jaws sought the body of the demon Set. Zarum noticed that some life was slowly coming back into his limbs. With a tremendous effort he looked above at the titanic struggle taking place between the two hellish monsters. He realized that the fight had somehow lessened the Stygian's power over him.

Zarum shot a look to Ja Nan. "Can you move yet, priest?" he asked as he furiously rubbed the numbness out of his aching arms and legs.

"Barely, but better," Ja Nan replied, as he forced himself to move his muscles as much as he was able.

Overhead the sounds of the battling hell-beasts came to Zarum's ears. Gripping the hilt of his sword firmly he picked up the still rigid form of the priest.

"Our only chance is to run and hope they both send each other down to the darkest pits of Hell, where they came from!" Zarum said fiercely.

Now carrying Ja Nan, Zarum ran with as much speed as his legs would allow. Though still weak, the terror of the situation had given him a strength he did not know he possessed. It is amazing what abject terror will do to a man. Above him the demons fought on. It appeared the dragon was losing. Its left wing was completely destroyed and quickly both beasts plummeted down to the earth. The dragon spewing flames on the face of the furiously hissing snake. The rider atop the dragon was not laughing any more, as the snake opened its jaws and clamped them down upon the reptile's throat. Flames burst forth. The snake bled a dark, foul smelling liquid from a dozen wounds, while a bright green fluid poured out of the hole where the dragon's left wing had been. This gross green gushing mess spewed forth from the beast's neck as well.

Zarum looked back and saw both beasts hit the ground with a thunderous smack, churning up rocks and dirt in every direction. It was like an earthquake when they hit.

The barbarian stopped in his tracks, and carefully watched the scene before him for a moment in stark wonder. He noticed that neither of the beasts moved now.

"Stay here priest," he said, putting down Ja Nan. "I'll finish them off and send them both to the bosom of dark Erlik."

With sword in hand Zarum strode carefully forward. He noticed that the snake lay atop the dragon and that both creatures appeared alive, yet remained motionless. He could not fathom it—if they were ever truly alive to begin with, he thought. The man in the black robe who rode the scaly hell-beast lay to the side, having been thrown in the giant beast's fall. Zarum walked over to him, sword ever ready. The man appeared to be dead. There could be no other fate for such a fall.

"Rot in a thousand Hell's, wizard!" Zarum shouted at the shrouded form, and he gave the lifeless body a brutal kick. Good riddance, the barbarian thought. He noticed that indeed, the neck of the man was broken. So much for one wizard!

"Zarum, both beasts must be killed now, before they waken," Ja Nan said as he walked towards the barbarian.

"Aye, priest, then we get as far away from here as we can," Zarum replied walking closer to the two lifeless monsters. Suddenly the giant fire-breathing dragon of Khaiti dematerialized before their eyes. In the blink of an eye, it was gone.

"The Grim Grey God and Mithra too!" Zarum growled anxiously.

Ja Nan looked at Zarum mildly annoyed by the barbarian's curse, but he thought it best to say nothing upon the matter just then. Instead he stood by Zarum and looked at the serpent's motionless body.

"The dragon is gone, but you must kill the serpent," Ja Nan insisted.

"Aye, Priest, but can such a great snake be killed?" Zarum asked somewhat hesitantly. He did not overly like this duty, but he knew it had to be done.

"Barbarian, this is not the black snake Set, not the god itself, it is but a stunned wizard of Stygia who has taken the snake-god's form. Did you not see yourself? You must act quickly or it will awaken."

Like one shaken out of a trance, Zarum shook his shaggy black mane and let out a gusty laugh. "The thing shall die!"

"You must act quickly before it awakens," Ja Nan repeated.

"Aye, but me thinks I have not met with so much foul sorcery in all my life. To me it all stinks," the wily barbarian growled as he quickly lifted his massive sword and hacked away at the middle of the snake, seeking to cut it in twain.

...he gave the lifeless body a brutal kick...

Ja Nan let out a shriek as he noticed the snake's movement when Zarum began his next sword sweep,

"Zarum, quickly now, it awakens!"

The barbarian had noticed the movement long before.

"Awaken Hell-beast and I will still hack you into a hundred pieces!" Zarum shouted at the serpent, now that it was fully awake and active, it reared its ugly head at the young barbarian.

Zarum, with all the strength of his massive northern muscles, dodged those venomous dripping jaws. In doing so he swung his mighty blade straight for the snake's head, caving in the bone and opening a large crevice that splattered him full of a sticky black blood-like substance. Again, the snake struck, and again Zarum moved quickly to escape mighty Set's ravenous jaws. Now Zarum struck with all the ferocity of his barbarian heritage. The results of his next blow completely caved in the skull of the hideous snake-thing.

When the snake came at Zarum again, this time its attack was more disconcerted and it was easier for Zarum to move away from its lunge. That the beast was dying, Zarum was sure, but whether or not it killed the young barbarian before it expired was another matter altogether. The damn thing was taking a most inordinate amount of time to attain its demise.

Suddenly in one mad rush the huge serpent was upon Zarum once more. Vise-like jaws clamped down upon the Norse warrior's chest and lifted him off the ground, shaking him violently. The fact that the warrior wore thick chain mail armor saved him from an instant crushing death, but he was still in a lot of pain. Blood rushed into the barbarian's head as he tried desperately to fight unconsciousness—an unconsciousness that he knew meant certain death. His chest ached and was cut with many small wounds that would have instantly killed a lesser man—or a man without armor. With both hands he used every ounce of his strength to force those mighty slavering jaws open. Then without a moment to spare, he pushed himself free, as the beast's jaws came crashing down upon the empty space he had been mere heartbeats before.

In terrible pain, Zarum tried vainly to fetch his sword where it had landed after the giant snake's attack.

"Here Zarum!" Ja Nan shouted, pressing the sword into the barbarian's willing hands. The priest looked at Zarum's wounds with awe that any man could sustain such injuries and still live. Then he thought of the serpent's deadly venom, and he knew that it did not matter.

"Zarum you must slay it now, for you have too much of the creature's poison in you," the priest warned. "Soon I shall not be able to save you, even if you do slay the beast."

Zarum growled and advanced upon the giant snake warily, rubbing the blood from his eyes. "This Hell-serpent is stronger than I realized. It is like it draws power from some unknown source."

Ja Nan said something to that but Zarum did not hear him. The barbarian saw an opening and rushing in, leaped upon the back of the snake's neck. Then he began hacking away at the back of the head of the giant thing. The snake hissed and screeched in pain and anger at the little man-thing riding upon its huge scaly neck.

Zarum began getting dizzy and weak from the creature's poison. He was being hurled and bucked, and was finally thrown off the creature to the ground. He knew he must work fast now, for if the snake did not kill him, he knew the poison in him would. He could feel it working on him already. So he came at the serpent once again and continued hacking away at its neck, trying to do as much damage to the thing as possible.

"If I cannot cut off your head, then I'll cut you in half, demon-spawn!" Zarum shouted in rage. Where he was drawing his strength from now he knew not—mostly his terror of sorcery, no doubt!

Ja Nan looked at the titanic struggle in sheer terror. He had never seen a man take such a beating and yet continue to fight. The beast's screams now became more numerous and at higher pitch while its movement was beginning to slow down and seemingly falter.

Fighting unconsciousness and waves of pain, Zarum let out with a monumental sword stroke that finally separated the horrid worm in two.

Immediately Zarum was thrown yards away unconscious. Quickly the last vestiges of life flowed out of the serpent, and it appeared to be destroyed. Just as quickly Ja Nan ran towards the body of the dying barbarian. From the folds of his priestly robes he withdrew the bright, blinding-yellow Star Stone that Zarum had given him earlier. The priest got to work and prayed to divine Mithra that he had enough time...

—————

In that secret chamber, around a large wooden table, five deadly powerful hooded figures sat. That they were not in any good humor was evident by the large scowls upon each and every face. One of their number was now dead.

"So then, we have lost," Tor Leh told his companions in an angry tone of stark resignation.

"Not exactly, not if we act quickly," Ujthol said rather more calmly. "We still have a chance."

"How so, Master? I thought the traitor Tijh Kih defeated our dragon and now has the stone," the one named Nor Arbret said, greedy hope again filtering into his eyes.

"We had not counted on this wild barbarian, and his great strength," Ujthol told the group, still feeling self assured in their mission. "It is true that the traitor Tijh Kih, working with that low Stygian son of a slut, Amon Thoth, slew our Khaitian dragon, and its rider. Through our stupidity we let the Star Stone slip through our fingers, but not all is lost. Not yet. The Barbarian, still has the stone, and at this very moment he is beginning to enter the land of Nemedia."

Tor Leh hit his fist upon the huge table with a resounding whack. "Damnation! While we and the Stygians fight each other—each supposing the other side has the stone—this damnable barbarian is calmly strolling into Nemedia with *our* treasure!"

"Hardly strolling, but…" Ujthol said with a deep grin upon his face now, "there is still time, if we act quickly. I am sure we will prevail. We always do."

Upon a jade throne carved into the likeness of a massive serpent, a man sat brooding. One single brazier lent light to the otherwise black bleakness of the large chamber.

Suddenly a dusky Stygian warrior appeared at the portal to the chamber. Nervous shaky legs walked forward bringing the warrior closer to the motionless man upon the throne. A strange terrible odor assailed the warrior's nostrils as he neared the motionless form of the master wizard of Stygia. He now knew that odor for what it was, the fetid stink of death and decay and he recoiled in disgust—but took care not to show his true feelings. And yet, there was something else there that was worse, and he realized that it was the noxious fumes given off by the *Rose of Exhumanities*. Seated in front of the warrior, still appearing as if a dead man sat the demon-wizard Amon Thoth, his glassy eyes starring off into who knew what demonic climes. Visibly shaken to the core of his being, the lone warrior carefully approached the wizard with his message.

"You dare enter my chamber unbidden!" a loud voice as if from another world spoke through the master magician's thin pale lips.

"Oh, Great Lord, I have important news for you from your General, Abor Kan. I am to seek you at any cost to deliver you his message," the warrior sputtered kneeling fearfully.

"Then speak!"

"My Lord Abor Kan has found both Mir Uj and Tijh Kih dead in the desert near the ruins of Zarf. He bade me tell you that your servant Tigh Kih, who had taken the snake form of Mighty Set, was found splattered in the sand, his body cut in two parts. Mir Uj, who took the form of a Khaiti dragon, was also killed. The barbarian, Zarum, now has the Star Stone. Together with another man, he is making his way to Nemedia. Abor Kan also says he and his force are on their way to Nemedia to recover the stone for you."

For a moment the eyes of Amon Thoth focused to reality. He looked at the warrior who stood so nervously before him and grinned an evil smile seldom seen this side of Hell.

"It shall not slip through my fingers again!" the wizard growled in anger. "I have been a fool to think that the Khaitians had the bauble."

The body of the warrior trembled, his face shocked. For all his warrior arts he knew he was at his master's mercy here now, and his master was not one ever prone to that particular disposition.

Much to the warrior's relief, the master wizard waved him away with an imperious dismissive gesture.

"Leave me," he commanded the warrior. Then to himself, Amon Thoth whispered, "I must leave at once to Nemedia."

⸻

For days now Zarum and Ja Nan had been traveling and living off the land. They walked for many hours, until coming to a small village where they were able to procure mounts. Then riding swiftly northwest, they entered a sparse land and now stood at the border of the Kingdom of Nemedia.

They had met no opposition along the way so that now Ja Nan was in high spirits. He was glad he was traveling with the big barbarian, and that he had been able to use the Star Stone to save the man's life from the great snake's venom. Zarum rode on as moody as ever.

"Why so quiet, Zarum?" the priest asked trying to make conversation with the naturally non-loquacious barbarian. He wanted to know what the man was thinking. They had been through much, but Zarum had never spoken about the past events, except to make clear his fear and disgust with all forms of sorcery.

"These wizards will not give up that easily," Zarum growled in answer.

"But surely if they could have taken the gem, they would have done so before now? I hope that we are in the clear. I think we are. We must be. Once we get to Nemedia we shall be safe—and the stone will be secure," Ja Nan said confidently.

"You believe that?" Zarum replied, he was unconvinced.

"Well, in another day we will be safely behind the walls of Nemedia, What's more important, the Star Stone will be safely in the keeping of the priests of Mithra, where no wizards shall ever get near it."

"Hah!" Zarum grunted dubiously.

"Do not despair, my friend."

"I still do not understand how you used that damnable stone to save my life," Zarum said, grumbling an oath, shaking his head perplexed. "I do not like that you used that wizard gem to save my life—but I do admit I like being dead even less. So, all in all..."

"Just so. The stone is not evil, my friend," the priest said smiling now as they rode along a lonely road to Nemedia. He had explained this once before to his barbarian friend but Zarum had only shrugged and grumbled. Zarum hated all things sorcerous.

"The Star Stone has a strange power," Ja Nan told his companion, "and while evil wizards will stop at nothing to get it, they shall not have it now. Without the stone, they and all like them could be forever weakened. It can blunt their power and magic. However, in their hands it will be a potent talisman, supplying them with enough power to enslave the world. But, Zarum, in the hands of good forces such as the priests of Mithra, it feeds upon the powers of the evil magicians and weakens them considerably. It is a present that has come from beyond the stars, from another world—from Holy Mithra. The stone must make it to Nemedia safely, even if it should cost us our lives. We have come too far on this quest to fail upon the border of Nemedia."

Zarum nodded in acknowledgement. He had no thought of giving up the stone to any wizards, and especially after going through so much danger to get and keep it. It also made him feel good to spite these wizards their sorcerous bauble. He knew soon that the real fight would take place, for these black magicians and evil wizards would never give up. However, the fact that they had not acted in some days nagged at Zarum's mind. It seemed unnatural. He knew something was coming and the fact that it was sorcerous in nature was reason enough for him to grow nervous. Each mile they rode, the barbarian's keen senses grew more alert and wary. He wished he could be done with this whole thing and be free to take in the lusty pleasures of Nemedia's drinking houses. Then the Barbarian realized that they were being followed.

As was usual, General, Abor Kan inspected the Stygian army camp. After waking a sleeping sentry, almost killing the man, he walked on back towards the tents. All the time he had the eerie feeling that he was being watched. Abor Kan turned around in surprise. And shock.

"Lord of Stygia!" the general whispered nervously. "I had not thought to see you here!" Who knew what the master wizard's actions would be now? How

Amon Thoth had come into the camp, all the way from far off Stygia, Abor Kan did not even want to think about—much less annoy his master by asking him such questions.

"The barbarian, where is he?" Amon Thoth demanded.

"One day out from Nemedia, Lord," Abor Kan replied, fear evident in his voice at dealing with this most dangerous and unpredictable of Stygian wizards.

Amon Thoth looked at the general with deadly menace.

"We will overtake him in a couple of hours if we ride hard," the general added quickly. "I am just allowing the men to rest."

"Then do so now. No rest! Order your men to ride out now!"

"I shall have the men break camp immediately, Lord," the general replied swiftly and gave the order.

The order given, the two dozen warriors were already taking down the tents and repacking goods.

"Enough of this! We leave the camp immediately!" the wizard ordered impatiently.

So ordered, Abor Kan gave the command to his men, "Leave it all! Mount up now, we ride immediately!"

Within moments dozens of Stygian warriors rode towards Nemedia as if they were being chased by the great serpent Set itself. At the front of this frantic command rode a dark hooded man, Amon Thoth, demon-wizard of far off Stygia.

———

On the borderland of Nemedia, the goatherd Matmos Som tended his small flock of sheep. The pasture lands around his home had not been good of late, so he had been forced to wander to this nearby country that he did not like overly much.

The man sat looking intently at the midday sun, and noticed strange shapes in the sky coming out of the southeast. Whatever were they? As they neared him he saw there were five in number.

Matmos Som grew very nervous, for he had never seen such flying creatures like these before. Quickly the five things came closer into the range of his vision, so that he could easily make out what they were—now from his hiding place. He was no fool and was scared. Looking up his heart jumped into his mouth, for the herd man now saw five men in long dark robes, each seated upon a small flat platform of some kind, that looked to him to be, of all things, a large rug or carpet—that flew magically through the air! He was astonished and amazed for this certainly seemed to be some strange form of sorcery.

The man had heard tell of the wondrous flying carpets of Iranistan, but until now he had never believed the incredulous tale. As the five men flew past him, hundreds of feet in the air above him, Matmos Som let out a long sigh of relief. Then he began running to the flock of his friend Frabros to tell him of the wondrous thing he had just witnessed. As he ran he thought of the poor soul that these mysterious magi might be after, and quickly wiped the sweat from his brow, thanking his god that it was not to be him.

———

Flying over the outskirts of Nemedia like a flock of Hell-spawned vultures, were the five Khaiti wizards. Around and around the city they flew like ominous birds of prey. Many were the terrified glances upward at this frightful apparition that the inhabitants feared spelled doom for their beloved city.

Sentries on the walls and gates alerted officers at what they had seen, who promptly ordered all men up to the battlements to the defense of the city. Archers were called up. The royal governor of the fear-struck city at once sent out riders to Belverus, and to the King of Nemedia for military help should it be needed. He did not expect any help.

The city gates were ordered closed immediately, trained warriors stood ready upon the battlements and rooftops, for they knew not what might be coming.

Suddenly, from up above, the scene changed, the mysterious magic carpet riders stopped their circling of the city and glided to a landing outside of the city. They were now out of sight from those in the city. It was soon after that, the sky, seemingly by sorcerous means, grew unnaturally black and the city slipped into darkest night—though it was only the middle of the day. The sun was gone. It was as if it had disappeared, and darkness reigned. The city populace was terrified by this with cries of fear and impending doom, as though it were the end of the world. Prayers and curses were vainly heard along the dark streets and avenues, while people huddled in their homes in terror. As the fear spread, some soldiers deserted their posts on the walls, though none dared leave the city. Looting had begun in the poorer quarters. Overhead, replacing the five flying magi, now flew thousands of large red bat-like creatures. They neither landed nor attacked, just soared around and around like harbingers of some ungodly doom.

———

In the city in the temple of Mithra, an aged man in a long flowing white robe moved hurriedly about. His benign face showed signs of nervousness and deep concern. Brushing back his long white hair and beard, he walked into another chamber. Here were seated dozens of younger men all dressed as he was. As he entered they all stood in a respectful salute to the chief priest of divine Mithra, Famar Khand.

"Brothers of Mithra we have waited a long time for this day," he began earnestly. "The time is now for us to take action. We must leave the city immediately."

—

Upon the vast plain before the city, two riders were moving as fast as their weary mounts would carry them. A few miles ahead Zarum could see the dark quietness of the city. His barbarian soul told him something was not right.

Quickly he looked back and from out of the trees he saw two dozen riders racing towards him and Ja Nan. Zarum had known that since the morning they had been followed but he managed to stay ahead of his pursuers. Now however, they were very close behind him, so both men urged their weary mounts to greater speed. It would be a close chase indeed, he thought, hoping he and the priest would beat them to the city.

The barbarian's chest heaved as he glanced skyward. There he now saw five flying wizards who were being transported through the sky by the magical carpets of Iranistan. He looked upon them and cursed.

The enemies were advancing upon Zarum and Ja Nan, closing the distance. Suddenly the lead wizard stood up and outstretched his arms in some manner of supplication—to what demon or force no one could tell. The barbarian saw a large bolt of white lightning shoot down from above right at him. Another bolt shot out at Ja Nan. As the bolt of fire hit the ground where Zarum *had* been, a small explosion came to his ears and he was thrown clear of his mount. Recovering quickly and standing up with drawn sword he noticed that his horse, or what was left of it, lay smoldering in the burnt ground. Likewise a similar bolt of power had hit Ja Nan's mount and he had also been thrown to the ground. Aside from being a little shook up, both men were unharmed, for the present. It was obvious the lightning strikes had not been aimed to kill them, but at their mounts to stop them from getting away.

As the mounted Stygians under General Abor Kan approached, the wizards of Khaiti landed their magical carpets and now moved towards the barbarian and the priest.

"Well, priest, it seems it is up to the sword now," Zarum grunted in resigned anger, hefting the cold metal of his deadly blade. At least this was something he could understand. "Here they come, like a pack of scavenging wolves."

Ja Nan drew a dagger from within his robe. Although not a warrior, he would sell his life dearly, before he allowed either of these groups of dark magicians to get the scared Star Stone. If he got the chance, he hoped, he would use his small ornate knife to good effect. Zarum's lips pressed into a proud smile as he noticed the determination of the armed priest.

"Good for you!" Zarum bellowed to his companion.

"I am afraid I will not be much help to you when the times comes," Ja Nan said sadly.

"It is of no matter. The very fact that you stand with me and will fight for your life, is all that matters," Zarum stated grimly, a slight smile crossing his lips.

Then the two groups of dark wizards closed in on the two men. Each group eyed not only the Calgarian and Mithran but the other group as well. Zarum could almost physically feel the hatred between the Stygians and the wizards from far off Khaiti.

Ever so slowly the Khaitians moved towards their prey.

"Hold still, Eastern dogs!" the sonorous voice of Amon Thoth boomed out in warning.

"The Star Stone belongs to us, Stygian filth!" shouted the leader of the five Khaitians, "and we intend to take it!"

The dusky faced Stygian's lips twisted into a loathing grimace. He eyed the Easterners with a mixture of hate mixed with some apprehension. He respected the power of these wizards from the East.

Motioning his warriors closer, the Stygian general was told to give the order for his men to take Zarum and Ja Nan into captivity. He wanted them both alive—for now. Carefully the Stygian warriors moved forward, weapons at the ready, for though they had vast numbers, they had heard of the ferocity of this barbarian.

"You will never take the stone if my good Turan blade has anything to say on the matter!" Zarum shouted in grim defiance. Then he let loose with a wild Calgar war cry.

"Take him!" ordered the Stygian priest. "He is but one man!"

"Try to take me, dogs!" Zarum growled as he quickly brought down his sword and clove the skull of his foremost adversary—a Stygian warrior who growing too eager, ran too far ahead of his companions. "That is the first one to die! Anyone else!"

For a moment the warriors stood back aghast. Shocked at the death of their comrade. Then their fear of their master naturally overcame their fear of the large barbarian who stood boldly in front of them. For at least the barbarian offered a natural sword death for them—as opposed to some demon-inspired death at the hands of the wizard Amon Thoth.

Zarum, however, did not allow his enemies to have even this slight respite, for with a wild barbarian war cry he quickly charged them with bloodied sword and dagger. He was on them instantly, a whirling, vicious, killing machine. They were certainly not expecting that action. Zarum was upon the Stygians cutting and slashing like a fiend, horrid were the cries as enemies quickly went to their doom.

Now the Khaitian wizards moved nearer. They watched the battle with intense interest. Their eyes blazed with a blue fire, their faces shone an ashen white.

Beads of sweat now glistened upon the face of Amon Thoth as he suddenly felt the blue beam of light encompass him now as well. The five wizards walked closer to Amon Thoth, oblivious of the terrific battle being waged between Zarum, Ja Nan and the Stygian warriors.

Zarum fought like a maddened bull. Slicing here, chopping there, while bodies were heaped about him. Ja Non too, although not of the warrior class made a good showing for himself by taking down one of the warriors and wounding another. The enemy grew to fear this priest of Mithra and his slim dagger of death.

Meanwhile, Amon Thoth stood by rigid and silent. The mysterious blue flame was more and more engulfing his form. He entire body was now soaked in sweat and began to shake, slowly at first and then more violently. Soon a single finger on the man's hand began to glow a violent malignant blue. Then ever so slowly, the rest of the body of the Stygian wizard took on the ghastly shade of violent blue flame.

"It is done, Tor Leh," the Khaitian leader said recovering with deep breaths from the power drain of the use of their magic. "The Stygian shall not interfere with us again."

"It all seemed so easy, My Lord," Tor Leh answered.

"He was but one and we are five! There could be no other result. Now we take the stone."

When Famar Khand, the chief priest of Mithra came upon the small battlefield he saw a grim play being enacted before him. There he saw the barbarian and Ja Nan, fiercely fighting many dusky Stygian warriors who now seemed most leery of getting too close to their deadly prey. He saw Amon

Zarum fought like a maddened bull.

Thoth, the master wizard of Set, engulfed in a blue flame, and he noticed the demon wizards of Khaiti walking confidently towards the battling barbarian. Then using magical gestures and words calling upon dark powers, the chief priest of Mithra caused the remaining assailants of Zarum and Ja Nan to turn into black willowy figures that became drifting smoke, to suddenly disappear upon the light breeze. In a moment all the Stygian warriors attacking Zarum were gone. The barbarian growled with delight at what he had just seen happen, and without a second to lose ran towards the wizards of Khaiti with a dark vehement hatred.

The five from the Far East were shocked and taken aback by the sudden head-long fury and imminent danger presented by the mad barbarian. With a mighty sword stroke he cut the head off of one of the fiends before he even knew what had happened, then with a vast backwards thrust sunk his blade deeply into the guts of one other. The wizards moved back in fear. So fast had been his attack, that he was able to kill two of their hideous number before they could employ their magic to save themselves, or to hold him fast. Now they held him unconscious.

"Do not kill the barbarian, Tor Leh! Not yet!" venerable Ujthol, leader of the Supreme Council ordered quickly. He looked at Zarum angrily, for two of his companions now lay dead at the barbarian's feet.

"After the Star Stone is ours, then we shall deal with this cur at our leisure."

A sinister smile came to the face of Tor Leh, as he quickly searched the unconscious form of Zarum for the stone. He looked up angrily, "It is not here, Master!"

Now all four remaining Eastern wizards converged upon the terrified figure of Ja Nan. The Mithran priest held his dagger out menacingly, there was Stygian blood upon his blade, and he slowly moved backwards.

"It is over now, priest. Give me the stone!" Ujthol demanded coldly.

It was then that Famer Khand and the priests of Mithra decided to show themselves. They had remained cloaked with invisibility until this moment. Now as they showed themselves, Ja Nan advanced towards them. It was then the Khaitians acted.

By now Zarum had regained consciousness and took in all that was happening in a glance. He found that now he was behind the wizards and could reach for his sword without being noticed. He did so most carefully and quietly while all the other's attention was occupied. He saw the wizards from the East and the Mithran priests with the nervous Ja Nan between them. Then he saw something else that sent his hair prickling the back of his neck.

Encased in an ominous flickering flame of azure stood the ultimate demon-wizard, Amon Thoth. He appeared to be motionless and frozen-like, but as Zarum looked upon him more closely it seemed he could detect a slight movement. So he was still alive.

However, now Zarum was too distracted to watch the form of the Stygian wizard, for just then with a horrible cry from Ja Nan, he knew the real battle had begun.

Turning from Amon Thoth, Zarum now saw that a new element had been added to the conflict. Screams rang out in hollow horror from both wizards and priests alike as Zarum saw a massive snake materialize instantly out of the air in front of them. It was exactly like the image of Set that Zarum had killed weeks ago outside the ruins of Zarf, excepting that this snake was much larger and looked to be much more formidable. Zarum was terrified – so were all the others. A hideous aurora of evil sprang from the thing, while a malignant intelligence glowed from its ghastly eyes. Zarum shuddered in terror for he now knew, as the others there also knew, that they were looking into the hideous eyes of the very snake god, Set, itself! Somehow it had been called to this earthly plane.

Those eyes! It was those horrid eyes! Red cobra eyes! They shone with a malignancy that every man there could feel. Here was purpose, cruel, cold, evil purpose. There was that doomed feeling of disgust as the coils slithered toward Ja Nan, and all stood petrified as the creature of the very gates of Hell itself, inched closer towards the Mithran priest. None could move, all were being held fast in the great serpent's power, and now even the mighty Khaitians seemed powerless.

As the beast moved closer and began to wind its coils around the helpless Ja Nan, the priest vomited in uncontrollable disgust as those loathsome scales tightly hugged his human skin. Quickly the snake-god from Hell completely encompassed the form of the man in its ever-tightening coils. A noxious odor permeated the atmosphere and a cloudy smoke rose in the air over the hideous monster.

Then the giant coils seemed to be unwinding, and when they did, it became apparent to all that Ja Nan was no more. His body gone. Not one vestige of the man remained.

If the horrid Hell-spawn lizard could smile, then the scaly facial expression surely would have shown such. Its utter contempt for human life was a terrible and loathsome thing to view, terrifying by all those left alive, still trapped motionless in its power.

Then slowly slithering forward, Set reared its ugly head up in evil pride. The fatty folds of its neck waved back and forth as it swayed slowly too and fro in some demonic hell dance. Zarum could see maggots and worms hanging from its eyes and scales, as the slimy tongue darted in and out of its foul mouth in a whispering hiss. Zarum had never seen such a creature, it truly was some kind of Hell-spawned nightmarish beast, even the one he had killed weeks ago had been nothing like this one. That one had been but an pale imitation of this vile thing, which Zarum knew was the original king of darkness itself. How it had been summoned here, was beyond the barbarian's understanding, as it was the Khaitian's and Mithran's as well.

Then Zarum heard the hissing grow louder, as the swaying of the giant snake became more pronounced and rhythmic. He tried to move, to free himself, but was still held in thrall by the creature's dark power, as were all the others. Zarum now thought that he heard speech coming from the scaly snake's lips.

The hissing whispers grew until all there could finally make out the slithering words.

"_Ssstar Ssstone!_" it demanded in a voice that mocked very humanity itself by its demonic sound.

Zarum had given the stone to Ja Nan, but if the evil snake-god Set did not have it, then who did?"

Horrid curses came from the frothing lips of the great snake, curses so seething in malignancy that Zarum wished he could cover his ears and get away from those terrible words – and the vile images they conjured up in his mind. The sound was horrendous! It was like all the tortured souls in Hell's depths writhing in one thousand unmentionable agonies. Fear and sweat covered every man's face as the snake from the bottomless pit slowly slithered forward, moving closer to the wizards from Khaiti.

The fear on the faces of the men from the Far East now was indescribable. The snake slowly, almost hypnotically, inched closer to the wizards and then stopped. The eyes of the scaly abomination glowed with a red radiance as it swayed with venomous jaws dripping noxious saliva. The odor was disgusting. Overpowering.

The eyes looked straight into the very souls of the Eastern wizards.

"Our... _our souls!_" they yelled out in agony.

"It is taking our souls!" another of them screamed in terror.

Soon the Khaitians fell to the ground with heart-rending cries of agony. No sooner had the bodies hit the earth than they became withered and then aged at an immense speed, until all that was left of the men were four small heaps of darkened ashes.

Now the snake-god slowly turned towards the priests of Mithra. A particularly vehement hatred came to the face of Set as its eyes looked upon these priests, who it knew were diametrically opposed to the rule of it upon the Earth. It had been hated men such as these who eons before in an earlier age of man had killed the Valusian serpent men, destroying the cult, and banishing Set's rule from this sphere of existence of the Earthly plane. Set hungered for the souls of such enemies as these!

Once more the serpent's eyes glowed a radiant red, the color of rich glowing blood. The eyes bore down upon the terrified Mithrans, even as they too, felt the power entering them and tugging at something that was not a physical nor mental part of their being. One priest, his lack of faith making him weaker than his companions, suddenly let out a cry of unfathomable pain and terror as he fell writhing to the ground. Soon his form was added to the other small heaps of dark ashes, all that remained when mighty Set devoured that which was mortal.

The other priests held on as well as they could, bolstered in their faith, but ever so slowly their will was being eaten away by this overwhelming force.

Zarum stood looking on in fascination at the priests, brave but helpless to move. Not one cry broke the lips of the courageous priests at the appalling sight. Try as he might, he could not move his great muscles. Though his giant frame shook in impotent rage, he could not as yet break this most potent of enchantments that had been placed upon him.

Suddenly Zarum noticed a dim yellow light pulsating on the ground where Ja Nan had last been standing, and a grim knowing smile came to the barbarian's face.

The Star Stone, Zarum realized! How had it come to be there? Ja Nan, certainly, had done it, somehow. Then he looked at the stone as he felt the presence of something inside his mind. It was not the seething evil of Set, but it was exceedingly powerful. A voice kept calling his name inside his mind, but seemingly from very far away, and under great strain. He felt the gaze of powerful eyes upon him, and now the voice was getting louder and louder. He turned and saw looking upon him the strained eyes of the chief Mithran priest, Famar Khand. He could now hear the priest's words. Suddenly with a screaming shriek another priest had his soul ripped out from him, to lay dead, a small heap of black ashes. Then the voice grew weaker and suddenly disappeared. One less priest alive had apparently diminished the voice that had been calling out to him. But what had it been trying to tell him? The presence in his mind had left him, and Zarum saw a look of hopelessness on the strained frozen face of Famar Khand.

Whatever it had been that the Mithran priest had been trying to tell him, Zarum would never know now. All his attention was riveted to the pulsating yellow orb which seemed to beckon him towards it.

"If I can not move and go to it," Zarum thought grimly, "then perhaps it will come to me!"

Immediately Zarum put forth all his strength of will into one unobstructed thought – calling the Star Stone to come to him.

Both the Mithran priests and the serpent-god Set were now too busy in their battle of wills and magic with each other to notice the Star Stone suddenly fly into the rigid hand of the barbarian.

No sooner had the stone come into his hand than Zarum felt the warmth of life-giving power surge throughout his motionless limbs. Suddenly he was motionless no longer. Immediately he was able to move once again. His first action, to retrieve his sword which was a few paces away. He grabbed up the weapon immediately.

Zarum now felt an invincible strength that ebbed from the stone into his body. Almost as immediate, evil Set realized that its hold upon the barbarian had now slipped, and reared its ugly head in rage. It turned around to see a defiant Zarum holding his bloody sword in one hand, and the glowing yellow Star Stone at arms length in the other hand. Slowly, with hissing jaws, the horrid abomination inched towards the barbarian, now ignoring the Mithran priests. Zarum gripped the stone and his sword as tightly as possible, ready for any eventuality.

If the face of the great serpent was capable of showing alarm, then surely its features were now twisted and bent into a parody of that fearsome expression.

The spell broken, Famar Khand and the remaining Mithran priests were now also capable of movement again, and they quickly moved to stand behind Zarum, as all Set's power over them had withdrawn at the sight of his new threat. The snake's ugly cobra head reared itself upwards over a hundred feet into the sky, as Zarum boldly moved towards it.

The big barbarian looked into the hollow eyes of Famar Khand, and the man replied to his unspoken question.

"It is impossible to kill the beast, barbarian, the most we can hope for is to banish it to its own plane of existence. To send it back to where it came from. You understand?"

"How, priest?"

"The Star Stone is our only hope, barbarian," the white-haired priest replied thoughtfully, now with a small flicker of hope visible in his old eyes. "This abomination was brought here by the Stygian wizard Amon Thoth, to help him take the stone. There are only two ways that Set can be forced out of our plane of reality. One is that the Stygian will order it away – most unlikely. The other, is that with the power of the Star Stone we may be able to force an impasse in the powers of magic. If we can render Set's power here impotent, we can then force it away. We must work fast, for even now the snake strikes and seeks to take the stone for itself."

Suddenly giant venomous jaws hissed down upon the large barbarian. Zarum, quickly handing Famar Khand the Star Stone, dove away from the attacking snake. Once away, he was immediately on his feet and let go with a terrible sword blow to the giant snake's sinuous coils. A stroke that would easily cut a man in two seemed to have no effect at all upon the demonic serpent.

Zarum cursed but defiantly stood his ground, continuing to fight and dive, cut and run, as the snake slowly moved closer to him. The barbarian thanked his lucky star that the reptilian god was so slow in its movements. That enabled Zarum to run in and attack quickly, to thrust in deeply, then escape before he could be touched. He was fast and the terror he felt at battling such a demon-spawned thing gave him incredible speed and energy.

The snake swayed forward in a slow rhythmic dance of hissing fury, eyes blazing a Hell-red color. Behind Zarum, the Mithran priests now shouted a slow sonorous chanting. In the eerie situation, it appeared that now Set danced, almost hypnotized by the strange chanting of the Mithran priests who were using the Star Stone to enhance their power. The priest's hypnotic chanting grew louder and more repetitious, slowly building up to an ear-piercing crescendo.

Famar Khand stood before the snake-god now. His arms outstretched, hands holding the Star Stone before him. The priest of Mithra walked closer until the rays of golden light from the stone shone upon the serpent's reptilian form. Now the gem's gold yellow light began to engulf the snake, covering it in a bright sun-like glow, as it stood there swaying in its own rhythm, with tongue darting in and out in anticipation. Soon the warm yellow glow from the Star Stone completely encompassed the huge form of the snake-god. It was then that the chanting by the Mithran priests, which had continued the entire time, suddenly grew louder reaching a new feverish pitch.

"Go back, foul demon!" Famar Khand now shouted at the huge beast, as the wind began to rise. There was movement in the atmosphere, magical and unnatural change. Darkness and light fought in the heavens. Great gusts of fetid air slammed the priest's face, but he held his ground. Zarum looked on in wonder as did the other Mithran priests. The sky darkened again and lightning flashed violently. Soon an unnatural freezing rain began to fall in massive windy drafts.

"Go back demon! I command you by the power of the Star Stone to return to the loathsome pit that is your vile home! Go down to the Hellish depths and loneness that shall be your fate for all eternity!" the priest chanted in a powerful voice demanding obedience.

What happened next was so unexpected that none were ready for it. The frozen blue form of the Stygian demon-wizard Amon Thoth slowly moved. He was beginning to work himself free from his magical prison. The blue flame was gone now, replacing it were blood red eyes of hate and the deadly corruption of abject evil.

Amon Thoth moved forward holding up a withdrawn dagger, and into the unguarded neck of the Mithran chief priest, he deeply sunk his blade. Blood gushed out in thick red spurts from the high priest, who instantly dropped down to the ground and was soon dead. The sacred stone falling from his fingers to roll upon the ground.

Immediately Zarum grasped up the gem in his hand. Then with his sword, he struck the onrushing Stygian wizard with the flat of his blade. He hit the man hard, and the wizard quickly fell to the ground unconscious. Zarum immediately turned towards the giant snake-god, Set.

In that one moment of chaos, the snake moved forward ready to strike at the barbarian, and the barbarian spit in defiant terror to meet it.

Zarum rushed upon the demon-god with sword held high and the Star Stone held tightly in his white knuckled fingers. He was almost transfixed by terror and his fear of the supernatural – but he was also a barbarian who would never admit defeat. So he fought on, attacking the demon-god. From behind him he heard the strange rhythmic chanting of the Mithran priests resume, growing ever louder.

"Back to where you came from, you filth!" Zarum growled savagely, in frantic shouts of rage and fear, as he used the Star Stone to shower its bright yellow light upon the snake-god. "This is one soul you'll never take! Your days are done here! Go back to whatever foul smelling pit you crawled out of!"

Once more the snake-god swayed in evil anticipation of attacking before the yellow glow of the sacred gem encompassed its complete form. Meanwhile the chanting of the priests grew louder and more powerful, reaching almost fantastical proportions. Sweat dripped down Zarum's body in tiny rivers, and he felt all the terror of the superstitious barbarian, yet he remained resolute. He would not surrender! He could feel that the stone was sending immense power through him, for without it, he would never be able to do what he was doing now – and what he was about to do!

Zarum carefully moved in front of the hideous swaying beast, as he noticed the chanting had reached some kind of climax and had suddenly stopped. That was the sign. The result was that now wild screams and screeches stung the barbarian's ears coming from the giant snake. The noise was incredible, almost a physical force. Suddenly the giant snake-god Set – shimmered in a yellow glow – and then it completely disappeared! It was now gone! Set had disappeared, as mysteriously as it had arrived, no trace being left to show that it had ever been there.

Zarum let out a deep sigh of relief and whipped the terror-sweat that was dripping from his forehead. Quickly he turned to see the form of Amon Thoth standing behind him, the wizard now spoke in a trance-like tone.

"You have broken my power, barbarian! You have sent Mighty Set back to the pit! The Star Stone is yours for now, and I can not hope to take it. Not yet. But I will have that stone, barbarian. Some day I shall have it, and then I shall have you also!"

"Rot in Hell, wizard!" Zarum spit. Then before he could swing his sword and cut the vile wizard in half, the form of Amon Thoth suddenly disappeared.

Zarum looked at the few remaining Mithran priests, who were now recovering from their recent frantic chanting and prayers. Here was victory, hard won and high priced, but victory nevertheless. A hardy grin crossed the barbarian's scared face as he put away his sword and thanked Mighty Crom he was still alive.

EPILOGUE:

Already a week had gone by and the small sack of gold coins was almost empty. A deep scowl crossed Zarum's face at the thought of all he had been through recently, and yet, it soon turned into a deep grin at the affections of the two young beauties who were seated upon his lap. The tavern was full and busy and he had plenty to drink so things had not turned out so bad after all. Slowly the big barbarian took a deep draught of the sweet Nemedian wine.

The barbarian's thoughts drifted to the sacred Star Stone resting safe in a vault deep within the temple of Mithra, and a small sigh left his lips. He could have bought himself a small kingdom with that gem, but he was actually relieved to be rid of it. Let the priests handle that problem from now on. He was happy the business was finally over with and that now his numerous wounds were healing.

Zarum took another deep draught of the Nemedian wine. To him it was the wine of victory and it tasted sweet. He gently squeezed the ample rumps of the two wenches upon his lap, and then stood up and walked away from the table and the young women.

"Zarum! Zarum! Where are you going?" one of his tavern wenches asked him sheepishly.

Without turning the big barbarian replied, "I tire of whoring and drinking. I hear they are in need of mercenaries in Aqualonia, something about a Pictish invasion. So it is there that I may go now. Or perhaps, not. I have not yet decided."

"Stay here! Stay with us!" the young women asked him, most passionately.

Zarum just smiled and walked out of the tavern, and soon was on a speedy mount riding over the windy plains towards Aqualonia and the gleaming city of Tarantia, the capitol city of the Golden Kingdom. And the capitol of his destiny! For a wizard had once foretold that he would become the king of that mighty kingdom, and he knew that some day he would go there to see if the prophecy was true or not. For now, however, he thought better of it and he turned his mount around and headed back to Agraphur, for he felt he still had unfinished business in the Kingdom of Turan.

THE END

THE BLACK HAND OF SET

Prince Yezdergrid of Turan was in an imperial fury as he briskly trod the long corridors of the royal palace in Agraphur, to the sumptuous apartments of his father, Yildiz, the King. At his side, trying his best to keep up with the royal youth, was Kaduthies, the court councilor.

"Ease your steps my prince," Kaduthies pleaded, striving to catch his breath as he followed behind his lord. "I am an old man and can not match your furious pace."

"Then be left behind!" Yezdergrid growled, never one to be considerate of others. He was full of rage against his imperial father on a subject that for too long had gone unspoken between them. "I mean to have this out once and for all and he'll not put me off again!"

"But think, My Prince," the councilor added between gasps of breath, "he is not only your father, but the king. It is risky even for a son to go against the wishes of a king."

"The matter is at a head now, and I shall see it through," the prince responded, as he imperiously passed members of The Immortals. These were the King's elite bodyguard, and were stationed at all intersections in the corridors throughout the palace. As he passed they came rigidly to a saluting posture. Yezdergrid passed them by without so much as a glance.

"We are almost there, sire," Kaduthies added quietly. "Will you not give this up until a more opportune moment? Perhaps when your mother returns from her visit in the south, then perhaps the two of you may join forces to sway the mind of the king to see things your way?"

"No! I will not be put off any longer. He promised me men—men and ships— that I could use in my conquests. Where are they, Kadithies? He has me cooling my heels here in the capital for almost a year, wasting my time in useless feasts and parties and the entertainments of his pleasure garden."

"My lord, are these not worthy pursuits for a young royal warrior prince?"

"For others perhaps, old man, but not for me. I grow weary of this idleness. I have the red hot blood of conquest in my veins and it must not be denied," Yezdergrid growled and his eyes seemed to stare off as if seeing into unknown realms.

The worry on Kaduthies' face deepened. Perhaps the rumored madness of the mother was also present in the son? If so the throne of Turan, unsteady at best, would be in even worse hands when the son became king. Kaduthies had no illusion as to Yezdergrid's reign, one of oppression at home and aggression abroad, and always conscription and burdensome taxation to bleed the people for ever more coin and men for his ever voracious conquests.

"Ever since Makalet, I have felt this destiny in my breast," the prince continued. Kaduthies eyed him carefully, then the prince added, "It is a fate to be written upon the book of nations. In the end know this Kaduthies; Turan shall be the world—and the world shall be mine!"

"I fear you talk too rashly sire, your ambition...?"

A large gloved hand slammed into the face of Kaduthies and he fell back with a gasp of pain and hurt that was more than merely physical.

"Dare you tell me of how I may speak! Hold your tongue old man, lest you loose it! My ambition is great, but it will be fulfilled," Yezdergrid growled. The torches in the corridor shone upon a sinister smile that played over moist thin lips, then with regal impatience he looked back to see Kaduthies rising and following him. "Come now. Be quick about it, we near the chambers of the king."

It had been a quiet night at the Griffin Shield. Most of the regular patrons of the tavern were out on patrol or had other duties as the sun rose lazily in the sky. There was however, one customer, a large dark-manned barbarian mercenary who now wore the uniform of a Turanian captain. He was seated quietly in a dark corner alone with his grim thoughts.

"More ale?" a shapely barmaid asked a bit apprehensively as she neared the sullen barbarian. He was young and wildly handsome and she was surely attracted to him, but she saw he was also very troubled—so she knew he could be trouble. She quickly put down another full tankard and was just as quickly gone.

Zarum, late of the vast northern Calgar Wastes, sat alone in moody contemplation. He had returned just last night past with his command. They had been searching the hills outside the city for a thief, or a group of thieves, who had stolen certain treasures from the Grand Library of Agraphur. What these treasures were, Zarum did not know, for they were said to be hidden in a sealed box of strange metal, a box forbidden to be opened under penalty of death.

Finally Zarum and his men caught the thieves after a short battle where all but one was killed. Zarum brought the single prisoner and the strange box back to the palace where he hoped to receive a small reward for himself and his men. At the palace he had been turned away by the King's Immortals, and did not even receive a thank you for a job well done. Worse yet, he was ordered to have his men ready that morning for a ride to Fort Ghorl, a ride of some distance with weary horses and exhausted men.

The barbarian was angry at being treated with so little respect. Even though he was a barbarian—and used to the contempt of others because of it—he was not used to having his pouch so empty of the pay that he and his men had justly earned. Traditionally the army paid the outlanders of mercenary companies last, and when funds were short because of some excess of the king—then often as not—payment was very slow in coming. If ever. This angered the big barbarian.

When Yusef, Zarum's lieutenant, entered the tavern, he saw that his commander was not in the best of moods. With a bit of caution he neared the still form of the grumpy barbarian.

"Commander?" he asked meekly.

Zarum looked at the youth. "Aye, lad. What is it?"

"It is now daybreak," he said, in an effort to remind his commander of their orders to ride to Fort Ghorl.

Zarum nodded, and was just getting up from his seat when he heard a loud gong reverberate in the distance. Soon afterwards came a whole chorus of more loud gongs and chimes which created a veritable din throughout the city.

"By the gods! What can that racket be?" Zarum grumbled, looking to Yusef.

But Yusef's face only turned pale as his eyes widened with disbelief and growing fear.

"What is it? Out with it, lad!" Zarum growled impatient, but he could see that temporally the youth was incapable of responding.

—

When Yezdergrid, with Kaduthies close behind, neared the huge ornate door that marked the entrance to the King's royal apartments, both men immediately noticed that something seemed wrong.

"Where are my father's Immortals?" Yezdergrid asked angrily. "Find out from the night captain who is to be on duty here, and I want them sent to the mines in the morning. Mayhap that will teach them something about discipline and duty."

"Sire, I fear that it is something more than that," Kaduthies whispered fearfully. "I would draw my sword if I were you, before we enter here."

Yezdergrid looked to the councilor and the smile on his face melted away as he saw the fear in Kaduthies features. The prince drew his sword and with a mighty boot, kicked open the door to the king's royal apartment.

All was quiet in the half-light of the enormous apartment. There was no sign of the two bodyguards who should have been at the door as the prince and councilor walked through the ornate sitting room and to the door that led to King Yildiz's private bedchamber.

Cautiously, Yezdergrid opened the door a crack so that he and Kaduthies could look into the room.

They saw that the great chamber was empty of any intruders, and that upon the bed snoring restfully was Yildiz, the king of Turan.

"There is no one here," Yezdergrid whispered curiously. "The king seems to be sleeping soundly."

"Aye, sire, so it appears. Still I like it not. Where are his Immortals?" Kaduthies asked. "You should call out the guards."

"They shall be found and dealt with for deserting their posts," the prince added with a crooked leer, amazed that palace Immortals had deserted their king. This was untenable. "I shall see to it myself."

"There is no one here and all seems right. Still I do not like it, sire. I have the feeling that something is dreadfully wrong."

Yezdergrid smiled imperiously, "Are you scared, old man? Very well, we will enter and investigate the apartment to ease your fears. Then I shall awaken my royal father and have this matter out between us."

The prince and Kaduthies quietly entered the bedroom, and having searched the room and finding that there was no one else there beside themselves, they moved over towards the bed where the king lay sleeping so soundly.

Kaduthies was about to advise his young prince about the disadvantages in disturbing sleeping monarchs, when suddenly he thought that his old eyes were deceiving him—for he saw a small shape moving under the blanket approaching the king's chest.

"Sire, the blanket moves!" he yelled out in warning.

Yezdergrid had also seen the moving shape and instantly grew alarmed. With the speed of a warrior's reflexes, Yezdergrid's free hand grabbed the blanket pulling it off of the sleeping king.

What the two men saw there sent shivers of fear through them.

"By Tarim!" Yezdergrid cried out in horror. "Can such a thing be possible?"

"The great god Tarim has very little to do with this, my lord!" Kaduthies mumbled as a cold fear gripped him.

For there, walking upon the body of the motionless king of Turan, was a horrid, black dismembered human Hand moving with a life of its own, upon its five fingers as if they were spider legs. Blood was evident on the stump where the member had been severed, and yet it moved upon its five fingers with a life of its own like some grotesque spider-like creature. Both men stared in horrible fascination as the hand slowly moved to a position over the king's heart.

"Kill it with your sword!" Kaduthies shouted in terror.

"I can not move!" Yezdergrid cried back fearfully, astonished and terrified. "My legs and sword arm are as if frozen!"

"Tarim preserve us from this!" Kaduthies whispered in horror. He found that he could not move either. "By the gods, the thing is going for your father's heart!"

Yezdergrid screamed in terror and rage. "We must do something!"

"I wish that I could My Prince, but this is a most powerful sorcery, one that I cannot counteract. I have heard legends of such a demon Hand as this, one that was called the Hand of Nergral, but I have read where the great wizard Skelos has written of an even deadlier one. It is called the Black Hand of Set!"

"Do something quickly! I command you! It will kill my father!" Yezdergrid howled, still unable to move a muscle in the king's defense.

In hopeless horror both men watched as the Hand—now positioned over the king's heart, used its long steel-like fingernails to bore down into the flesh and bone—into the very chest of the aged and motionless king. Relentlessly it groped about inside so that for a moment only the severed stump was visible, and then it withdrew in its large fist, a red mass of pulsating flesh.

"It has taken your father's heart!" Kaduthies cried in horror. "By all the gods, what manner of sorcery is this that has befallen us?"

Yezdergrid watched then as the hand moved off holding its terrible prize in a tightened fist. Then to both men's amazement the Hand suddenly disappeared.

It was gone!

Now able to move once again, the prince and Kaduthies rushed to the side of the dead king.

"What do we do now?" the prince asked in shock.

"It is not for me to say, sire," Kaduthies said quietly, his mind swirling in fear and confusion. "It is up to you to decide. You are the King of Turan now!"

Zarum was fast loosing his patience with the lad, Yusef. He grabbed him roughly by the shoulders and shook him for a bit to gain his attention. Yusef started as if coming out of a drunken stupor.

"I asked you, lad, what is the meaning of all this noise?" the barbarian commander repeated now that he had his full attention.

"It is the funeral chimes."

"So some old dog of a noble has died, eh?" Zarum asked gruffly. What did he care?

Yusef lowered his head as if in contrition, "It is the king. King Yildiz is dead."

For a moment Zarum stood silent. He did not really like the fat little old man who sat upon the Peacock Throne, but he knew that with the old king gone, also went the old laws. Perhaps even *all* law? He knew Yidliz's son, Yezdergrid, from a few years back and he knew that his rule would be much harsher than that of his father. Zarum thought about it, tough days coming in Turan, for sure. Then he shrugged it all off. What did it matter to him of the rise and fall of kings, so long as he did not fall with them. He would take his pay and then leave if things became too hot for him.

"Cheer up lad," Zarum mused with a sly grin. "Things can not be that bad, mayhap this new king will see fit even to pay us our back wages."

Yusef quietly walked away and Zarum followed him out into the street. Once outside Zarum could hear the wailing and screams that were heard throughout the city. He saw women walking by, heads covered in black scarves and bowing, singing sad dirges to the god Tarim for the blessing of their dead king.

Zarum grunted skeptically. Yesterday the people hated the king, many was a man—and woman too—who would have slit his royal throat had they only the chance. Now they mourn him as they would have a lost lover. Civilization does strange things to people, Zarum thought, as he quietly walked to where his men had gathered.

When one of the warriors saw him coming, he broke from the group, and ran to his commander.

"Captain, our orders have been changed. You are ordered to go to the palace immediately and see Minister Kaduthies."

The big barbarian growled unhappily, "What now?"

—

Once at the palace Zarum found it in a state of curious pandemonium. There was a primal fear flooding in the air, and the courtiers and soldiers-at-arms were seen whispering with nervous apprehension. He heard hints of rumors, half sentences that told of the king dying—and by some horrible and foul means. Dark sorcery of the foulest sort was mentioned a number of times, and the barbarian could feel the hairs on the nape of his neck prickle at the very thought of such unnatural things.

On being stopped and questioned by a guard, Zarum told the man of his summons by Minister Kaduthies.

"Aye, so you are the barbarian we have been hearing so much about?" the guardsman said more to his fellow than to Zarum.

"I am the one," Zarum said with grim impatience.

"I hear this one's a real fighter, Ahmed," the other guard told his mate with a smile of contempt. "Well you'll not get a station in the Immortals for all your pain, my friend. We do not trust outlanders, nor barbarian dogs here in the palace. They have filthy manners."

"I'll show you dogs manners!" Zarum barked and quickly whipped out his sword. The speed of his movement was so rapid that it took both guardsmen aback. "Well what are you waiting for, dogs? Though you call yourselves Immortals, I'll wager I can make you bleed and die like anyone else!"

Ahmed's face paled, but a crowd had now formed wanting to see the fight and he had no choice but to draw his sword also. As he did so, an officer came over and dangerously stepped between Zarum and Ahmed. The man quickly held up his hands in a gesture of peace.

"Hold your fight, barbarian!" the officer pleaded, calmly. "My friend has a loud and stupid mouth, but I have no wish to see you spill his blood. You are here to see Minister Kaduthies, so you had best go about your business. You will find Lord Kaduthies through those doors yonder."

With a grim smile Zarum sheathed his sword as the other guardsman did likewise. Then with a brisk trot he walked to the indicated chamber, opened the door and entered.

Inside the lavishly furnished room, seated at a large desk was an old man, about him were a dozen yammering courtiers and officers. Zarum stood with folded arms a few feet away from his desk until the old man looked up and saw him.

"Aye, barbarian, so you are here," Kaduthies said showing some relief. "All of you leave me now; I wish to be alone with this man."

When the chamber was finally emptied Kaduthies offered the barbarian a seat. He pointed to an ornate flask upon his desk.

"Wine?" Kaduthies asked in a friendly enough manner.

"I'll take a goblet. Thank you," Zarum replied gruffly, wondering what this man wanted of him. When he had the wine he took a sip and then looked intently at Lord Kaduthies. Lowly captains are not summoned into the palace to speak to royal ministers for no good reason. He knew he must be careful here. "Now what did you want to see me about? I am to leave with my men soon for Fort Ghorl."

"Forget about Fort Ghorl," Kaduthies replied hastily. Quickly he tried to size up this barbarian before him. That he was big and strong and a good fighter there could be no doubt. There was also a quiet smoldering intelligence lurking behind those cold blue northern eyes. Perhaps this was just the man that Kaduthies had been looking for after all?

"You know, of course, that our great king, Yildiz, is dead."

"I'll take a goblet. Thank you."

"I heard," Zarum replied wondering how he was tied up in any of this.

"And you know that his son, Yezdergrid is now king?" Kaduthies added, "One Thousand Blessings Be Upon Him!"

"So I have heard. It is what he always wanted after all."

Kaduthies' face reddened. "You are full of impudence, barbarian. I would watch my tongue if I were you."

"Thanks for the advice. Now let us get on with it. What is it you want from me?" Zarum asked sternly.

Kaduthies took a deep breath and held his anger in check not a little because of his fear of the giant before him. "Yezdergrid has sworn vengeance for the death of his noble father…"

Zarum grunted, then smiled, wondering what that had to do with him.

Kaduthies frowned, "You smile barbarian. No, Yezdergrid was not responsible for the killing…"

"That is a surprise!" Zarum said with a wider grin. "He is an ambitious lad."

"Be that as it may, the king—the new king—wants the heads of all those involved in his father's death."

"That I can understand."

"Of course."

"So just how was Yildiz killed?" Zarum asked carefully.

"By the foulest means possible," Kaduthies replied unable to hold back the fear of what he had seen with his very own eyes. Then he told the barbarian of what he and Yezdergrid had seen in the old king's bedchambers.

Zarum listened intently, the chill of dark sorcery unnerving him more than a bit.

"You are sure about this Hand?" Zarum asked quietly.

"I can see that it scares you too, barbarian. I too felt horror when I saw it; with my own eyes slay our king. Yezdergrid is near panic, and wants his father's killers caught before they decide to do away with him also—perhaps even in a similar manner! It is not a pleasant way for a man to die, barbarian," Kaduthies added with a deep sigh.

Zarum could see that the minister was not far from panic himself at just the thought of the events he had seen last night. He had seen a vision from Hell and it was now indelibly etched into his mind. The terror was very real.

"What do you want from me? And more importantly, what do I get out of it?" Zarum asked firmly. "And even if I decide to help you, where do I begin? Do you even know who is behind the sorcery that moves this Hand?"

"As to your price, if you succeed, you can name it from the king. Does that not please you?"

"Aye, it sounds right enough," Zarum replied thoughtfully. "We'll talk of that later. Now what of this Hand?"

"It is called The Black Hand of Set. It was once the hand of a young King of Stygia called Tothimedies, who began to forsake the worship of Set and instituted a different religion in its place. Well needless to say, the priesthood took offense at this infringement of their power and a civil war soon broke out. While the king's army was small, great was their fighting ability, and in a short time they began to take an upper hand in the war. Faced with defeat, the Stygian ring rulers turned to desperate measures, and they brought forth into the world the power that now resides within the Hand. That ancient Stygian king, so says the legend written in Skelos, one day dug his own hand into his chest and pulled out his beating heart with his very own blood-drenched fingers!"

Zarum was silent but looked intently uncomfortable.

Kaduthies sighed deeply and continued, "The Stygian king's men at arms, in rage and horror at what his offending hand had done, scornfully cut it off. Later they sealed it in a small metal box and hurled it into the sea. Upon its lid, carved in all the Hyborean languages, was a dire warning not to open the box on pain of terrible death."

Outwardly Zarum listened calmly, yet his insides were now a seething cauldron of intense emotions. Could it have been the same box that he had just rescued from the thieves? Is that the thing that the box contained? Zarum visibly shrank back, as though he had come into contact with something unclean.

Kaduthies' eyes narrowed and he looked at the barbarian intently. Did he know something? It seemed so. Quickly he described to him the strange box as it was described in the book of Skelos.

"What do you know, barbarian?" Kaduthies said curiously. "You can not fool me. I can see it in your eyes."

Zarum smiled grimly, "It may be nothing, then again…"

"Tell me!" Kadithies ordered.

"My mission. A day ago I was commanded to take my company and track some thieves and recover what they had stolen. Of the stolen items I brought back, one such item was a box of strange metal like you describe. I was ordered upon pain of death not to open it. Not that I did not try, but thought I broke two good blades upon the seal, the box would not yield."

"It is sealed by sorcery, and can only be opened in that manner," Kaduthies said surprised that the barbarian had even tried to open the box, but relieved that he was finding out some facts. "But this is wonderful news! The box is here—so who did you deliver it to?"

The big barbarian looked intently at the minister.

"What is it? Why do you look at me like that? Now tell me, who did you deliver the box to?"

Zarum replied calmly, "I delivered it to you. Do you not remember?"

Kaduthies looked shocked, horrified, "Me! Are you insane? Me, barbarian! Do you know what it is that you are saying?"

Zarum smiled, shrugged, "I brought the stolen goods and one prisoner to the palace. The box was with me also. The captain of the guards, Alem Kan, ordered me to turn my prisoner and goods to him to hand to you—or a man who looked just like you. At the time I did not know who you were. He told me that you would be very happy that your property was back safe with you once more."

Kaduthies looked aghast. "Why this is unbelievable, someone has stolen my form, my image! Traitors in the palace itself!"

"Hah!" Zarum laughed grimly. "If they could kill a king in such a way, this does not surprise me."

"Right you are, Captain," Lord Kaduthies said quietly. He was beginning to form a keen respect for this wily barbarian. Ah, if but all soldiers of Turan were like this man, then surely Yezdergrid might have all his dreams of empire come true.

"Of course you know that these goods were stolen from the Royal Library."

"I figured as much. Or the palace. They were not your average rich noble's trinkets. Most of the things looked like junk to me anyway, and I was glad to be rid of them."

"One thing puzzles me," Kaduthies asked rubbing his chin contemplatively.

"Only one thing?" Zarum laughed.

Kaduthies allowed a slim smile, "If these goods were stolen from the Royal Library as I believe, and it appears that is the case, then where did the box with this horrible Hand come from? For certain I know we had no such demonic item hidden here. Oh, there is a copy of the *Book of Skelos*, and a few other items of mild magical interest, but never would any abomination such as this Hand be allowed to enter the precincts of the palace without my knowing."

"You are sure about that?" Zarum asked with a skeptical leer. His curiosity too was now piqued.

"Dead sure, barbarian. Such a portent is too dangerous to even keep in the capital here," the councilor admitted. "And unthinkable in the palace."

"I think then, that these thieves I tracked down were working for the original owner of the Hand. It was probably stolen from some wizard originally, and he tried to have it stolen back."

"And you took it from his men, and gave it back to the original thieves who used it to kill the king?" Kaduthies asked at last. He did not look overly happy.

"It looks that way, but I had my orders," Zarum stated, as a matter of fact.

"Very good reasoning," another voice whispered from a dark corner of the room. Here there were long hangings that stood draping magnificently down to the ground like a mass of shadowy and mysterious shapes. A man could easily hide behind them.

"Who is there?" Kaduthies demanded, while Zarum drew his sword and cautiously walked over to the hangings.

"Come out of there, or I'll cut you down where you stand!" the barbarian warned with firm and deadly meaning. There was no hint of fear in his fierce words—it was dire death he was promising. Kaduthies inwardly trembled at the thought of ever having to go up against this barbarian giant.

Carefully with his sword point the barbarian parted the large hangings to reveal to his astonishment that there was no one hidden behind them. There was no one there.

"I am over here!" the voice now whispered in a fierce tone from behind Zarum and Kaduthies. Both men turned instantly, to view walking from behind the large wall hangings at the other end of the room, a tall man enshrouded in a dark hooded robe.

"Be not alarmed. You are not in any danger from me. Be assured that if I wanted either of you dead, you would even now be laying lifeless upon this floor."

Zarum swore, "Wizard, you move quickly!"

"It was but a trick, barbarian," Kaduthies said regaining his composure. "The man obviously has a talent for throwing his voice. He can be hidden in one place and make his voice seem to be coming from another."

"Aye sounds like sorcery to me," Zarum growled in anger. He did not like this kind of thing. He still hung on securely to his drawn sword.

"Not sorcery, but a well learned trick," Kaduthies repeated calmly, hopefully. However, he could see the man was a Stygian, and that surely meant sorcery. Often, sorcery of the most foul kind. "What I want to know is how long this Stygian has been hidden in my chambers, and what he has heard of our conversation."

"Aye, wizard, or whatever you are," Zarum barked. "Who are you and what do you want here?"

The tall lean figure stood rigid and silent for a long moment. His hood and floor-length robe of black completely obscured his features. All that was visible to the two men were the two red eyes that stared at them from beneath the overhanging cowl, and the long, boney dusky fingers that were covered with a wealth of strange jeweled rings.

Kaduthies had no idea how the man had even entered the palace, much less his personal apartment. He was thinking of what the man had heard. He was also thinking that he was going to have all the floor-length hangings removed from the palace immediately. He was thinking of calling the guards, but was too scared to do so. Then the intruder finally spoke.

"My name is unimportant," the tall robed figure stated with confidence and impatience. "And as to how much of your conversation I have heard, rest assured I heave heard enough. It may interest you to know that I arrived here but a few moments before the barbarian did."

Kaduthies looked uneasy, so that meant he knew everything. "Then what is it you want? Answer me, before I call the guards!"

"Your guards will not answer your summons. They are under my control for now. Forget them. What do I want? I want what was stolen from me and my Brothers of The Ring. Return to me the Black Hand of Set!"

Zarum was thinking of gutting the intruder with his sword right away, but the minister motioned him to ease up on any violence. For now.

"If you have heard what we were saying," Kaduthies replied nervously, "you will know that I do not have the hand, nor do we know who does."

"I know that," the mysterious figure whispered.

"Then if you know who does have the damned Hand, why do you not go and take it yourself?" Zarum asked boldly. His own hand still grasped his sword tightly; he did not trust wizards and was ready to run this one through. Or at least, to die trying.

A sound of grim impatience escaped from the lips of the intruder. "The talisman was stolen by a thief; it must be recovered by a thief. If my brethren and I were to become involved in its overt recovery it would cause the unleashing of certain forces that might prove detrimental to the delicate power balance in our world. I can not make you understand the caution and delicate action that is required here. The very gods themselves could fall, to be replaced by...well..."

"You wizards are so powerful!" Zarum barked. "Do it yourself!"

There was a snake-like hiss of contempt from the figure in black. Both Zarum and Kaduthies took a fearful pace backwards, not knowing what would now come of all this.

"Fool of a barbarian!" the intruder whispered in disgust. It was more a statement of fact than insult. If the wizard was getting angry, well then, so was Zarum also. He held on tightly and meaningfully to his sword, awaiting only the command from Kaduthies, for him to slay this vile wizard. But the command did not come.

Lord Kaduthies regaining his composure walked forward a few paces, "Sir, wizard or not, we shall help you in any way we are able, if you can show us how both our interests may be served by doing so."

Zarum looked at the minister aghast, growling a curse at devious political scheming. Always scheming.

"Very well. My Brethren and I have been the possessors of the Hand of Set for more years than you would care to count. It is a reservoir of power that we rarely use, but must be in our possession, for our power and influence over magical events will begin to wane if we do not possess it."

"So good, let your powers wane and then disappear!" Zarum growled defiant.

"Halt your aggression, barbarian!" Kaduthies ordered firmly.

Zarum nodded, acceptance of the minister's words, but he did not like it.

The wizard hissed and continued, "The talisman is now in the hands of an Eastern wizard called Aldakar, an Iranistani, who resides in this city."

"Aye," Kaduthies remarked with a nod of his head. "I have heard the name. So he is the murderer of our king whom we seek?"

"No, he is but the device that moves the Hand," the Stygian wizard continued in a harsh voice. "The man who ordered your king's death is a captain of his personal bodyguard, Alem Kan."

"So it was he!" Zarum growled. "The very captain I entrusted my prisoner, and the stolen goods to. Including the box with the Hand in it. Damn him! I never liked him!"

"The very same, barbarian," the wizard now replied to the Northman. "But this imperial conspiracy grows deeper and twists and turns like the mighty coils of sacred Set himself. For brave Captain Alem Kan also receives his orders, orders from another, who is high in the Royal household itself."

Kaduthies looked mystified at this revelation and did not like where it might lead, but he knew he had to know. Finally he blurted, "So who is it? Give me the name?"

The Stygian ordered simply, "First I want the Hand from Aldaker the Iranistani, then I shall give you the name behind the death of your king. Do not be fooled because Aldakar is one man, with the power of the Black Hand of Set, this impudent cur is a power equal to the Brotherhood of the Ring itself! Such a battle of equals will avail us naught, whereas if a lone thief could gain entrance by stealth and steal the Hand, it would be unexpected and perhaps even succeed. Had we but the right man to do the deed."

"Aye," Zarum growled, so now it came to him. "And after all, one more dead thief is nothing so long as your precious hides remain safe—and you obtain what you desire!"

"Take care with your words, outlander," the Stygian warned. "It is help and information that I offer you. Be wise, and take it."

"Wizard help!" Zarum spit out the words.

"Any help, from any source, is valuable, fool!"

"We help others best, when we help ourselves," Kaduthies offered wisely.

The Stygian smiled at the remark. "Barbarian, listen to Lord Kaduthies. Aldakar has a castle on the outskirts of Agraphur. It is guarded by things natural and supernatural, but I shall give you what aid I can."

Then from within his robes the wizard brought forth a dull medallion upon a long chain which he held out in his long bony fingers.

"Take this small item of magic, barbarian. Place it around your neck and it will ward off all guardians and demons summoned from the Ninth Plane. These are the creatures which Aldakar uses in his service, for the most part."

Zarum looked at the dull medallion and chain being offered to him in the outstretched hand of the Stygian. His hatred of all things that smacked of sorcery was easily seen in his manner and he hesitated to take the proffered gift. In fact, he took a step back away from it.

"You cannot secede without this medallion," the Stygian countered with a grim leer. "It will offer you at least some protection against those things you may fear most. The Ninth Plane is not a particularly pleasant place and its inhabitants sometimes prove difficult for even the followers of mighty Set to control."

With practical reasons, or in abject fear—or a combination of both overtaking his reluctance and hatred of sorcery—Zarum snatched up the medallion and placed it around his neck.

"Very good," the Stygian said assuredly. "Now, when the middle of the night arrives, you are to seek entrance into the abode of Aldakar. Where the Hand is hidden I do not know, but you should try first the library on the second floor of his manse. I will see to it that Aldakar will not be at his home for two hours this night. Be warned, barbarian, a time of two hours is all that I can promise you!"

"Well, Zarum?" Kaduthies asked quietly, thoughtful. There was no way he could really blame the barbarian if he did not want to do the job. Kaduthies knew that even had he the youth and strength of Zarum, he would never do such a thing. It was far too dangerous. Even foolish. "So what have you decided?"

Zarum said not one word.

"I am sure that King Yezdergrid shall reward you —-" Kaduthies offered but was quickly cut off by the barbarian.

"King Yezdergrid hates my guts! Who do you think it was who gave him the scar on his face during the siege of Makalet?"

"He is rash and impulsive—but he is a king now and..."

"And a damn brat by his actions. Why if he knew that it was I in this chamber with you now, he would send a hundred of his much vaulted Immortals here to separate my head from my shoulders!"

"I did not know this, barbarian," Kaduthies said quietly. "Then I know not what I can promise you for such a risky venture."

"Perhaps, barbarian…?" the Stygian began in a silken whisper.

"I will take no sorcerous reward!" Zarum replied nervously. Then he looked once again to Kaduthies, "Give me and my men the back pay that is ours by right, and a hundred Turanian Eagles each, along with the time to spend it."

Kaduthies' face brightened, for this was nothing. The barbarian must be mad. He asked, "And that is all, Zarum? Why, you could ask for a small dukedom of your own!"

"Aye, I could ask for the treasury of the Royal Palace, but I know what I' will get from Yezdergrid!"

Kaduthies smiled, he knew his young king only too well. "So be it, Zarum."

Silently the huge barbarian strode out of the chamber.

⸻

The moon rose full in the heavens over the house of Aldakar the Iranistani. With so much light, Zarum knew that this was a bad evening for any thief to go about his work. However, perhaps on a night such as this, when no thief in his right mind would risk the bright light of the moon's revealing rays, would be the exact time when such action would be unexpected. Then perhaps, it might be the best night after all for the dangerous business at hand. Or so he hoped.

The abode of the wizard, in reality more like a small fortress, was barely discernable behind a high wall that encircled the house and its grounds, effectively hiding all that went on inside from the inquisitive eyes of any wandering passersby.

Zarum watched the area intently for a time. He noticed that the house was two floors in height, and that the top floor was absent of all windows or openings. That would be his destination, the library of Aldakar. On the south side of the house's wall was a small gate. The only exit or entrance that he could see at that wall. It was guarded heavily by a dozen armed mercenaries. These were hardened sons of the desert. By their look these fellows knew their business, so he could not seek entrance there. He would have to find another way.

On what looked like a deserted area at the northeast corner of the wall, Zarum decided to attempt his entrance. Uncoiling his rope, one end of which was attached to a four-pronged grappling hook, Zarum readied himself for the toss. The barbarian was lucky, his first toss held fast atop the thirty foot wall.

"...you could ask for a small dukedom..."

Silently, just as he used to climb the tall bleak peaks of his native homeland, Zarum easily ventured up the wall to its top. Quickly he looked down inside the compound.

There were a hundred yards of sward and bushes to transverse before he could reach the windows on the ground floor of the house. So far he saw no one, and in a moment he had lowered himself to the well manicured grasses to once more cautiously gaze about him for any inkling of danger.

To his surprise Zarum could see no danger yet, the full moon lit up the area fairly well, but he saw no guards or beasts in evidence. It was almost too easy, and a nagging fear began to tear at the barbarian. He knew he must be very careful of his steps now. Cautiously he walked with drawn sword towards the house, wisely testing the ground before him with every step that he took. He came upon no traps or staked pits, nor any other protective devices, and for a moment he began to wonder if he might have had the wrong house. Of course that idea was foolish, but Zarum was a well versed thief who had broken into the houses of the wealthy and powerful before. He knew that not even an Aquilionian money-lender guarded his treasures more carefully than a practitioner of the sorcerous arts. The idea that this huge manse lay seemingly unguarded, but for a gang of thugs at the main gate, went against all that he had learned from a long and active career of thievery. Curiously, Zarum wondered about the medallion which he now wore about his neck. Did the Stygian wizard speak the truth? Zarum wondered about that. Slowly he lifted the chain that held the dull medallion off of his neck.

Immediately, the barbarian let out a gasp of fear followed by a lusty curse. For all around him suddenly came dark and monstrous shapes of half-human, half-bestial creatures. Horrors from legend and other monstrous images too terrible to mention swarmed foreword in a massive wave of seething, hissing, fury.

Zarum immediately put the medallion back around his neck and all the images disappeared. With a vast sigh of relief, the barbarian whispered reluctant thanks to the nameless wizard who had given him the protective talisman. It had certainly worked. Much shaken now, but recovering quickly, the barbarian resumed his movements towards the house and soon neared a ground floor window. Peering inside through the ornately designed red stained glass, he saw only quiet darkness within the room.

With his sword point, he pried the frame of the window open and quickly eased himself into the inky blackness of the room. With all senses alerted to a feverish pitch, Zarum looked around the large room. Aside from a huge oaken table, some chairs and a desk, the sparsely furnished chamber seemed empty. He also noticed that there were no guards in attendance, and that fact further piqued his curiosity. In fact, it made him more nervous than if he had actually come upon guards.

The barbarian was puzzled. He had surely thought to meet some kind of opposition to his errand, but it almost looked as though the place was deserted. Cautiously, he crossed the room to an opening that led into a lighted hallway. As he did so, he passed the rear of a large, ornate, high-backed chair.

Instantly Zarum's senses were alerted for he realized that the sunken form of a man lay sitting in that chair. With drawn sword he rounded to the front of the chair to confront its occupant.

"I was wondering when you would get here, barbarian," the man in the chair spoke up calmly. Even with Zarum's huge sword scant feet away from his face, the seated man showed no fear at all.

"Who are you?" Zarum muttered, angry with himself at being found out so easily.

The seated man smiled, and rubbed his hands contemplatively. "My name is Mulay Aldafeir El Nabastrum."

"That is a mouthful of name," Zarum grunted, waving his sword in a menacing gesture. "Is it supposed to mean something? What are you doing here?"

"Well might I ask that same question of you, barbarian. You see, this is my house. I am the one known as Aldakar."

Zarum was afraid that surprise showed upon his face. Should he cut the man down quickly before he had time to give alarm? With all probability there surely were guards with knocked arrows watching him this very moment.

"I see you debate what action to take?" Aldakar said quietly, showing a wrinkled smile. "Your first instinct is to kill me right away, but you are a wise man who knows that I would not expose myself to you like this if I were not suitably protected."

"It seems likely," Zarum grunted disappointed. He did not like being outfoxed; he liked it even less when done by a wizard.

"You have nothing to fear, barbarian. We are both quite alone here," Aldakar replied.

Zarum looked at the man closely, skeptically. This Aldakar was known as a wily rogue. "You want something of me. What is it?"

Aldakar laughed. It was a deep, freezing cold laugh that had a haunting sound all its own. "From you, barbarian? Now what could I possibly want from you? No, what causes my humor is that I have something that you want. And you want it very badly. Am I not right? Something that you would brave the dangers of my house, to steal from me."

Zarum gripped his sword more tightly. He was determined to lop that wise head from its withered shoulders should the man sound any alarm.

"Well, barbarian? Why do I not receive any answer from you?"

"I do not know what you are talking about," Zarum muttered.

"Forget the feeble pretense. I know you were sent here by the Stygian, to steal the Black Hand of Set."

Zarum lifted his sword menacingly, but more for protection, then he admitted, "Well, what of it, wizard?"

"Well, then you may have it," Aldakar said simply.

Carefully, for Zarum watched the old man ready for any trick, alert as the wizard withdrew a small metal box that lay on his lap hidden by the silken folds of his long robe.

"Here is your prize, barbarian. Take it away from me, and be gone."

Zarum looked at the man in utter surprise. "You are giving it to me, without a fight?"

"Yes! It is yours! Now be gone, and take that horrid thing away from me!"

"Wizards do not so easily give up their treasures, especially ones they have gone through so much trouble to steal in the first place. What kind of trickery is this?" Zarum asked angry now, his fear growing.

"No trickery, barbarian. I only wish that it were. Like a fool I misinterpreted the scant knowledge about the Hand. With it you may kill anyone wherever he be; but there are certain conditions. For each murder committed the Hand seeks payment with the soul of he who uses the Hand. The cursed thing is now after me! I want it out of here and far away, back in Stygian where it belongs."

Now the barbarian smiled. He had no sympathies for the troubles of wizards, but he could not help but see a grim irony in this wizard's dire situation. If it were true?

"All your kind play with powers you do not fully understand," Zarum grunted with contempt. He looked at the fear on Aldakar's face and gave him a wicked leer, "Suppose I open the box now!"

"The Hand will kill me," Aldakar said quietly. "And then it would come after you. For opening the box, you then set it out on its new mission. You would become the next victim."

Zarum's cocky smile melted away.

"It is not so funny now, eh, my barbarian friend?" Aldakar asked with a wry grin. "Leave me now. Give the Hand back to the Stygian, and pray we may both save ourselves."

"Yes, Zarum of Calgaria, give the box to me!" demanded the mysterious voice of terror from the other end of the room.

Zarum turned instantly and saw that it was the Stygian. Somehow he had gained access to the house and was now walking toward him. His long robe seemed to flow with an unnatural breeze, eerily haunting for no wind blew within the chamber.

"The Stygian!" Aldakar said in alarm, standing up now and facing the advancing figure.

"And you are the Iranistani," the Stygian whispered back to him in his hissing voice. "You know, that if I could, I would kill you for what you have done."

"Well do I know the Stygian ways," Aldakar answered with a hateful sneer, but he regained his composure quickly. Then with a grim smile he added, "But to do that Stygian, you must use the Hand, and I believe you fear the power of it, even more that I do."

The Stygian said nothing but it was evident he agreed with the Iranistani. Slowly he walked closer to the nervous figure of Zarum. "Give me the box, barbarian!"

Zarum deftly held out the box to the Stygian's grasping hands, glad to be rid of its terrible contents.

"Here, it is yours now, enjoy it!" Zarum stated boldly.

"Be gone, back to Stygia with that foul Hand," Aldakar whispered in mounting terror.

"Fear not, I shall leave soon, Aldakar, but before I do, I have some unfinished work to perform. Then the Stygian fingered the intricate patterns upon the sides of the metallic box. "You desired this so intently, you who call yourself Aldakar! Now *you* may truly have it!"

The face of Aldakar constricted with terror as the Stygian slowly opened the lid of that doom-laden box and brought out in his hands the squirming horror called the Black Hand of Set.

Zarum's face tightened and a low bestial growl escaped his lips as he looked for the first time upon the horrid abomination. He had never actually seen it before, and it put the dread fear of doom upon him. He saw it was a dark-skinned human hand, covered with congealed blood, and cut off at the wrist. The Blackened stump dangled with pieces of putrid flesh and loose veins, the sight sent a shiver of fear through the barbarian's giant frame.

If Zarum was scared, Aldakar was in a state of absolute terror. With eyes bulging in grotesque fascination and panic he watched as the Stygian approached him with the thing held in his outstretched hands. He stood there motionless as if unable to move.

Zarum stared at what was happening with a tight grip upon his sword. Did he see a slight movement of one of the Hand's fingers?

"Take it away!" Aldakar screamed terrified.

Zarum could see that the man tried to move away, but he appeared to be held in place by some unknown force. He eyed the sinister Hand fearfully as the Stygian moved closer.

"You are helpless now, Iranistani," the Stygian wizard whispered sinisterly. "The power of the Hand can overcome any defense that you might muster against it."

"Leave me be! I beg of you!" Aldakar pleaded now. "Leave me be and I will be your slave for life."

The Stygian smiled under his masking hood as if considering the deal. Then he slowly shook his head. "I fear it is too late for that."

Aldakar screamed, and Zarum watched, ready to do whatever need be done.

Then the Stygian began to mutter words in his strange tongue, words that intensified into a sinister melody. As he chanted his strange sing-song, one of his hands began to fondly stroke the back of the severed demonic member. It was a ghastly caressing motion that the Stygian performed while his voice crooned softly, almost lovingly to the grotesque abomination. Zarum was nauseated by what he was witnessing, but he could see the performance—bizarre and eerie as it might be—was having its effect. For slowly, almost imperceptibly at first, the horrid Hand began to flex its dusky fingers with imitative movement as if coming to life.

Zarum fell back and raised his sword with a curse.

The Stygian turned to him quickly, "Do not interfere, barbarian! My quarrel is with this worthless one, not you—do not make it your fight also!"

"I'll not stand here and see a man killed before my eyes, not in such a way as this!" Zarum shouted as he spit upon the floor before the Stygian to emphasize his disgust.

"So be it. Then you are a dead man, barbarian!" the Stygian cried out, and before Zarum could reply, the Stygian charge him in a headlong attack of insane fury holding out the Hand before him.

"Die, barbarian!" The Stygian screamed as he charged wildly.

Zarum immediately brought down his huge sword upon his attacker, in a great blurring motion that sliced through the neck of the dusky Stygian. Zarum saw the head fly across the room where it rolled upon the floor, while the headless body propelled by the fury of the attack, landed upon the barbarian.

Zarum let out a grizzly yell as the force of the still animated corpse knocked him to the ground and soon lay lifeless upon him.

The barbarian grunted in disgust as he dragged the bleeding corpse of the Stygian wizard off him. He had killed the Stygian, but how had he done it? Then he realized that it must have been the power of the medallion that had saved him. He still wore it around his neck. He sighed deeply, relieved. Then to his horror, he lifted the remains of the Stygian from him, and saw the Hand of Set grasping the folds of his shirt.

"The Hand, barbarian!" Aldakar yelled in warning. "Get it off you quickly!"

Zarum needed no urging. Instantly he grabbed for the Hand and tried to pull it off of his stomach, but it was as though the thing was of enormous weight. No matter what he tried, the Hand would not release its icy grip. All the time it slowly, inexorably, began its spider-like walk over his belly to his chest, to reach the heart of the helpless barbarian.

"Help me, wizard!" Zarum growled, the terror apparent in his burning blue eyes as they helplessly watched the movements of the grotesque Hand crawling upon him. "Help me, or you'll be the next one to feel the weight of this demon-thing!"

Aldakar straightened up, a new terror brought home to him by the wrath and threat in the barbarian's words. Much against his will, he realized that if the barbarian did not win against the Hand, then it was just a matter of time before he too would succumb to it.

"Well, wizard!" Zarum shouted in rage. Sweat broke out in rivers from his forehead as the Hand slowly inched its way upward on his body. Furious now, Zarum used every ounce of strength in his mighty frame to move, but it was all to no avail. He lay pinned upon his back seemingly as helpless as a babe in the woods.

Aldakar fearfully stepped closer, his eyes never leaving the noxious horror that lay moving so slowly, yet ever upwards upon the Calgarian's massive chest.

"There is one way, barbarian," Aldakar said nervously. Even as he uttered the words a frenzied fear gripped him and he tried vainly to cover his face with his folded arms.

"Well then, hurry dog!" Zarum's voice strained in panic.

"I will invoke the spirit of the Hand. Because it has a prior hold on my soul, it may leave you for the moment to take me. When it does, you must rise up and kill it!" Aldakar said in fearful haste. "Do you understand, barbarian? You must drive your sword through the back of the hand. Only one of your strength can do it. I see you are wearing the medallion, so you should be safe from much of its power."

"What of yourself?" Conan asked quickly.

"My time is at and end, but there may be a chance for you. You must drive your sword as deeply into the hand as possible. When it lays still, take both the hand and sword together and set them in the fires of that great brazier burning yonder. Place the Hand in the flames. It is your only chance, barbarian."

"Hurry then, wizard!" Zarum yelled as the Hand moved to the center of his chest. He could feel the long-nailed gory fingers perambulating towards his rapidly beating heart. Soon the great nailed fingers were beginning to position themselves in anticipation of the strike. Aldakar quickly moved to the barbarian's prone form. With a swirl of his majestic robe he began to utter a bleak incantation from age old antiquity which sounded like the growling of frenzied animals to the barbarian's ears.

At first the words appeared to be having no effect, but then a strange thing occurred, the Hand stopped its movement as though it had some uncanny intelligence that was deciding what it should do.

Zarum stared at the Hand in bug-eyed terror, then suddenly it flew from his chest onto Aldakar's chest, knocking the old mage to the floor with a hard thump. Aldakar cried out like a terror-stricken child as he felt the icy strength of the Hand holding onto him.

Zarum, finding he was now able to move, quickly lifted his sword. For a split second he hesitated as his blade hovered over the form of Aldakar.

"Strike now, barbarian!" Aldakar murmured hopelessly. "Save my soul from the Hand! Strike well with your blade!"

Zarum tightened his hands on his weapon and then drove it with all the force of his mighty muscles into the back of the horrid hand.

To the barbarian's amazement, his sword was deflected, while the point imbedded itself in one of the wooden floor boards.

"Do not stop, barbarian!" Aldakar screamed as both men saw the long nails of the Hand's fingers getting ready to strike. Within seconds those grim harbingers of death would begin their terrible burrowing into the old man's chest for the treasure that they sought. Aldakar pleaded hopelessly, "Strike now barbarian!"

Zarum grasped his great sword positioning it over the back of the Hand, and let loose with a monumental lunge using both hands to literally bore his sword point home. It was working, for he could feel that the hard, putrid flesh of the Hand was giving way ever so slightly. With each passing heartbeat he drove his sword point deeper into the nauseating horror. Zarum was finally rewarded by the feel of his weapon hitting the soft inner material. A great gush of bloody putrescence sprayed the barbarian, as his sword worked its way ever deeper into the hard bones of the demon Hand. Soon it went altogether in a quick burst that caused him to bury his sword down to the hilt into the thing. Unfortunately, Aldakar also received part of that massive sword stroke.

Aldakar let out a sharp sigh and then shuddered in death.

Zarum withdrew his weapon. It still had the ghastly Hand impaled upon it like some terrible trophy, and with great speed he put both sword and Hand into the high fires of the brazier, as Aldakar had ordered him to do. He scraped the Hand off his sword and then used the weapon to push the horrid thing deep into the raging flames.

Aldkar...then shuddered in death.

Fearfully, the barbarian watched as the flames enwrapped the impaled Hand. Cautiously he stoked up the flames with his sword, so as to make them ever hotter. Hoping that the cleansing fire would do its work faster.

Zarum watched with amazement as the Hand began to burn. The flames attached themselves to it, eating away at the ancient parchment-like skin, even as the burning gave off noxious fumes that threatened to make even the strong innards of the barbarian retch with loathsome disgust.

It was all over within moments. Once Zarum was satisfied that the deed had been done properly, and that the Hand was destroyed, he quickly left the dead wizard's house. He stopped long enough only to lay Aldakar upon a silken divan, where he looked much like a man in slumber. There was peacefulness in the old mage's face in death now, and Zarum knew that Aldakar had not lost his precious wizard's soul to the thing that hungered after it so greedily.

═══

When Zarum reached the palace at Agraphur, he was not in anywhere near a pleasant mood. His fight with the Stygian, the horrible experience with the Black Hand of Set, and the death of old Aldakar were heavy thoughts upon his mind. He had not yet figured out all that had happened entirely, but he was still alive, and for that he was thankful.

As he trod the steps that led to the portal of the palace, he was challenged by the two guards on duty.

"Ho, barbarian!" one called out in a coarse order. "Stop there! What business do you have in the palace?"

At times like these Zarum's impatience knew no bounds. With a massive fist he struck out at the nearer guard, sending him to the floor with a loud pounding to the head. The other guard, having drawn his sword, no sooner neared the enraged barbarian than Zarum had disarmed him with a trick that he had learned long ago in the Shemite meadows cities. He flung the unarmed guard against a wall, in disgust.

"Stand back! I have important business with Kaduthies!"

The first guard moved off to help his companion to his feet.

"We know you, barbarian," an officer came over and shouted at Zarum. "Go and pass, but King Yezdergrid will hear of this and it will not make him happy."

"I care little what makes Yezdergrid happy!" Zarum grunted. Then he was in the quiet confines of the palace and on his way to the offices that Lord Kaduthies used on the first floor.

Zarum came to the door, knocked it open, and entered. Kaduthies looked up from his desk startled by the intrusion.

"Ah, Captain Zarum," the minister said with surprise and some trepidation, rising from his seat. "It is good to see you alive."

"I see we meet again," another voice said from a seat in a dark corner of the room. Then a tall lean figure rose, and walked slowly into the light. Zarum recognized the hawk-like features of the man's face instantly.

"Yezdergrid!" Zarum said in surprise.

"King Yezdergrid! Barbarian!" The imperial youth corrected.

"Aye, yes then, King Yezdergrid." Zarum added carefully. He felt as though he had jumped from the frying pan, into the fire. He spoke up quickly, words he knew should never have uttered, "It has been a long time since…Makalet."

"I still wear the memento you gave me," Yezdergrid said in a rigid tone that did not bode well.

Zarum could see the long scar that ran from eye to chin upon the young King's face, it seemed to redden with the imperial youth's rage.

"That was a long time ago, Your Majesty," Kaduthies interrupted firmly, trying to focus the mind of his vain and impetuous master. "We have more urgent business to speak of today than past events. This barbarian is the man I was telling you about. He may have some information we need. What did you find at this Aldakar's house, Captain?"

"Yes, tell us," the king asked firmly.

"More than I bargained for," Zarum replied grimly. Then he gave his report, telling of all that had happened the past night.

"And are you sure that this damned Hand was destroyed?" Yezdergrid asked quite nervously. He was obviously relieved when Zarum told him of the destruction of The Black Hand of Set. Much relieved that he would not now be the next victim.

"Aye, it is destroyed!" Zarum grunted.

"Good work, barbarian!" King Yezdergrid replied, now once more the royal brat, but his tone was full of respect for the barbarian, or more precisely, for his prowess. There was also an idea being born in the young King's eyes as he observed the barbarian.

"And what of this Stygian?" Kaduthies asked curiously. "I had no idea he was going to appear at the house. Did he say anything about the murder of King Yildiz?"

"No," Zarum replied carefully. He slowly walked over to a table and poured himself a flagon of wine. Kaduthies eyed him suspiciously. The young King remained curious.

"You know something, don't you, Zarum?" The royal minister asked.

"Aye, I know who your killer is, but the royal brat here may not want to hear the answer."

"You speak dangerously, barbarian! Dangerously for you!" Yezdergrid warned, his face flushed. "I am grateful for your help to me in this matter, truly, but do not over tax that gratitude."

"Who is behind the murder, Zarum?" Kaduthies asked quietly.

Zarum smiled, savoring the moment. He did not relish giving the hot tempered king the unhappy news. He was about to speak when the door to Kaduthies' chamber was thrown open and a dozen armed warriors of the palace Immortals entered with drawn swords. In their van was Alem Kan, Captain of the Immortals, the elite Imperial bodyguard.

With a snicker of triumph on his features he walked through the pathway created by his men. Once Kan was in the chamber, Zarum and the others could see another who walked securely behind the captain.

Kaduthies let out a gasp of astonishment, "Queen Kallia!"

"Mother?" the young king asked curious. He had no clue.

The queen was young. In fact she appeared the same age as Yezdergrid, though she was many years older, and she had a look in her eyes that did not bode well for anyone in that room.

"It seems that I interrupted your speech, barbarian," Kallia said tossing her gorgeous head as though in some sexual frenzy. "Please continue. You said you know the identity of the killer of that old sloth, Yildiz?"

Yezdergrid stood shocked, angry but fearful. He saw all the guards standing obediently behind her. Where were his own Immortals—the king's personal bodyguard? Surely they were on the way...

Zarum said nothing. His eyes wandered to the face of the royal brat, Yezdergrid. The scar from Makalet was now livid red as realization and then rage dawned upon the youth's features.

"You!" he stammered in angry disbelief.

Queen Kallia just laughed showing an evil temper.

"Murderer!" he cried. "You did it! My own mother!"

Kallia sighed gaily, "Watch him, good Alem Kan. If his Royal Highness comes any closer, you have my permission—to kill him!"

Shock overcame the young King's features at hearing this order and he swallowed hard.

"You heard the order of the Queen, boy!" Kan said to the king in dire warning. "Stand back!"

"Why, Kallia?" Kaduthies asked in shock. His body seemed to sag as he tiredly sat at his desk. He had not yet accepted or understood the full import of all that had happened.

She leered at Kaduthies, "You should know, old one. Does not the same blood flow in my veins as in the royal brat yonder? Is my lust for power any less than his own? The useless sloth, Yildiz, was in my way."

"But he was your husband, you loved him. And I am your only son," Yezdergrid said meekly, trying to understand.

"Love? Loved by that pig!" Kallia replied in poisonous rage. "I hated him with all my heart. You have no idea of the length of that hatred. Of how I was taken by him when still a young virgin! Of rape on my wedding night, and all the other indignities,…"

"But I am your son!"

"By rape and of that same evil seed! We are much alike, too much alike, son of mine. I can not rule in safety knowing that you live, for I know that some day you would kill me and take the throne. Am I not right?"

King Yezdergrid nodded quietly, and a deep rage and hatred overcame his features. Without warning the young king drew his sword and charged his mother with murderous intent.

Quickly she stepped back and Alem Kan rushed in to fill the void and meet the boy's reckless attack. With drawn sword he fought off Yezdergrid's wild swings easily.

Soon the youth was disarmed, and with a rough kick from Alem Kan, he was thrown to the floor. Weak and bleeding. Was he crying?

The other men at arms who had come into the room with Alem Kan took it all in good humor, laughing at the humbling of any such privileged royalty.

Zarum smiled too, Yezdergrid had deserved this for some time.

"You cannot do this! You will cause Civil War, Kallia!" Kaduthies stated firmly. "You will tear the empire apart!"

"What care I for Yildiz's old empire? I will build a new one, greater than the first. And as for Civil War—if there are no leaders to oppose me—then who can the people follow?"

"And that will be that," Kaduthies said matter-of-factly.

"It is really quiet simple. At the last moment Aldakar refused to use the Hand once again, for some reason or other. It was to be my gift to my son. I think the old wizard was afraid of its power. No matter, it only delayed the inevitable. By this time tomorrow, all opposition to my takeover will have been eliminated. Captain Kan here has quiet a remarkable group of warriors; already they have imprisoned most of the royal family and any ministers loyal to Yezdergrid. It helps that my son is not overly loved by our people."

With that said, Queen Kallia imperiously walked out of the room. Passing Alem Kan, she whispered, "Have your men be quick about it."

Alem Kan nodded and motioned his men closer. All had drawn swords and were ready now.

"I have no wish to loose good men against you barbarian. I am told you fight like Tarim himself. Submit peacefully, and all your deaths will be quick and painless. I promise."

Zarum spat and drew his sword. "You promise! Come and get me!"

Alem Kan motioned his men to advance. Four of them were to go up against the big barbarian, the other four closed in on Kaduthies and Yezdergrid, who had now armed themselves and stood ready to fight for their very lives.

"Move in on them! Be quick about it!" Alem Kan ordered his men as he went to leave the chamber to join his Queen. "When you finish bring the bodies to me in the cells beneath the palace to be burned."

"Well then, come on dogs!" Zarum bellowed in a bold warrior taunt, "My blade is hungry and eager to taste your red Turanian blood!"

Warily the murder squad advanced. These were no green troops to go headlong into battle against a man like the barbarian. They all had heard the tales of his prowess with the blade. They moved on him most carefully, and reluctantly.

Zarum growled in defiance at his attackers. Then with a speed that few men would have believed possible, the barbarian ran to the huge desk of Kaduthies, picked it up over his head, and quickly hurled it at the advancing warriors.

The heavy wood hit three of them with a resounding thump sending them to the floor of the opposite wall in a heap of broken bones and confusion.

No sooner had Zarum done this than he was upon the remaining warrior, and with a savage slash to the gut disemboweled the man with a surprise move learned in Poitain. The warrior was dead instantly. Now to the others.

In a lighting move the big barbarian next flung himself upon the backs of the four men fighting Kaduthies and Yezdergrid. Kaduthies, with a slim dagger tried to guard his king, and Yezdergrid now with a curved Hillman sword, fought furiously against an opponent who threatened to get past his guard and gut him at any moment.

Zarum came upon the attackers like a mad dog, cutting and thrusting with such precision and speed that in a moment three of the attackers lay dead upon the floor. The last man remaining was pressing in on the young king, ready for the killing blow that would make him a champion of the Queen. Instead, he did not see the mighty sword stroke of Zarum, which cracked his helmet and skull. The warrior's head fell to the floor, the face frozen in a mask of grotesque and utter surprise.

Kaduthies stepped back from the barbarian in fear; he had never seen a man fight so furiously before. He was more terrified of the big barbarian, than he was of Alem Kan's killers. In an instant it was all over. Zarum stood covered in the blood of his enemies.

King Yezdergrid eyed the barbarian suspiciously. He was even more fearful of this man's power now, realizing as he did the superiority of him to himself. This barbarian was a born king, and Yezdergrid was going to see to it that he did not make himself a lord of Turan. If he got through this alive—after he killed the rebels—he was going to hold on to his kingdom. No one would ever take it away from him. Not even his own mother!

Suddenly there was the rush of boots from the corridor without.

"Alem Kan and his men!" Kaduthies warned from his watch place near the door. "They must have heard the fight and judged we were putting up too much resistance."

"Good, let them come," growled Zarum in a mighty rage. He was ready. "You both know what you are to do?"

"Aye, Zarum." both men replied.

When Alem Kan returned and entered the chamber with Queen Kallia and a few of his men, he saw a strange sight. By the doorway lay the bodies of Kaduthies, Yezdergrid, and the barbarian as though dead, while thrown in a heap at the opposite wall were his eight killers, just as dead.

"What has happened here?" the Queen asked.

"This is most strange," Alem Kan said as he investigated the corpses of his men. Then without warning they were set upon by three wild fiends with swords and daggers.

Zarum quickly cut down Kan's two warriors in the confusion and surprise, and to his wonder he saw that both Yezdergrid and Kaduthies each dropped a traitor also.

That left only Alem Kan, Queen Kallia and a couple of men. The fight went on. Yezdergrid accounted for another man, and Zarum quickly slew the other, but Alem Kan drove his sword deeply into Kaduthies, who was vainly trying to bar Kan and Kallia's exit from his chambers. Kaduthies fell to the stone paves with a short cry that alerted Zarum.

Zarum saw Kaduthies slump to the floor and his eye caught a movement behind him. Instantly he turned, just in time to ward off a killing blow from Alem Kan. As he passed the barbarian, Zarum quickly returned the blow with a mighty sweep of his blade that gutted the Turanian captain. He fell down to the floor writhing in pain and soon died.

Queen Kallia, drawing a long dagger, instantly charged Zarum, after seeing the horrible death of her lover. Over the unguarded back of the unwary barbarian, she ran to plunge her weapon down into his unprotected neck, but was stopped in mid-stride.

Zarum heard her slight cry and turned to see her hovering hand bare inches from his throat—then he noticed the sword hilt that extended from the body of the Queen. With a shriek he saw her body hit the floor.

He looked over at King Yezdergrid, who had plunged his blade into his own mother's back. He had saved the barbarian's life. Now the king was holding the dying form of Kaduthies in his arms.

Zarum went to the boy to thank him for saving his life, but Yezdergrid hardly knew he was there. He held the dying form of Kaduthies in his arms almost lovingly. At least for him.

"Do not leave me now, old man," the young king begged.

Zarum was surprised to see tears in the King's eyes.

"I need you to help me. Who will look after me?"

Kaduthies coughed blood, "I am sorry, My King. I have done my best to serve you. Be a good ruler, try not to be so ambitious, it is the best advice I can give…"

Kaduthies' aged form then slumped lifeless and King Yezdergrid carefully laid him down.

"He was a great man, barbarian," King Yezdergrid said with genuine sadness.

"I could see that."

"I saw it too late. That is my short-coming. I seem to have many of them."

Zarum did not reply. Then do something about it, he thought, but he did not say the words.

"Is my mother…?" the young king asked.

"Yes. Dead," Zarum replied quietly, but he did not regret saying it. That woman was a witch of a bitch! She had almost taken his life!

It was all over now. Zarum made ready to leave. He hoped. It all depended upon the king now. The thought of all this civilization he had seen lately made him sick. A wife murdered her husband in the foulest way imaginable! A mother would kill her own son! Then a son kills his mother! Even though it was to save his own hide, Zarum wondered at what type of lad Yezdergrid was, to so easily kill his own mother. Then again, what kind of woman was Queen Kallia to so ruthlessly dispose of both husband and son? Zarum would never understand civilized people; they seemed more vicious than the wild animals of the forest. Northern barbarians never acted civilized. He thanked Crom, his grim grey god of the north, for that. Zarum was glad he was a barbarian.

The big barbarian watched as King Yezdergrid looked down upon the body of his mother with a mixture of wonder and hate.

"I never really knew her, you know?" Yezdergrid admitted, more to himself than the barbarian. There was a strange sadness in his voice, but also great relief and triumph. "She was a great woman, but a very strange one."

"And a very dangerous one," Zarum added, trying to bring the youngster back to reality.

Yezdergrid looked at Zarum carefully. "Yes. So what will you do now, barbarian?" The king asked the important question thoughtfully, and intently watched closely for his answer.

"I have had it with so-called civilization. It is too much like living in a Zamoran cesspool," Zarum muttered in moody response. "I think I will go back to the northlands for a while. The snows of Calgar call to me for some reason."

"That may be wise."

Zarum noted the king's relief at having him go to a land as far away from his kingdom as possible. Such a powerful man as the barbarian would only mean trouble for King Yezdergrid in the future. Far better to be rid of him now—one way or the other.

"Yes, I think so. I will leave right away, if you permit it."

"A good idea, barbarian," King Yezdergrid replied in better humor now, and with evident relief. "And to speed your hasty exit, I will give you a sack of good Turaian gold to liven your journey."

Zarum allowed a wry grin, and then just nodded. Why not? Well, he had planned to leave anyway—but did this twerp think he could stop him if he truly wanted the throne of Turan? No, not if Zarum wanted that throne, but he did not want it. Not yet.

Two days later the big barbarian was on the road to the far frigid northern Calgar Wastelands, with a good horse and a heavy sack of Turanian gold for company. And no regrets.

The End

THE SNOW MAID

Zarum awoke startled and bewildered. Was something wrong? He grasped his mighty sword and cleared his sleep bleary eyes immediately. The crisp chill of the mountain air was seeping into his body as he gathered his sleeping furs about him more tightly. This frigid mountain air was much like that of his native Calgaria, in the Northlands. Nevertheless, it was brutal and froze his bones with powerful gusts that howled through the craggy passes with such wicked strength. Warily, the barbarian looked around as he grasped his sword and rose to his feet. His boots sank with deep crunches into the ancient hoarfrost as he strained his eyes to investigate the darkness. Although his keen eyes saw nothing moving, he could not help feeling the presence of an intruder. Something did not seem right.

"Damn and bedevilment!" he muttered annoyed, as his sharp eyes scanned the area around him in vain. "I know I heard something moving about. I am sure of it!"

Quickly the barbarian's eyes looked to where his comrades were bed down for the night. He saw that they were all in sight and sleeping restfully, nothing seemed amiss. Nevertheless his nape hairs prickled at some premonition of impending danger.

Zarum looked around for the sentry. As he did not know the hour, he was not sure who the man on duty should be, but surely someone should be guarding the camp? Yet the ever suspicious barbarian could see no one on guard. That did it.

He did not waste time looking for the sentry, and was about to awaken his men with a lusty oath, when he heard a faint rustling behind the rocks. Instantly he choked a hold more tightly on his sword handle as he cautiously stalked whatever it was laying hidden. Upon investigating he heard a low, soft whisper coming from the shadows behind him. It was the voice of a girl. But what would a girl be doing in a wilderness like this? Perhaps it was a trap? He had heard of demons who lured off fighting men using a woman's sweet voice— with all manner of sweet promises. His blood began to grow cold as he moved closer to investigate.

"Do not waken your men, Zarum," a youthful female voice whispered. It sounded like pleasant laughter to the barbarian's ears, and his fear grew, for he knew now that this was not the voice of any ordinary girl. There was a charm about it that was distinctly non-human and it evoked strong feelings deep within the man that he could not describe yet.

"Who are you, woman! If true woman you be?" Zarum asked with bold contempt and suspicion. He was taken aback by finding a girl in this stark cold wilderness of hills and bleak forests, and had grave doubts whether this was truly a woman or merely some clever deception. It could be a trap, and if so, Zarum would be ready for it.

The woman did not answer him right away.

"What is it you want?" the big barbarian growled.

"Do not waken your men. They are safe, and in any case they sleep under the spell of the *Rose of Exumanities*. I will wake them later, but for now you must come with me. Have no fear, I am alone and all your questions shall be answered once we leave the camp," the woman's voice said this in an enchanting whisper. It was a voice unlike any other, full of a soothing calmness, at the same time offering wild promises of luscious ecstasy. She spoke up once more, "Have no fear, Zarum, your men shall remain safe, this is no trap."

"Then show yourself. I'll not follow you until I see who or what you are," Zarum demanded with the patience born to a mountain warrior, though suspicious and skeptical of everything.

"So be it," the girl's voice replied simply. Suddenly a female form withdrew from the shadows to stand boldly into the flickering half light of the small fire where the barbarian has his first view of this strange incredible young woman.

Zarum gasped, this was no ordinary woman! She was beautiful beyond compare, possessing an enchantment and lushness that could easily beguile the most willful of men. The barbarian thought of the mysterious girl he had chased through the bleak snows of his native land so many years ago when he had been a lad. That other had been of the Kiatali, the Frost People. Now as his eyes devoured the form of the girl before him, he could see that there was a definite resemblance between these two mysterious women.

His eyes roved over every inch of her marvelously pure ivory skin, so perfect and sparkling, it glowed with an unnatural and enticing aura. Meanwhile her face was certainly that of a goddess, with that type of enigmatic smile which has haunted men from time immemorial. Her hair was sunshine blonde and exceptionally long and radiant; it danced over her full rising breasts and hugged the rest of her body ending in a delicate twist at the curve of her silken thighs. Enticingly dangerous, he knew. She wore the thinnest translucent white silk, having it draped about her in a most alluring manner, but for this, she stood before him boldly naked. She did not seem to notice the snow or the terrible cold at all, and at that moment neither did Zarum.

The barbarian finally noticed her bare feet standing in the frozen snow, yet she showed not the least sign of discomfort from the blistering cold. The barbarian shuffled his furs about him to better keep out the cold, and then followed the beckoning girl out of the rocky camp and down a sharp defile. He walked on until he came to a little valley nestled between two greater peaks, here the barbarian let out a lusty oath for he realized that when he and his men had passed this way hours before there had been no such valley here at all.

What astonished the barbarian more was that this was not your bleak snow-covered mountain valley as expected; this was a land that was lush and full of greenery, as the tropical lands around Punt and some of the Wild Kingdoms. Zarum shook his long black mane. A valley such as this could not possibly exist in these cold and inhospitable climes without sorcerous aide, and once more the barbarian moved with deliberate caution, for where sorcery is involved, danger can never be far away.

As Zarum walked he closely watched the girl before him, and his mind filled with an over powering desire to have her. The more he was with this girl, the stronger his urge became. It was a powerful longing, and at last the Calgarian had begun to fear that the girl had somehow bewitched him. If such was the case, there would be little he could do but wait until she told him what it was she wanted. Yes, he knew she wanted him for some reason, Zarum smiled grimly—but there was something he wanted from her also.

Finally the pair reached a small promontory at the valley entrance and the girl pointed to a huge castle that was situated many miles in the distance. It was a glittering edifice that shone with a bright gold glow. Even the stark blackness of the moonless night could not diminish the glory of that wondrous structure.

"Now Zarum, I shall answer your questions. You want me! You want me more than any man could ever want a woman! Your desire burns deep and strong in your mighty loins, but before you may have me, there is a task that you must perform."

Zarum watched the girl and drank in the heady wine of her beauty. He did not doubt her words at all; in fact he was entertaining the idea of taking her there and then, and the hell with her tasks. However, before he could do so, she laughed merrily, anticipating his thoughts.

"Do not try to take me now, barbarian, for you shall not live to claim that reward which you desire so dearly," then she held out her hands and from the fingertips sprouted great waves of burning flames. Zarum could feel the tremendous heat and stepped back astounded and fearful. He had never seen anything like this before, but it was not natural at all, and careful fear now took hold of him. He stepped back, cautious.

"That is better. Now are you ready to listen?"

Zarum grunted, but listened intently to what the girl had to say.

"In yonder castle lives the ancient mage Denethor, who binds me as his slave and concubine. The castle is protected by a great dome of sorcerous gold which is impervious to all powers but one. There is no Earthy entrance. For me to be free of this monster the castle must be destroyed and its contents scattered to the four winds."

Her hand opened and in the palm was a small pulsating stone no bigger than a hen's egg. "Take this jewel. It is the only talisman for which I can focus my magical powers to destroy the castle, and Denethor. You must attach it to the castle portal and then depart quickly. But be on your guard, Denethor has a servant that roams the grounds, and it can assume many form. You are not the first I have sent to destroy Denethor, be careful of his servant. Once you place the jewel, return to me here and I shall give you that which you so strongly desire."

"Why have you not placed this jewel yourself?" Zarum asked, and as he watched the girl he felt his senses reel as those of a drunken man. His eyes narrowly followed the curves of the girl's enchanting form. "Are you a goddess or a witch?"

"My name is Alyia, some call me the White Witch."

Zarum had heard the tales while seated at the fires of the hill people. The White Witch, who through all the ages had been held prisoner by a great sorcerer—how although she was a woman in bodily form, she was not altogether human, but belonged to an ancient pre-human civilization. Until now, Zarum had thought these tales mere myth, but now he knew there was reality behind those old stories and that he might be in great danger. For Alyia and her kind were said to live off the life force of other beings, most notably men, which they lured unto them with enticing promises carried out at the expense of the poor victim's life and soul. The hill people called these women succubus. It was rumored that to have one for a night of pleasure was the height of a man's sexual fulfillment, while the cost was a horrible death that lingered for insufferable eternities. Zarum grew wary, he wanted to sample this girl's glorious charms, but he did not want to loose his life or soul in doing it.

"I have been in Denethor's power for untold ages and can become free only when a great warrior sets this power jewel at the portal to the monster's castle. The jewel radiates a pulsating energy which will react with the sorcerous gold of the castle to cause its complete and utter destruction. It would be impossible for me to deliver the gem for Denethor's servant will find me out as it has upon numerous occasions. This servant has a power that is attuned to my own; it can always be warned of my presence and stop any move that I may make. Please Zarum, be my champion, help me! Help me to be free! You will not find me ungrateful."

Zarum could not decline her offer, although his judgment told him to do so in a heartbeat. A deep well of obsession clouded his mind until he could only think of Alyia and the time when he would have her all for himself. At the though of Denethor's name a fierce rage came into the man's mind. He had never met the mage, and yet the barbarian hated him with a deep passion. Zarum knew that a hatred such as that was not natural and that Alyia's sorceress powers might be at work influencing his mind to take action against the wizard, as though it were the barbarian's own fight, and not her own. Then Zarum looked to the girl and thought of his reward, and that took predominance in the thoughts within his swirling mind. By the Frozen Gods, Zarum thought, he would live to claim that reward!

Zarum took the proffered jewel from Alyia and examined it closely. It pulsed in his hand with a life all its own. Quickly he stuffed it into his belt, then without a word he began the long climb down to the floor of the lush valley below.

For what seemed many hours, Zarum walked across the dense jungle floor. He saw many exotic birds and wild animals whose hides and feathers would bring a good price back in the markets of the western cities, where the idle rich seemed to value such things so highly. Hah, thought the barbarian, there's wealth aplenty here for any trader, let the rich Zienumbrans come and get their soft furs and multicolor palms. They are all here, ready for the taking; the barbarian let them all be.

Zarum walked onward past thick woodlands. He had met with no trouble, everything appeared peaceful until he reached the castle of Denethor. Here he saw the magnificent golden dome atop the manse glowing and shimmering before him like some wicked Trantorn star, but his senses alerted him that there was danger near, so he tore his eyes away from that grand sight of the castle of gold.

Alyia had warned him of the servant of Denethor which lurked in these grounds, so that Zarum's eyes and ears were alert to a fever pitch. To be surprised in these woods would mean a very quick death indeed. What type of a servant was he to meet? She had told him that it was one that could change shape at will, which could appear in one of a thousand varied forms, and that would prove extremely dangerous. Nevertheless the more that the barbarian thought of the slim girl Alyia, the more determined he was to defeat any and all obstacles in his path to attaining his reward from her. Zarum's heart raced with anticipation, but soon his amorous thoughts were distracted by a loud roar that was coming straight towards him.

The barbarian drew his sword and waited with the patience of the Northern hill men. Finally, he heard a great roar behind him. Instantly he turned and saw a gigantic fur-covered creature, less than five yards from where he stood.

It was an enormous rat, but this was like no rodent-like creature the barbarian had ever seen before, for this rat was standing upright upon two huge hind legs to the height of almost fifty feet. Its great blood-red eyes glared down at the tiny man thing before it—then to Zarum's utter amazement it spoke in a sharp rasping voice.

"So I see Alyia has found another fool! I hope you furnish me greater sport than her previous champions."

Zarum grunted, but he was terrified. There didn't seem much for him to say, and then the creature moved towards the wild-eyed barbarian. Zarum advanced upon it, using his sword to hack incessantly at the rat's two front paws, but to no avail. Finally those front paws picked up the man and brought him up to the creature's great slavering jaws. He could smell the fetid breath, which came at him like a foul wind from that mouth full of hideously long teeth.

Zarum hacked away madly at one giant forepaw, as the foul breath of the beast continued to blow upon his face and it tried to bite him in the neck. Finally, with a massive blow, he was able to sever the huge rodent's paw completely. Instantly the monster let out a wild shriek of ponderous pain and dropped the barbarian with a loud thump to the hard ground below.

"By Braga's Beard!" Zarum growled astonished. "Come any closer, and I'll cut off your other paw as well!"

This time the huge rodent did not advance, it just stood there shrieking in miserable pain, but between the wailing, Zarum thought that he heard strange curses and prayers to some horrible unknown god.

Zarum carefully walked around the wounded beast so that he could get to the doorway of the great castle, but then the rodent came at him again. This time it was a full charge, and the rat hoped to trample the man into the ground, but through much luck and skill, Zarum managed to dodge the murderous advance. At the same moment, the big barbarian cut with a vicious sword stroke to the rodent's hind quarter. There was another cry of pain and the splattering of much blood, and the man smiled grimly. Now he could go on the offensive and finish off this lumbering brute! Zarum ran with surprising speed for one so large, sheer terror spurning him ever onward, and with an agile leap, he alighted upon the furry back of the huge creature.

No sooner had Zarum landed upon the great rodent's backside, that he realized the creature had now changed its shape. He now found himself seated upon a huge horn backed lizard. Zarum looked at it full of astonishment, realizing this battle was going to be harder fought than he realized, for he noticed the creature's new form did not carry the wounds that Zarum had inflicted upon the previous rodent creature.

Zarum hacked away madly...

Zarum immediately found himself shaken off the lizard creature's back, to land upon the ground with a loud smack. Then the huge snake-like tail of the great lizard—as long as a pirate galley—began whipping wildly all around him. He dodged it as best he could, but he was still hit once, the shock stunning him while the rough scales of the beast's tail shred his skin. The barbarian knew that he must get away from that lashing tail and face the beast head on; otherwise he would be cut into ribbons before he even had a chance to use his broadsword.

Zarum dodged and rolled upon the muddy ground until he was finally in front of the lizard. Its massive jaws were distended widely, showing huge pointed teeth, while all the time a great forked tongue darted in and out with a horrible hissing whisper.

"Die barbarian!"

Zarum could hear the lizard say these words in a barely audible hiss.

"No, you die!" Zarum shouted.

Then the creature charged.

The barbarian dived and rolled to get out of the way with lightning speed. He moved out of his attacker's path, and now lay in a ditch as the creature passed by over him. Zarum quickly shoved his sword upwards and into the creature's soft underbelly as it passed. He shoved the weapon upwards with such force it went in all the way to the hilt. There was now some four feet of the finest northern sword blade inside that damnable lizard beast.

However, before Zarum could withdraw his weapon, the great tail lashed him, sending him flying far away. He fell down stunned, but shook the feeling off to quickly get to his feet. He saw the lizard roar, shudder, and then once its small eyes had located him, the creature charge again. This time it missed the barbarian completely. Zarum saw that his sword was still imbedded deeply into the creature's belly, and that the deep hole it made was gushing blood all over the small clearing.

There was no way to get his sword back now the barbarian thought, so he drew his dagger. Though reeling from exhaustion, he awaited the next attack.

The giant lizard did not charge this time, but stopped and began changing into some other shape. The barbarian watched the transformation with amazement. This time it became a huge feathered bird. It flew up into the air, and with a grim smile Zarum once again noticed his sword still hilt-deep into the creature's belly. Then the hawk-like bird dived down at the man with its sharp beak and wicked talons extended.

Zarum let fly with his dagger as the great hawk came at him. The weapon hit the beast's huge head so hard that it sank completely into the animal's skull. Seconds later, the hawk fell end over end in the air, and then plummeted downwards to the ground.

Zarum watched the creature cautiously now. It did not move, but just lay there motionless, as if dead.

The barbarian walked over and carefully retrieved his sword, pulling it out of the creature. It felt good to have the weapon back in his hands again. Then he noticed the creature was changing its shape once more. Now it took the form of a giant two-headed wolf-like creature. Zarum had never seen the likes of this animal before and its sight sent shivers of fear through him.

"Night's Devils!" Zarum growled as he stepped a few paces back in sheer terror. The barbarian eyed this strange wolf carefully, and noticed that the creature did not move at all. A grim smile crossed his face as he took a few confident steps forward.

No sooner had he neared the creature than it changed its shape yet again. This time it became a giant white-horned ape, such as the type that the hill men in far-off Eastern lands say inhabit the passes in ancient snowy mountains.

Zarum cleaned the blood and mire from his blade and then put his sword in his scabbard. Then he looked on as the beast changed to the form of a large bulbous snake. Within another moment the form changed yet again, now to become a sinister giant black mantis.

Zarum stood by in opened-mouthed wonder and watched as the servant of Denethor changed shape many more times. There were many beasts, some of which had no home upon the planet Earth. Some shapes were truly horrible to look upon, and twice the barbarian almost retched at the sight of foul monstrosities that he saw materializing before him that were visions of Hell itself.

Finally, the guardian went through its last transformation and there was only a great mound of black, fetid dust that remained.

Zarum now walked towards the huge glowing portal of the castle of Denethor. He withdrew the small jewel which began to pulsate in his hands. Quickly, yet carefully, he deposited the bauble at the foot of the portal, then went away from there as quickly as he could run.

Within a short time, and at a full run, he had traversed the steamy jungle valley and stood upon the hill besides the beautiful witch-woman, Alyia. They both watched the golden castle, then Alyia muttered some strange incantations and afterwards there was a sudden monumental explosion that shook all the surrounding hills and mountains.

Debris flew in all directions, one small chunk landed before the feet of Zarum and Alyia. The girl picked up the golden shard and gave it to the barbarian, who promptly put it away in his picket pouch. Sorcerous gold it might be—but gold nonetheless.

Zarum looked longingly at the girl besides him. He felt his amorous desires returning.

Alyia, as if sensing his thoughts, turned and looked upon the wounded, bloody barbarian that was near her. With a wave of her hand, all of the wounds and filth upon the man's body began to instantly disappear.

"I have healed your wounds and cleaned the fighting filth from your body," Alyia said in a sultry whisper, "And now, I shall show you more of my appreciation."

Slowly, like a heated panther, she walked toward Zarum and put her arms around his massive neck. He responded by wrapping his mighty arms around her lithe form and quickly pulling her to his lips. Within a short time they lay together upon a bed of soft sleeping-furs. The big barbarian's hands grasped at the slim gal and...

Zarum next felt a violent nudging of his body.

"Wake up! Wake up, Zarum!" a warrior said pushing at the barbarian. "Zarum!"

The barbarian's eyes quickly opened and he looked around him to see what all the commotion was about. He was now lying in his furs, in front of him burned a small fire, and on all sides of him were his men. They were moving about making ready with their morning routine. Some of them looked at him curiously.

"Trebgazi, you slimy dog!" Zarum barked loudly. "What do you want? Is it morning already?"

"Aye, Captain," Trebgazi replied, and he gave the barbarian a very confused look. "You ordered us to break camp early so that we may get a good start on that bandit dog Nafestrum."

Zarum looked at the man curiously, "Who was the sentry last night?"

"I was, for the first four hours," Trebgazi replied carefully. "Abul watched the last four hours."

"Abul!" Zarum barked. "Abul! Get your dirty carcass over here!"

"Aye, Zarum," the warrior said as he ran to answer his captain's summons.

"Both of you stood watch last night. Answer me one question, and on your lives, I want the truth. Did I leave my sleeping furs at any time during the night?"

Both men looked at each other in evident surprise. They eyed Zarum strangely, then both replied that he had slept soundly all night long, and that in fact he had never moved from that one position all night. His snores loud and as usual.

"Are you both sure?" Zarum insisted, perplexed, and growing fearful again. "Not even to take a piss?"

"Dead sure, Zarum," both men replied perplexed by their commander's strange questions. "We sat by the fire all night, and our faces were upon you. You slept in one spot all night long, never even moving."

"You both lie! I was up during the night, and could not see anyone on guard! One of you left his post!"

Trebgazi and Abul looked at the big barbarian with terror in their eyes. Then they looked with suspicion upon each other. Neither, however, seemed to be lying to their captain. He could sense what was going through their minds. These were good, loyal men, his two best officers. Now they must surely think him mad.

Zarum growled a curse and stood up. As he did so, he felt a sharp pain in his side. He reached in his pouch. Quickly he pulled out a large shard of glowing gold. He knew right away what it was. Immediately he walked to the edge of the camp and looked out into the valley below. He saw only bare trees and snowy desolation. Then his eyes fell upon an area at the far end of the valley. Here he noticed there was something quite different.

"Trebgazi! Abul! Come here!"

The two men came running; both hoped that the barbarian's madness was not of the violent type.

"Did we not pass through that valley yesterday?" Zarum asked with a grim smile.

"Aye, Zarum," both men replied, not understanding what he was leading up to, but hoping that it was not any dangerous act.

"Then tell me, did we also pass through those black ruins, or see the huge crater at yonder far end of the valley?" Zarum asked.

Trebgazi and Abul looked to the far end of the valley. When the mist had cleared a look of surprise and horror were written upon their faces.

"Mother of us all!" Abul gasped. "We saw no such ruins there yesterday!"

"What has happened?" Trebgazi added fearfully. He did not like any of this; it all stunk of the supernatural.

"Zarum, let us leave this place immediately!" Abul managed to whisper.

"I do not understand. What has happened here?" Trebgazi asked trying to understand that which is not understandable.

"Some day, I shall tell you an interesting story," Zarum replied with a grim smile. Inwardly he let out a deep sigh in relief—that he was indeed not mad after all. He nodded, then shouted his orders to his men, "For now, we break camp and ride to the Fort. Now hurry, you lazy dogs. See to it that the men are ready!"

Trebgazi and Abul needed no urging. Within moments they were gone, making the troop ready to move far faster than it had ever moved before.

Zarum withdrew the golden shard and looked at it carefully. He wanted no part of sorcerous gold, one could never tell what influence it could hold over its owner. With much reluctance he heaved it over the mountainside, watching as it bounced down into the snow-covered valley below.

"Come on you lazy dogs! Let's get moving!" Zarum barked in annoyance. Once more he felt in command and that felt good. What had happened had all seemed like a terrible dream, and yet it had seemed so real. And the shard of gold from the castle dome now told him that it had indeed been real. Zarum did not understand any of this at all, and tried to put it out of his mind. Instead he thought only of a young tavern wench who said she would await his return to the fortress. The events of the previous night he would not even try to explain, even if he could understand their meaning.

And if the girl at the tavern looked too much like the snow-maiden Alyia, then it would not matter all that much after the fifth or sixth tankard of good stout ale that would dull his grim thoughts and ally his fears.

THE LION OF THE NORTH

Arsk the Bear grunted with lusty delight as he watched the gyrations of the young wench dancing nakedly upon the dusty ground before him.

"More ale, by the sea god's slimy beard!" The Bear yelled, throwing a bronze coin disk from Turan at the woman's feet. Before it hit the ground the wily wench scooped it up and deftly placed it in the small hide bag strapped to her side—the only bit of covering that she wore. The other men, all rough and lusty freebooters, roared their approval.

The woman, a young Kushite wench, danced ever more wildly, even as the ale flowed more heavily. The serving girls, all comely gals taken from captured ships and sacked sea towns, were hard put to keep up with the demands for more and more ale—as well as their loose affections.

Arsk walked toward the Kushite dancing girl who called herself Sarana. The other pirates roared out their approval for the vile deed they saw growing in their leader's eyes.

The girl's dancing now slowed, she saw what was in his heart as well, and she backed away nervously. Arsk, drunk and unsteady, ambled forward with greasy grasping hands outstretched surrounding her. The girl yelled in fear and then staggered backwards until she fell into the hands of the pirates. Those men roughly grabbed at her and with a loud roar of laughter, pushed her to her feet and towards their leader, Arsk the Bear.

The Bear let out a lusty growl as he grabbed Sarana's long hair and roughly jerked her closer to him, where they stood face to face.

"You shall serve me tonight, woman!" Arsk commanded with fetid drunken breath and foul temper as the girl yelled, squirmed and pleaded for mercy. She struggled to escape his massive arms. The Bear only grunted, somewhat amused. Then he slapped her twice, savagely at the thought of being refused pleasure from a mere slave. A few drops of blood dripped from the girl's mouth. Crying now, she wiped the blood away with her free hand and then spit full into the face of her tormenter. There was stunned silence for a moment. Then the crowd of rough pirates roared with gruff laughter at this insult to their leader. Many of his men wished that they could have done the same thing to the Bear—and some had—but none had lived long afterwards.

Arsk turned red with rage at the insult. His lust had now been replaced by a desire to hurt and humiliate the girl. He had never been so insulted by a mere woman before, and now he would make her pay.

"We will see if I can not cure you of that overabundance of pride, woman!"

he snarled at her. Then with one great push, the girl landed upon the ground and Arsk drew his sword. It was a huge dirty weapon unclean with dried blood and he aimed the point of it at the helpless girl's throat. She was pinned and could not move.

"Take her lads! Stake her out, and we'll all have a go at her! No one can say that Arsk the Bear is not generous with his women, eh?" he bellowed, looking down at the girl with a wicked grin, enjoying the approval of his men. Then he looked at the wench again and whispered, "Afterwards we will cut you up and feed you to the sea beasts!"

The pirates laughed, all followed Arsk's lead and grinned with pleasure.

"At least," one pirate shouted out, "we will all get a piece of this beauty instead of Arsk keeping her all for himself!"

Arsk the Bear only grunted at those words, took another drink of ale and shouted, "Aye, mates, not one of you that can say I am not generous with the spoils, eh?"

The pirates cheered.

Stakes were brought and hammered deeply into the soft sandy ground. Sarana was then roughly thrown on her back and her arms and legs were forced apart and outstretched and then bound to the stakes in painful agony. She fought them like a champion, but her plight was hopeless.

Sarana screamed in rage, anger, then in terrible fear, all to the further amusement of the drunken pirate louts who stood by laughing and cracking rude jests as they waited for the evening entertainment to begin.

Arsk, now drunker than ever, stumbled over and bellowed in laughter. He poured the contents of a full bottle of wine upon the girl's writhing form. Sarana begged and pleaded for mercy, but there would be no mercy here. What was to come, Sarana knew to be inevitable. She could not hope for pity from such men as these.

Sarana, and these pirates, were alone on a small island in the dark West, thousands of miles from her home in Kush, where she had been born and raised, and her later home in the seraglio of the King of Argos. She was a prisoner, a slave, a newly taken pirate captive. As such, she expected to have to submit to men. She had done so on numerous occasions before, but because of her vast beauty, always to her own advantage and with men of her choice. Now it was different. Now she would be toyed with and used brutally, and when her captives grew tired of her, she would be thrown to the tender mercies of the ravenous sea beasts. She would never see her home in faraway Kush again and tears now came to her eyes at the hopelessness of her plight.

Quickly torches were fired and brought over to shed light on what was to occur. Soon all in the tiny pirate camp circled about the weeping girl with ravenous looks. Dirty faces drooled in anticipation as Sarana, now in stark horror, fainted away into merciful unconsciousness.

═

There was a man lying upon the wet sand of the beach. How long he had been there unconscious he did not know. He awoke slowly and moved his massive body carefully, his head was an aching cauldron of pain and his skin was caked with dry blood. Whether the blood was his, or someone else's, he did not know—nor care at that moment.

He was a large giant of a barbarian, and yet he had a lithe and trim figure, which denoted the agile, well trained fighting man. He was perhaps in his late twenties, yet looked younger, with heavily hewed muscles and a long mane of thick black hair, parted down the center of his head as was the style of the Northlanders. His name was Zarum and he was originally from the vast cold northern Calgar Wastes, but lately had seen much travel to lands in the warmer southern climes, where he was a pirate known as The Lion of the North. He stood up tall and bold, flexing his strained limbs and then he walked a few paces to retrieve his massive long sword. He had been able to hold onto that grizzly weapon of death until he had been thrown upon the beach. He sheathed the mighty weapon and looked about him at his new surroundings. He knew he was upon some island somewhere in the western ocean, but exactly where, he did not know, for the storm could have blown him many leagues off course. He could be anywhere. He was ravenously hungry and began to walk into the forest above the beach to hunt for food.

The barbarian warrior had been trailing a particular buck for the better part of an hour. It had taken him towards the other side of the island, where he heard the sounds of rough laughter coming from a small glade above the beach, in an area that was far from the place he had been washed ashore. This was surely something to investigate.

Men, probably pirates, he thought, as he stealthily moved forward to get a look at just what was going on. Far off in the bay, he saw a ship anchored and was now sure that he was on one of the dozens of small pirate islands. Below, in a clearing, he counted perhaps a hundred stalwart sea rogues drinking and laughing. He also noticed a beautiful dark haired wench dancing seductively in the full moon's glow. She was slim and large breasted, with brown sweat-glistened skin that shone as her body twisted into positions that the man could not believe possible. That she was a harem girl was evident, yet how had she gotten here among these pirates? He decided to sit and watch the dance and enjoy it. Later, when all the pirates were drunk and in deep slumber from drink, he would make his way into their camp and take what food and drink he wanted from them. Perhaps he would also take the girl, he thought with a grim smile. She certainly looked to be worth the effort. As he watched from his point of concealment, he saw all that transpired below. He heard the yells of the girl as a large warrior pirate, evidently the leader of the group, grabbed the unsuspecting girl. Then he saw her spit fully into the face of the drunken sea dog leader. The hint of a smile came to the watcher's grim features. He admired that spunk in a gal. He would take this girl, he thought, but then events changed rapidly for the worse, as the girl was slapped down and held helpless at sword point. He saw the stakes brought and the girl outstretched and tied to them. He heard her cries for mercy mixed with the cruel laughter of the pirates, and he knew what was to come.

———

Arsk the Bear shouted out to a fat greasy Zingarian across from him, "Balthas, you shall be the first to sample our dancer's friendliness. But be careful that your ponderous weight does not crush the life out of the delicate little fawn, for all these other bold lads want a go at her before we feed her leftovers to the sea monsters."

The pirates loved this cruel humor and reeled with drunkenness and laughter as their large four hundred pound brother stepped eagerly forward, wiping the froth of drink from his grinning lips.

Within a minute Balthas was standing in front of the girl, looking down at her as he licked his fat lips in anticipation. He was ready and anxious and unable to hold himself in check, he moved closer to the helpless girl, but within another moment he was staggering with a knife sunk deep into his chest. He fell backwards dead with a heavy thump—instantly all was chaos and confusion in the pirate camp. Weapons were drawn, curses flew and eyes roved frantically about to find the slayer of their brother. No enemy was in sight, however, for them to vent their anger and violence upon. Arsk ambled forward with drawn sword. His bleary eyes looked around at the wall of forest and the thick trees surrounding them.

"Come out dog, and prepare to die!" he shouted into the trees. "We know you are there!"

There was a rustle of the foliage to the left, and suddenly a large black-mane giant stood defiantly in the glow of the full moon.

Arsk, upon seeing that it appeared to be just one man alone, walked towards him in bold confrontation. While he could see the newcomer was a barbarian, and a very tall giant of a man, Arsk himself was just as large and powerful, so he did not fear. The pirate chief could not make out this interloper's features too clearly, but whoever he might be, he surely was a fool to venture alone into a pirate camp. In his drunken state, Arsk could not think too clearly, yet there was one thing that he understood, this could be a trap and this man might have armed friends hiding among the trees. He motioned for his men to get into positions of defense. They did, waiting. Then the pirate leader walked forward to the barbarian. He knew it was best to go with caution at first; then this interfering dog could always be taken care of later.

"Who are you, son of a pig?" Arsk shouted out boldly at the man, all the time his eyes quickly checked the perimeter of the clearing for any movement among the trees. He saw no one. Could this fool really be alone? "Why did you kill our brother, Balthas?"

"I am Zarum, of the Calgar Wastes from the far North. I want food and water for three days, and I want that woman tied at the stake."

"You do not want much, do you?" Arsk barked amused. Then he eyed the stranger more carefully at his bold words. If this fool was alone as he appeared to be, then he had to have the guts of a god, or would soon be a dead fool. Arsk motioned for his men to draw closer to the interloper.

"You are a fool to confront us, Barbarian! You killed our brother! I see that they make them big and stupid in the North! No matter, you are a dead man already," the pirate blurted confidently.

Zarum stood by silently as Arsk, now with renewed bravery, stalked forward to the newcomer. The pirate leader was anxious to put this bold fellow down and was in advance of his fellows, for it was the ale that was giving him courage now—the ale, and the knowledge that this was but one man alone—an easy kill.

Before Arsk could make a move, however, the barbarian leaped upon him with a swiftness that belied his massive form. He was young and agile and fast. Within an instant, Zarum's sword point lay at the Bear's throat, little rivers of blood dripping onto Arsk's chest.

"Who is the dead fool now, pirate!" Zarum growled to the now cowering Bear. "Have your men release the girl and bring her to me. Otherwise you are the first to die here tonight."

Arsk thought fast. He did not want to die and it looked like this barbarian meant business. He would wait for the right time to kill him, but for now he would reluctantly obey.

"As you like, barbarian. No need to get personal, what care I for one troublesome wench," he answered in a manner to try to ingratiate himself with his captor. Then he barked out to his men, "Zleygar, Frothmar, release the slut and bring her here!"

Both pirates scabbard their swords and then ran to the bound girl. They quickly untied her bonds, revived her, and then brought her quickly to Zarum in a very cautious manner. Waved away with an angry gesture by Arsk, the two pirates withdrew back to where their mates stood watching the drama, wondering what was going to happen next.

Zarum bellowed with laughter. It had almost been too easy.

The pirates did not like his manner and drew closer with their weapons, but Arsk ordered them to move back, before Zarum's blade pressed ever deeper into his throat.

"I'll cut you into a thousand pieces for this barbarian!" Arsk promised.

Zarum ignored his captive and looked down at the shivering girl sitting upon the ground before him. She was free now but still terrified. He had been right about her, she was extremely beautiful. He threw her some clothing and she quickly put them on.

"Come with me girl, we're getting out of here."

Sarana stood up, rubbed the numbness from her limbs and walked beside the big barbarian. She looked at the giant in a strange light, not knowing what to expect from him. Was he a savior, or merely a new captor? As she walked over to Zarum, she gave Arsk a sharp kick right into the man's privates. The Bear doubled over and growled in pain while some of the pirate onlookers heartily laughed at her action.

Zarum's eyes burned into the face of the Bear, "Tell your men that if they want to see you alive again, not to follow us."

Arsk the Bear did as he was told, hoping against hope that his scurvy crew were loyal enough to him to do as he ordered.

———

On the other side of the glade dozens of pairs of beady red eyes starred down from the great trees at what was transpiring below them on the ground.

"Flesh, Goro Yan!" one whispered to his mate in a guttural tone. "May the great Dark God of Blood be blessed for delivering them to us. The sacrifices shall surely flow tonight!"

Goro Yan licked his saliva flecked lips and drew his blood-stained sword. The others about him drew their weapons as well. Quietly they crept closer and closer to the unsuspecting men below them.

Zarum, with his sword point strategically held at the throat of Arsk the Bear, walked back slowly with the girl, Sarana, at his side. He had armed her with a dagger, which she held most dearly. Within a few moments the three had quickly disappeared into the dense growth of the island's jungle. They were gone almost instantly and were not followed. However, before they had gone far, they heard the screams of dying men and heated battle that came faintly to Zarum's ears. The barbarian looked at Arsk questioningly for a moment, and then a grim smile came to his lips. Arsk the Bear had heard the sounds too and let out a flurry of frantic curses.

"The seadogs fight over my captainship, by the gods! When I get out of this I'll still slit your throat barbarian, and then I will go back and chop up the bloated bodies of Zleygar the Kushite and that bow-legged Argosean pig, Frothmar."

"You'll not get out of this corsair, unless it be with my sword through your ribs, or slit across your fat neck!" Zarum taunted his captive as they moved through the jungle. The Bear grunted his displeasure but decided to bide his time for now.

"Come on dog of a sea pirate. Move faster! We do not have all day! We have a ship to capture. I have no wish to stay on this stinking island any longer."

"No! Not my ship!' the Bear bellowed understanding what the barbarian's words meant.

"Quite, pirate!" Zarum ordered as he slipped his sword point a bit deeper into his captive's bloody neck. For the first time in his life Arsk the Bear actually was speechless. Who was this damnable barbarian? How could he walk into the camp of a hundred of his deadly seadogs, and steal his beautiful slave wench? Not to mention his gall at dreaming to steal his ship all by himself! Arsk grunted to himself as he was being shoved forward; always a sharp point being pressed firmly now against his back.

"Damn barbarian!" Arsk complained in a low tone. "Slow down, I am no Turan pack horse that I must be driven so hard!"

"Would you rather die by the hands of those who follow us?" Zarum informed him, as he pushed the pirate to greater speed.

The pirate looked at the barbarian with great contempt, but the girl seemed to understand and held her dagger more tightly.

"My men will not harm me," Arsk laughed.

"It is not your dim rogues who follow us," the barbarian said with calm assurance, a grim smile playing upon his lips as he noticed the pirate's evident confusion.

"What do you mean?" Arsk asked.

"Then who is it, barbarian?" The girl, Sarana, spoke up carefully, voicing the same question that was on the Bear's lips.

"I do not know, they are little men, but they are very deadly. Move now, the both of you. We must make the ship right away!"

Both Arsk and Sarana looked to Zarum for more of an explanation, but the barbarian ignored their inquiring looks and he just pressed them on to greater speed through the jungle. Twice Sarana stumbled, for by now she was near the point of exhaustion. On the third time Zarum had to help her up and carry her for a short distance upon his massive shoulder. She protested, saying that if she could but rest a short time she would be fine. Zarum replied by saying that they did not have any time to spare. Suddenly the three heard the yelling frantic voices from behind them now, getting closer.

"What is that?" the girl asked nervously.

"Leave the woman, barbarian!" the pirate said to Zarum as he shot an apprehensive glance behind him. The man was terrified now. Zarum would not answer the pirate leader; he just kept up the quick pace, all the while pushing Arsk ahead of him with his sword point.

They had been running for a short time longer when they came to a high bluff and cliff, the sight of an anchored pirate vessel below them in the water. Here Zarum set down Sarana upon the ground, while he and the pirate looked longingly at the listing sea craft.

"By Ibar's Groin, there be my worthy ship!" Arsk bellowed in triumph, but soon a dark scowl crossed his face. "Where are my men? Where is Corath and the Kushite, Emua? I left them onboard as guards."

Zarum nodded, and looked steadily downward at the empty ship. His sharp eyes searched every bit of the vessel. He was brought to the alert when his ears heard the trampling of the jungle growth behind him. He knew he had to move fast, for soon their relentless followers would be upon them. Immediately he grabbed the unsuspecting body of Arsk and threw him off the cliff, down into the water below. They were not so high up, so he knew the pirate should be able to take the fall without death or injury. Arsk went down to the water with a stupendous yell.

Next Zarum quickly grabbed up the semi-conscious Sarana. "Time to take a swim, girl. Try to make it to the ship. I will help you if I can," then he set her down off the cliff and into the water. She screamed all the way down.

Zarum saw some small men hiding upon the deck of the pirate ship now. If in fact, they were men. Zarum was not really sure what they might be. Well, at any rate, it was time for him to make his move and so he jumped off the cliff into water as well.

No sooner had Zarum dived off the cliff and hit the water below then a flurry of little forms came darting out of the jungle onto the cliff edge. They gibbered and yelled a high pitched blood curdling scream of anger and frustration.

Sarana heard them and closed her eyes as she tried to swim and stay afloat.

The barbarian was already swimming in the water, his well-trained muscles gave him power to help the weak girl and keep her afloat.

He just kept up the quick pace.

"What sort of hell creatures are those?" Zarum said in growing fear. The creatures, half the size of a real man and resembling the fearsome Picts of the West in looks, stood upon the cliff and jumped up and down in frustration. More and more of their numbers were streaming out from the forest. As yet they were not jumping off the cliff to get at Zarum and his two companions below, but the barbarian knew that they would make it to the ship in time.

"Where are my guards?" Arsk spoke up, more to himself than to Zarum and the girl. All three now made their way towards the pirate ship. "I called out their names, and yet I hear no one answer. Did you kill them, Barbarian? Did you kill them before you entered my camp?"

Zarum just shook his head, eyeing the ship closely as they swam towards it. "The ship is our only chance now, swim faster!"

The trio swam furiously for all they were worth, for they saw swarms of the little bestial men behind them climbing down the cliff. The attacker's faces were twisted into horrid grimaces of anger, while they brandished their weapons with deadly intent.

Zarum stayed close to Sarana and had to help her at times to keep her head above water, for the arduous struggle of swimming against the current was taking its toll upon her already weak condition. It seemed that Arsk was also having his own trouble in the water. Only Zarum, his muscles as powerful as ever, kept up a quick and steady pace. Both Arsk and Sarana had to be aided at one time or another by the barbarian.

Zarum reached the pirate ship soon and was the first over the gunwale. He saw no one aboard, nor were there any signs of a fight having occurred—yet he had seen some of the little beast men on the ship from the cliff. Where were they now? To all intents and purposes, it appeared that Arsk's pirate guards had just vanished. Zarum had a nagging fear that he could not rest easy until he found out where these men had disappeared to.

Quickly he helped up Sarana onto the ship, and then reluctantly Arsk, who did not want the barbarian's help—even though he needed it to the embarrassing point of getting back aboard his own ship.

Once onboard, Arsk voiced his displeasure by mumbling a few hollow oaths. Then he called out the names of his men once again. The pirate chief, after getting no response, used some fine curses that even Zarum had never heard before. The barbarian wondered where the beast men where hiding, for he was certain he had seen some of them aboard the ship. As the barbarian watched Arsk, a grim smile crossed his lips. Arsk noticed Zarum's grin and spit out a particularly vile curse about the parentage of certain barbarian outlaws. Zarum only grinned more deeply with the intent to make Arsk even more furious.

"You have brought me to this fine fix, outlander. All to save a mere woman. Good then take the woman! Just give me my sword and let me get back to my men!"

"You fool! Don't you understand?" Zarum growled angry now. "You can not go back. You'll have to fight through hundreds of those beast men!. Did you not see them? They are all over. They are even here, on your—I mean, on *my* ship. Somewhere."

"*Your* ship!" Arsk growled in anger, but he had temporarily forgotten about the little demon men. He looked back up at the cliff and saw the small creatures swarming down it, a dark pall crossed his face and all the fight went out of him.

"What are they, barbarian?" he asked nervously.

"I do not know," Zarum replied.

It was then that Sarana called out. She had been walking about the ship, exploring, and had found the two pirate guards. Both Zarum and Arsk were soon at her side.

"By the gods!" Arsk growled. "Who would do such a thing?"

"I think I am going to be sick," Sarana said walking toward the gunwale to throw up.

Zarum just eyed the bloody remains gloomily. There was not much left of the two pirates. It was obvious that the beast men had killed them, and taken the choice cuts of the meat with them.

"Cannibals," Zarum said quietly, fearful for even he felt the horror of that word.

The pirate chief looked at him in fear, "The eaters of the living!"

Zarum slowly nodded, and then withdrew the sword that he had taken from Arsk earlier. Then he handed the weapon to the Bear, who eyed him curiously and with evident surprise.

"Take it. You may need it, pirate," Zarum added wryly.

Arsk the Bear understood and nodded, slipped the sword deftly into his scabbard, a scabbard that for too long had been empty. Of course, he thought of slipping his blade deftly into the heart of this big barbarian, but under the circumstances thought better of it. Those little demon men scared him greatly—and the barbarian said that some of them were here on the ship! Somewhere. Where? He looked around suspicious. Fearful.

"My thanks, barbarian. You'll not regret this act of kindness, even if you be the cause of all of my troubles. At least when my time comes, I shall die like a man, with a good sword in my hand," the pirate said boldly.

"Good, and try not to slip your blade into my back when I am not looking, eh? Or I shall be most disappointed in you," Zarum said grimly.

"Not for a time, barbarian. At least, not for a time."

Zarum laughed in an uneasy voice, "Well, that time may never come, pirate. Take a look at the shore."

It was the little Pictish beast men. There were hundreds of them now, and they had somehow brought out strange canoe-like boats, the bows and sterns carved with demonic shapes and faces, and they were busy rowing out to the ship. They chanted eerily, as they rowed furiously closer and closer to the pirate ship.

———

Amar Kahn looked upon the foam-specked waves and breathed a deep lung full of salty sea air. He stood out upon the poop, alone, as his first mate walked over to him.

"Lord, we must put into this island. We need fresh water and whatever meat and fruits that we can find."

"Provisions are that low? If it is at all possible, I would not like to put into any island in this part of the sea. I was among these islands years before, Korthus, and they are damnable places."

The first Mate Korthus saw the fear in Captain Amar Khan's face. He was surprised, for the face of the Sea Hawk never had shown any fear in all the years he had served him. Fear could not help creep into the countenance of Korthus as he looked at the small island ahead and wondered just what terror awaited them there.

"So be it, Korthus," Amar Khan ordered reluctantly, "but make all haste." Then he whispered in a barely audible tone, "Keep a sharp eye out for flying creatures. Watch the sky!"

Kortus's face went blank, while his captain slowly walked away to stand alone, a solitary figure, seemingly reliving past nightmares that were full of some mysterious horror.

The pirate lieutenant had never seen his captain in this worried manner before, a caution, bordering upon fear, now clouded his own thoughts. He bullied and pushed the men to the fastest speed, and as a result, the ship was anchored and the boats were lowered very rapidly. He was in charge of the landing party, a thought that now, he did not relish very much. He had heard stories about these jungle islands and the naked native woman that lived upon them. He had at first thought that a landing party to gather provisions would not be such a bad idea, and if they happened to run into a few pretty island women while near the beach, then so much the better. Now it was a different story. Whatever it was that had put fear into the fighting spirit of his captain, he did not want to meet on any desolate beach or shrouded jungle on this island.

There were two boats, with ten men in each. Korthus was in the fore part of the lead boat, with both hands tightly clinched about the shaft of his massive spear. The men, all seafaring rogues used to danger, could almost taste the fear that was thick in the air. They noted Korthus's mood and it made them all uneasy. There were no salty songs or spirited talk at all as the little party rowed moodily towards that bleak shore. Only Gorus, an old seadog of many years, spoke, and what he said only soured the mood of the men more. He told a tale of his youth in which he and a group of men had come to this island—or an island just like it. In his tale he mentioned terrifying flying demons that feasted upon human flesh. He also spoke of some powerful, unholy god that ruled the island and watched all that occurred. It was not long before Korthus, voicing a sharp oath, ordered the old sailor to be silent.

It was a gloomy, fearful party that nervously pulled up their boats onto the lovely clear white sand of the island's beach. Korthus called out to Gorus, and the old man ambled over in a speedy but uneven gait.

"You and one other stay here and watch the boats. Keep a good eye out and look towards the *Seahawk* and note that all's well aboard her."

"Aye, sir! That I will surely do. You just hurry up those lazy lads though, for I like it not being upon this beach alone."

"You are not alone, you will be with Talen," Korthus stated in a firm tone.

"Hah, being with Talen, is like being alone!" Gorus stated sarcastically.

The pirates laughed.

"Hey!" Talen shouted feigning hurt.

"Sorry, boy," the old sailor said to the callow youth.

"Would you rather go into that damn jungle with us you old dog?" Korthus asked Gorus, angry now.

"No, sir," the old salt answered softly. "That I would surely not want to do."

Gorus and the young lad, Talen, stood their nervous guard by the boats as they watched the small band of pirates enter the jungle above the beach. The old horrible tales spoken by Gorus had so shaken the young Talen that he now walked away and sat alone in dark contemplation. It was Gorus whose loud shouts brought the youth's attention back to the real world.

"By the gods! Lad, look, yonder to the ship!"

Amar Kahn had been in his cabin trying to work on lists of shares for each man's pirate booty, but it was to no avail. Haunting nightmares sprang up from his memory of long ago to shrivel his bold fighting spirit. He left his quarters and went back on deck even more distraught than he had been before, cursing the necessity that had prompted his vessel to this damnable isle in the first place.

He looked far off at the island's shore. He could plainly see the two boats from the *Seahawk*, but not a man at all was visible. Where were the guards? His stomach tightened at the sight. Surely Korthus would have left behind a guard over the boats?

Then the ship lookout shouted a shrill cry, "We are under attack!"

Amar Kahn's eyes instantly flashed upwards and he saw a heartrending sight, a sight that he had first seen many years ago. It was a sight that he had prayed he would never see again. Upwards of hundreds of feet in the air, coming at the ship with great speed, were a dozen giant dark winged shapes.

⸺

Upon the beach, Gorus and Talen saw the large black shapes flying towards the *Seahawk*, and quickly ran into the jungle to reach Korthus and their men. They had been in the bush not very long when they were set upon by a dozen little beast men who fell upon them from the trees above.

"Run!" Gorus shouted frantically.

Talen let out a terrified shriek and ran away for all that he was worth.

Meanwhile, Gorus went down under four of the bestial little men. His heart beat savagely as his knife cut in every direction with maddening thrusts. The little half-men came at him with a wicked fury, a bravery, or fool heartiness that was more fanaticism than anything else. Four of their number dropped from the quick, accurate slashes of the old sailor, so that it was then only two others who were upon him—but that was enough by now. Within moments Gorus lay dead, cut and slashed into a heap of bloody red meat that his surviving captors quickly picked up and put into a sack.

Talen, who had run off, was being followed closely by two of the beast men who grunted and growled as they came upon him. The youth was scared to death and in pure panic but he drew his sword and with a sudden surprise gesture he turned to meet his attackers. The two half-men jabbered together in surprise as Talen was upon them in a mad charge of rage and terror. With sheer panic taking hold, he let lose with two monumental strokes of his sword that cut both the beast-men in twain. With the warm blood of his enemies splattered all over his body, Talen seemed to awaken his bravery and continued his mad rush through the small island jungle.

⸺

Korthus and his band of men had not been in the jungle long, but even that small amount of time seemed like ages. They were en route to an inland lake that Amar Kahn had told him about where fresh water could be obtained.

The small group walked on in caution and fear. Every jungle sound now seemed magnified and took on an ominous meaning. They walked onward, weapons in hand until they came to a small glade. Here they saw the body of a young man, with torn clothing and covered with blood. They wondered what had happened to him.

Korthus and his men walked toward the body and turned it over in shock.

"It is Talen!" one of the sailors blurted fearfully, confused.

"What is he doing here?" another asked Korthus.

"If he's here, dead—then the boats must be taken!" one man said fearfully.

"We're trapped here!" another said in terror.

"Shut up dogs!" Korthus ordered angrily as he looked over the body. All the blood made the injuries look worse than they were. "The lad's not dead. Not yet at any rate. Most of this blood is not his own. We'll revive him and find out what has happened."

All the while little red eyes peered down at the small party of pirates from the hidden places in the ponderous trees above.

═

"Men to arms! Men to arms!" Amar Kahn yelled to the crew of the *Seahawk*. "Come on you lazy dogs, we're being attacked!"

Shouts of horror and terror sprang up from a hundred dry throats.

A dozen giant flying shapes came ever onward towards their ship. They were huge, and as Amar Kahn looked more closely he saw that they were giant horned bats. Their jaws were open wide in ferocious anticipation of a feast, and great pointed ivory teeth gleamed in the sun while horrid cries issued from their throats. Within moments the bats were upon the tiny ship and the crew, a horrid mass of talons and teeth which furiously cut and rent all in their path. Dozens of men went down to a vicious death. Amar Kahn fought like a fiend, yet the noble captain went down during the first attack. The rest of the men remaining alive looked on with icy fear as the giant bats now lifted some of the men into their gapping jaws, and then flew away with their ghastly trophies.

Cretis, one of the sailors remaining, cursed as he saw one of the bats grab up the bloody pulp remains that had once been Amar Kahn and then take to wing with it. Cretis cursed again when he saw that more black shapes were dropping from the sky upon the ship.

"By the gods!" he roared out in rage and terror. "More bats! Stand firm lads, there must be dozens of them!"

The next wave of the flying monsters came upon them instantly and furiously. Dozens of the giant creatures fell upon the ship and cut down the pirates. In moments it was over. All that remained of the crew of the *Seahawk* was a sheet of wet red blood covering the decks.

High upon a mountain Naga Yaro stood with outstretched arms and called his flying creatures back to him. Each fearsome beast alighted nimbly upon the rocky shelf. Then, one at a time, they ambled over to Naga Yaro who lovingly patted their bloody beaks and spoke soft soothing words to them. The flying monsters dwarfed the little man, and yet Naga Yaro was always in control. The creatures fawned upon him like a dog seeking a master's affection. Then the huge fearsome bats ambled onward, dropped their load of fresh pulpy flesh, and flew into the great caverns nearby.

Zarum looked upon the face of Arsk The Bear and saw nothing but cold icy fear.

Within moments hundreds of jabbering beast-men would be upon them. Sarana screamed hysterically and the barbarian had to slap her face once to keep her quiet and sane. It was then that Zarum noticed a dozen huge dark shapes flying far away and above the boat. As they came closer he could see they went into a dive towards an area of the sea that was far away from them. What were they? Where were they going? Zarum could not tell, for a jutting of the island blocked his view, and he just thanked his mighty Norse god that whatever they were, they were not coming for them.

"What the hell was that?" Arsk grunted fearfully.

"Pray we do not get close enough to find out, pirate," Zarum replied grimly. He did not like wizardry, and this stunk of wizardry.

Zarum and his two companions on the ship noticed that the half-men also saw the huge creatures too, and almost instantly they turned around their canoes and headed back to the shore. Zarum and Arsk stood by amazed while Sarana whispered her thanks to the goddess Mithra.

Once the little man-beasts reached the shore, they all began jabbering excitedly in their uncouth tongue, running into the jungle. They left only a dozen of their comrades on the beach to watch the ship.

"What do we do now, Zarum?" Sarana asked now that she had been able to

What were they? Where were they going?

regain her composure.

Zarum looked at the girl. She was dirty and had been through much horror, yet a fierce and intelligent glow still shone from her eyes. She was still very beautiful and had held up surprisingly well; and he told her so. He respected that as a warrior. As to what they were to do? He had no idea. He only had one thought in mind and that was to leave this trice damned island as soon as possible.

"Pirate, you still have your sword in hand?"

"You know I do, Barbarian."

"Then go about and cut the line to the anchor. There are not enough of us to run this ship, but we are getting away from this island as fast as we can. The stench of sorcery is too strong for my own good. We'll cut her ropes and let her drift out to sea. Then we'll take our chances."

Arsk did not like taking orders, especially from a barbarian on his own ship, but he wanted to get away from that island even more than Zarum did. So he did as he was told.

With the last line to the anchor cut, the ship floated gently away and out of the tiny cove. The weather was mild for now and the current lazily drove the ship around a jutting mass of the island and then into another small cove—where they were surprised to see anchored a sleek fighting ship. It was a warship for certain—and most probably being in these waters, a pirate vessel.

Arsk the Bear grunted with displeasure, "I know her. 'Tis the *Seahawk*, a Turan vessel turned pirate. A black-hearted dog called Amar Kahn captains her. What are they doing here?"

"We will find out soon, foulest of luck, for the current is bringing us towards her," Zarum said. Then he added, "But that must be where those black shapes we saw earlier flew towards."

"It may be where the beast-men went to also," Sarana said cautiously.

Zarum grunted, he now wondered if he had just gone, from the frying pan and into the fire. As their ship neared the dead *Seahawk*, he noticed that rivers of red blood were streaming through the scuppers and down the hull.

<hr />

When Korthus revived Talen, the lad told a horrid tale of how he and the old seadog, Gorus, had seen dark devil-shapes attack the *Seahawk*. The boy told of Gorus's fight and death at the hands of swarming beast-men, and how he had bravely fought his way through dozens of the nasty creatures to reach Korthus and his men. That last part was entirely fictional, yet seemed more believable than tales of flying monsters. Or so he hoped.

Korthus had seen no flying creatures as of yet, nor had he, or any of the men with him, come across any small men—beast-like or otherwise. Yet he remembered his Captain's words, while his men recounted the strange tales that Gorus had told. Now Gorus was dead. Korthus and his men did not laugh; in fact, many of them shook in their boots with terror. What made those men literally fly out of their boots was the weird uncouth cry they now heard coming from the trees around them. Then within moments, dozens of small bestial pre-human men were down upon them with daggers, swords, and even war clubs of heavy knobbed wood.

"Make to the boats, men! Make to the boats now!" Korthus barked in fury as he and his party of pirates tried their best to fight off the small bestial creatures that were coming at them in a furious rage. "Hurry, lads, to the boats, then the ship! It is our only chance!"

The men did not have to be told again, for no sooner had the beast-men appeared than the pirates were running full speed into the dense forest growth to find any place to hide. Nor did they stop running until they reached the beach. Once upon the beach, they saw both boats destroyed so badly that they could not be used. Four of their numbers had been killed, and even now the beast-men were still on their heels.

"Swim! Swim for your life! Make for the *Seahawk* now, lads!"

It was then that Korthus was surprised to notice another ship alongside the *Seahawk*. That was odd. However, he found himself much too busy fighting and running to do much thinking about what it might mean. All the pirates soon noticed the new ship, but none gave it much thought, for at that moment the only thought paramount in each man's mind was getting off that damnable beach and away from those horrible shrieking beast-men, and their pointed blood-stained weapons. If there would have been five hundred Argos slave traders on their ship, they would have happily welcomed them.

Korthus and the dozen men that were left to him swam for all that they were worth to get to their ship. The beast-men did not follow, and many were the praises heaped upon the gods for that fact. As Korthus and his men neared the *Seahawk*, they noticed that there did not seem to be anyone on board. Nor did they see anyone upon the new ship which was also a pirate galley, called *Triton*. This was a very strange occurrence. They did notice one thing; however, blood was dripping profusely from the deck of the *Seahawk*. It was a veritable stream that ran over the side as the ship gently rocked to and fro in the mild waves. Korthus called to his men and banded them into a group centered at the ship's hull and once they were ready with weapons in hand, they prepared, rather reluctantly, to board the *Seahawk*.

Zarum and Arsk, using large grappling hooks, pulled the two pirate ships close together. Soon they had them tied off and were ready to board the other vessel.

"She's a dead hulk now," Arsk said sadly, for this had been his own ship. "Look at all this blood, it was shed in buckets. No one can be left alive. What the hell happened here, barbarian?"

"The gods alone know, but you are probably right. It looks like no one can be left alive here, but let us check anyway."

"Why? Whatever killed my men might still be on board," Arsk said with a nagging fear in his face that he tried to hide. Oh, he was scared. Very scared.

"Shut-up, and follow me," Zarum barked a command to the pirate in a nervous tone. Arsk's words might be correct. The big barbarian had seen the horror and destruction that had been done aboard this ship, that had killed off its entire crew. He hoped that whatever it was—was no longer on the ship now.

"By the Great Whore's Teat!" Arsk bellowed fearfully. "There be blood aplenty here, but I'll be damned if I can find even one body that remains. What happened to them?"

"They must all be dead," Sarana ventured nervously, "and someone must have killed them and then thrown their bodies overboard."

"Not all of them," Arsk replied cautiously. "I think someone must have taken them away."

"Aye, pirate, someone—or some *thing*," Zarum growled thoughtfully.

"Some *thing*, barbarian…?" Arsk asked in a haunted voice.

Zarum made no reply; he was doubting the wisdom of coming on board this ship now. It was a death ship, and his barbarian instincts made him suspicious. One thing was for sure, there was no help to be had here for them. If anything, it appeared that they were in an even more dangerous situation now.

"Let's get off this damnable ship, barbarian, and when we get to Argos I will introduce you to my wife's sister. She be a fine enough piece, and willing, even for an uncouth barbarian such as yourself."

Zarum looked at the pirate and just laughed. Who was calling who, uncouth? He had not expected such words and because of them he had not laughed in many days. It was a big, boisterous laugh. A curious look came to Sarana's face also at the pirate's friendly words. Neither of them seemed to believe what they were hearing from The Bear.

"Why the change of heart, pirate? Your wife's sister!" Zarum asked him incredulous, shaking his head dubiously.

"What do you say, Zarum?" Arsk asked almost good-naturedly—for him, at least. This was a hard thing for him to do, and it attested to the fear that he felt. Right now he did not care about what had gone *before*—he only wanted there to be an *after*...with life for him. And for that to happen he knew he needed to win this grim barbarian to his side—or more accurately—his good sword arm.

"We will go below and check the living quarters first," Zarum ordered firmly.

"Damn barbarian! You press me too hard!" Arsk shouted in exasperation, his recent good will now short-lived. "I am not going down there!"

"Yes you are!"

"Some day I will cut your heart out with a dull rusty knife while you still live!"

"You need not use a dull knife, pirate, use a sharp one, but for you to take my heart will cause you much trouble. In the end you will only die, for you are not fast enough, nor shall you win against me by trickery."

Arsk grunted a foul oath and let his mind wander to the wondrous tortures that he would perform upon the barbarian once he was in control of him. However for now, as he eyed the ship's bloody deck, and then the face of the fearsome barbarian, he grew suddenly pragmatic and decided to do as he was told.

Sarana followed as Zarum and Arsk descended the companionway to the deck below. The girl trembled in fear, and the pirate trembled in rage, bidding his time. He had wanted to kill this barbarian for what seemed to be the longest time now, yet he knew that he needed the man—two good swords being better than one. What was worse, he knew that the big barbarian knew that for now, he would do nothing and obey as he was told. For Arsk could do nothing against the man, if he wanted to get away from this accursed island with his skin intact. He cursed his ill fate as he nervously crept down the dark companionway.

Soon a horrid stench came to his nostrils, the stink of death and decay. Both men found wall torches and lit them. They walked into the empty living quarters, but found nothing but dust and the ever-present rotting odor. The three looked about the deck, but found no one, not even any remains. At some points the soaking blood from the upper deck had dripped down upon this deck. Zarum could smell the danger.

"Let us go now, there is no one here, thank the gods!" Arsk said in a much relieved tone, eager to leave.

"We will see the captain's quarters before we go," Zarum ordered.

"You never give up, do you, barbarian? You will get us all killed yet. At least if you do not care about risking your own hide, and mine, think of the poor girl here."

The girl just laughed at his fake concern for her safety.

"Sarana, you can leave. Wait for us above on the top deck," Zarum told her.

The girl left happily. She was glad to get out of those cramped, dreary quarters. And the terrible odor—of death!

Meanwhile, Arsk the Bear, grumbled to himself.

"What did you say, pirate?"

"I said, that you have been a curse upon me ever since I first laid eyes upon you."

Zarum smiled at that, then he admitted in an amused tone, "You are probably right, pirate. Now come on, we are going to investigate the captain's cabin—and lucky you—you are going to enter the room first."

Arsk stopped in his tracks; quickly he raised his sword to the barbarian's back. Before he could bring his blade down, however, Zarum turned in a swift movement using his own weapon to knock the sword out of the pirate's hand.

"Kill me then, barbarian! For I would rather die by your hand, than by some un-human thing that may be behind that door."

"You are a fool, pirate—and a coward! You do not even know if there is anything at all beyond that doorway."

Arsk the Bear just cursed every one of Zarum's ancestors that he could possibly think of.

"Pick up your sword," The Norseman barked so forcefully that Arsk had no choice but to obey, "and enter that room! And if you ever raise a sword to me again, I'll separate that ugly head from your fat shoulders."

With a sword in one hand and a torch in the other, Arsk the Bear warily entered the dark room that had been Captain Amar Kahn's cabin. He looked about him fearfully, but to his great relief, the room was empty. He thought of the barbarian waiting outside in the hallway, and a hateful snarl curled on his thin lips. Now he saw a chance to reward that barbarian dog! Now he stood behind the door with upraised sword and a vicious smile played upon his lips. Then he called out:

"Barbarian, you can come in now. It is safe. Look what I have found!"

When Korthus and his few remaining men boarded the *Seahawk*, they found no trace of any human beings. There was a lot of blood and a horrible rotting stench of death—but not even one body remained—alive or dead. Korthus and his men had mixed feelings of fear and curiosity.

"Where have our comrades gone?" Talen asked of no one in particular.

"Shut your mouth, boy! I heard something," one of the men warned.

Korthus looked up. He had heard it also now. It came from forward, from one of the companionways that led to the quarters and holds below deck.

Korthus motioned his men to silence and had them conceal themselves about the hatchways. They stood armed and ready, sweating with fear, as they heard footfalls from below. Something was coming up from the lower deck, but they knew not what it might be.

In the dim shadows the pirates could see nothing, but within moments they saw a head covered with lovely long raven-dark hair.

═

As Sarana came up towards the upper deck, she had a bad feeling that something was not right. Her fears were justified when she saw a dozen grimy pirates stand up and stare at her. For a split instant both sides looked at each other in evident surprise. Before the pirates stood a beautiful woman—and with her two comrades below and not discovered yet—grasping pirate hands were upon her. Korthus soon had his dagger at her throat.

"A woman?" Talen asked incredulous.

"Where did you come from?" Korthus demanded.

"Please do not hurt me," Sarana said.

"Who are you and what are you doing here?" Korthus asked forcefully.

"A witch! Kill her!" one pirate shouted fearfully.

"Shut up, fool!" Korthus said cuffing the man to the floor. "Answer my question, girl, and be true if you value your life. Is anyone else with you?"

"I am Sarana. I was a captive on that ship yonder, the *Triton*. It is Arsk the Bear's pirate ship."

"We know that. Is anyone else here with you?"

The girl did not say another word, and it would have gone badly for her but for the bold forceful voice that spoke up at that moment.

"I am with her, you Turan dog! Now what do you want to do about it?" Zarum growled as he came out of the aft hold with his massive sword in his hand ready for absolute carnage. He had heard the footsteps above, and knew that the girl could not have been making all of those heavy steps. He ignored Arsk, and quickly went up to investigate and found about a dozen seadog warriors, disheveled and worn.

His sword was drawn and ready for action, but he was not attacked by the pirates. Zarum eyed the men more carefully. They were of Turan, and very far away from home waters. He had done some work once in Turan years before against a group of wizards and priests who were seeking the fabulous Star Stone. He thought these men must be outcasts or renegades, seemingly a Turanian warship turned to these waters to ply the trade of piracy on the high seas. As Zarum eyed them he noticed something else as well. These men seemed to have no will to fight left in them. They were tired and worn. They just stood by motionless, with bloody swords in hand. The fearful expressions on each face told the barbarian that all the fight had been scared out of them. On this damnable island, Zarum knew that could easily be possible.

Korthus let the girl go and stepped forward, sheathed his dagger and then continued to come towards the barbarian.

Zarum watched him carefully and waited, patient.

"I am Korthus. This my ship now. I am captain. I have put down my weapon. Let us speak. Now what are you doing here and who are you?"

Zarum nodded, sheathed his sword, "Very well. We will talk."

Then the two men spoke together for a short time. At times tempers rose to feverish heights, but they subsided just as quickly. Soon they made an agreement to join forces and work together to get away from the island.

"I have one more man below deck. He has not come up yet, but he will be here soon. Can you give me some assurance that you will be true to your word and not take us captive? There are a dozen of you and only two of us, with the woman."

"You have my word, Zarum," Korthus replied firmly and Zarum could see that the man seemed a trustworthy fellow—at least to a certain extent. "My word is all I can give you. I lead my men, but they often do what they want…"

"Fair enough," Zarum replied, showing his bloodied sword to the pirate crew.

Korthus explained, "We do not want captives, or to fight, we just want to get off this island."

"That is good enough for me, Korthus, for that is what I want as well. But I warn you, any tricks and you shall be the first to taste my sword—and it has a very thirsty blade," Zarum warned, even as he decided to keep a close eye on Korthus and his Turan pirates. He also had to keep track of that damn troublemaker, Arsk. Now where was he? Still in the captain's cabin, no doubt. Zarum allowed a slight grin. Did Arsk really think he would fall for that simple ruse? Zarum had had a taste of the word of civilized men before, so he knew they lied as often as they took breath.

Suddenly Arsk the Bear came up to the top deck from below. He was bellowing with rage.

"Barbarian! Where are you? Damn, barbarian!" Arsk shouted, but then he stopped in his tracks when he saw the men all around him. He drew his sword, "Who are these dogs?"

Zarum and Korthus told him.

Afterwards Arsk said, "Now maybe we can get underway. We have enough men for a crew now."

"...it has a very thirsty blade."

Arsk was not happy about things after he had been told how things would work now. It was agreed that both Zarum and Korthus would captain the *Seahawk*. This was made easier, since both men acknowledged each other and there was also a certain amount of respect. Meanwhile Arsk fumed that both these men now controlled the ship. As the ship was underway the men began to talk together and soon spirits rose; all but Talen's. He sat apart from all the rest of his mates in a gloomy mood. The only one who he spoke to was Arsk, who pressed himself upon the lad so that he had to listen to what he was saying. Soon the two men were conversing in soft whispers. Zarum noticed the rogues' friendship and warned Korthus to keep an eye on the two.

Sarana went about getting water for the crew, for Zarum would not allow the men to drink any type of spirits. It was an order that Korthus readily agreed with because it made sense. If they were to get out of this situation in one piece, they all needed to keep their wits about them. Korthus and Zarum also agreed that the *Seahawk* was the more seaworthy vessel, and they had just enough men to form the barest of a working crew.

Quickly the decks were washed of the blood and rotting remains. Then the ropes to the *Triton* were cut, and the sails unfurled. The two captains stood at the poop and looked at the small jungle island as their ship moved out into the sea. Both were relieved that the ship was slowly moving away from that island.

"That's the last we shall ever see of that damnable place," Korthus said now feeling a lot better that they were underway.

"I hope you are right, Turanian," Zarum replied grimly. All the time the wily barbarian's eyes scanned the island for any signs of pursuit. There was none, so far.

However, it was not long thereafter that Talen, up in the lookout nest, noticed a large group of black shapes flying towards them from a mountain at the opposite end of the island. Zarum, Korthus and Sarana, all noticed the ominous flying shapes at the same time.

"Put on every inch of sail we have!" Zarum barked to a swarthy sailor named Mumet, who had been given the job of First Mate. Mumet replayed the order and the men ran aloft, but soon it was evident that they could not outdistance their pursuers. The dark flying shapes just kept coming, closer and closer.

"We will not get away, will we, Zarum?" Korthus asked, his hope of only moments before now already gone.

"No. It will not be very long until they are among us, Korthus," Zarum replied drawing his sword. "Tell the men to make themselves ready."

Harsh cries rang up from the doomed *Seahawk*, as the giant hybrid bat creatures dove downward towards the luckless vessel. None on the ship had ever seen such creatures before and all were utterly terrified. All but Arsk the Bear. He lay outstretched upon his stomach asleep in a drunken stupor, upon the aft side of the poop deck.

Zarum walking nearby gave the drunken pirate a rousing kick and then walked away to lead the ship's feeble defense, vaguely wondering where Arsk had found the wine.

Arsk awoke with a start, his rage, however, was instantly replaced by stark fear when he saw the huge black bats begin diving towards the ship with dripping fangs and sharp talons outstretched. Arsk was petrified. Here was a sight even more fearful than those hideous little beast-men—also from that damnable island. His hands gripped the small carved black rock that hung about his neck and mumbled a quick prayer to the pirate god, Ibar.

Arsk stood still now, holding the black rock, when Zarum came up to him. The barbarian was about to curse the pirate, and make the coward draw his sword to join the fight, when he heard dozens of hellish shrieks from above. Within moments, Zarum, Arsk, and the ship's crew watched in open-mouthed wonder, as the creatures suddenly flew away. In moments they were gone. Zarum knew that whatever sorcerous power that held these vile creatures under its control, had now suddenly disappeared. The creatures flew away. He wondered what it could mean.

Then Zarum was surprised as his eyes fell upon Arsk the Bear, and the carved black rock that the pirate withheld before him in tightly clenched fists.

⸺

Naga-Yaro was old. How old, no one could even guess. He had been old in Quaga Nus' boyhood, and that had been almost sixty suns past. Every ancestor of Quaga Nus had known Naga Yaro to be a very old man. Everyone feared him, even the great chief Quaga Nus, the king of all the savage Bantuli peoples.

Naga Yaro had great power, a dark mysterious power, and he used it often. Often with horrible results. He also had an army of the beastly Mgor-Tus, the gigantic horned black bats that did his bidding. They had for all ages terrorized the sub-human tribes of the Bantuli. Ever since the memory of the Bantuli's could remember, the old wizard had lived alone, atop a mountain called Blackslope, with none but his horrid servants and his great horned bats for company. His house, a great castle-like fortress, was always avoided. Even Quaga Nus dreaded to go up to that place of ghosts and demons, but when he was called on those rare occasions, he always went. He had no choice. It would be sheer folly not to heed the command of the old wizard, and he had seen the results given to those who did not do as he told them to do, and it was never pleasant. This was one more time when Quaga Nus had been sent for by the old man atop the mountain. A slave had come to his hut and now led him up the winding path to the monstrous black stone castle.

Quaga Nus saw the mist and steam come up from the fire-god, and felt the horrid sticky heat. Although the height of this peak was such that snow should form, it never did up here, not since Naga Yaro had come, or so the legend said. However, the little beast-man king of the Bantuli had more to worry him than old stories, as he looked around him. There was a small stream that flowed blood red, and when Quaga Nus realized it was human blood that flowed in that stream, he felt dizzy with sickness. The Bantuli king was certainly brutal and had butchered many in war, but this went beyond even mere brutality; a dark suffocating evil permeated the entire atmosphere. Quaga Nus grew fearful, for he was petrified of disobeying the old wizard, and of the consequences that would develop should he disobey. When he was called, he went. He had to. He had not the courage to find out what would happen to him if he did not do as he was ordered.

Quaga Nus passed by high piles of human flesh. The remains of the bodies were somewhat familiar. They were the bodies of the big men he had seen come to the island on the big boats in days past. Today, they lay heaped in high piles of ghastly reeking flesh with a horrible decaying stench. He saw some of the dreaded Mgor-Tus fighting over a particular bloated body. They scratched and clawed each other away, all the time reducing what was left over of the mangled corpse into a multitude of tiny debris. He saw others of the great beasts locked in the caves, and breathed a deep sigh of relief.

As he walked up the path, he came upon dozens of men, both big men and some of his own smaller jungle people, hanging from poles and ropes so that their feet dangled above the ground. He winced as he came in hearing range of their piteous cries and pleas. Other men were alive and hung suspended in large metal cages. As Quaga Nus walked onward he could almost feel a twinge of pity, which was unusual for him, but it was all he was capable of feeling. He knew what would happen to these captives and in haste he redoubled his pace. He wanted to enjoy the coming blood feast—not be it. He just hoped that it would not happen to him.

The king was soon ushered into the castle by the slave who had led him up the mountain.

Naga Yaro was furious for the first time in eons, for his magic had somehow been subverted and interfered with. Diverted. The giant Mgor-Tus' sent and directed by his command had somehow wandered and ignored his commands. He had lost all control over the mighty beasts. What was worse—some of the big men—the pirate scum whose ship had wrecked upon the rocks, had escaped their cage. One man had even ransacked his castle during Naga Yaro's short absence. All the big men had been captured and punished, but for one of them, the very one who had dared to enter his castle. That one swine had taken something of great importance. It had great power, and Naga Yaro knew he must have it back.

"Listen closely, dog-king!" the old wizard's tongue hissed vehemently. "Something has been stolen from my castle. One of the big men, a pirate from the ship that was wrecked upon the coastal rocks. He is a large man, and he took a small black carved rock. I want that man and I want that rock. Send all your warriors to search, and you had better find it! Now be gone!"

Quaga Nus needed no more words to hasten his departure from that chamber. He ran out of the castle and down the mountain path, and he did not stop until he reached his village. Quickly he called forth all the warriors together and told them what they must do. Then he sent out runners to all the other villages, giving the wizard's orders to each headman.

Meanwhile, Naga Yaro stood alone using the powers of his mind to locate the whereabouts of the stolen rock that in reality was the powerful Eye of Beel.

Zarum eyed Arsk the Bear curiously, looking at the small carved black rock that the pirate held in his hand. It glowed and pulsed in the pirate's trembling hand. Zarum knew it for what it was; some type of sorcerous talisman. He also knew now that it was that talisman which had saved the ship from the huge flying horned bat creatures. Somehow it had called the creatures away from the ship.

Zarum had never really noticed the carved piece before now, for it just appeared to be a dark dusky thing of little value. The image of some heathen god. It looked like any other common rock, almost. It was badly carved in some image he could not clearly make out. Now as Zarum looked upon it more closely, he saw that it was indeed glowing and pulsating—so it was a very special kind of rock.

"Where did you get that, pirate?" Zarum demanded as Korthus and Sarana both came over to him.

"It's mine! I...found it!"

"Liar!" Sarana said spitting at the feet of the pirate.

Arsk the Bear growled, he had forgotten about the girl. Then he smiled a wide toothless smile. What mattered if he told the truth now anyway? The girl knew it and if he lied again she would surely tell all she knew. He knew it could go badly for him with the barbarian. What cared the barbarian how he obtained a simple rock?

"Well, Arsk!' Zarum demanded forcefully.

"He stole it, from a man on the island," Sarana replied. "From a tall black man we found tumbling in terror through the jungle one night…"

"Aye, barbarian," Arsk continued the narrative, as if he had no care and nothing to hide. "He was some Black, called himself Nikagi, I think."

"Nikagi of Kush!" Zarum said sharply, his face burning red now in anger. "What did you do to that man?"

"Well? What did I do? Well, I killed him, naturally. Then I rifled his pockets, but all he had on him was this interesting rock, so I kept it. Before he died, he told me that it was a powerful charm that he had stolen from some old shaman on the island named Naga Yaro. He said that it was the Eye of Beel, whatever that might be—but I thought it was a carven image of the pirate god, Ibar. So I took it. Anyway, he told me I could keep the rock if I spared his life and gave him food and protected him from the Bantuli. That's what he called those little beast-men we've been fighting. Naturally, I thought his price much too high. So I killed him, then I took the rock anyway."

Zarum's face turned a deep raging scarlet now. Quickly his hands grasped Arsk's throat and tightened inexorably. Arsk choking, tried to yell, surprised by this sudden action. The barbarian's hands were incredible vises as strong as the metal of a sword. Arsk tried to reach for his own sword, but it was knocked away and instantly he saw the blade of Zarum's dagger at his throat.

"Filth of a pirate! Son of a sea slut!" that man you killed, Nikagi, was one of my crew, and a friend. He was First Mate on my ship, *The Lion of the North*, wrecked upon the rocks of that island many days ago!"

Zarum had had enough.

Arsk's eyes opened wide in surprise and shock with growing fear as Zarum held the pirate up against the bulkhead and then thrust the blade of his dagger deep into the pirate's neck. The Bear let out a horrid scream, then gurgled some unknown words mixed with blood, to soon slump down to the deck in a slippery pool of crimson.

"No, Zarum!" Korthus shouted out too late. "We needed that man. We're too short handed as it is to run this ship."

"Shut up!" Zarum barked, still full of rage. "Nikagi was a friend of mine. That man killed him like a dog!"

Korthus remained quiet, then nodded, accepting the judgment.

Quickly the big barbarian lifted the bloody corpse of the pirate, ripped the black carved rock from about his bloody neck, and then threw the body into the churning water below. Arsk the Bear sunk beneath the waves and was gone in a moment.

Carefully Zarum looked at the strange rock in his hand, and then let it fly with a mighty heave into the ocean's foamy spray, "No one will command those flying monsters ever again."

Sullenly the barbarian walked away and sat alone by himself. Korthus and Sarana eyed him with awe and amazement.

"All right, you sea dogs!" Korthus bellowed taking command now. "You have seen your show, now move! Get to work! Let us take this ship away from here. Now!"

While Korthus was occupied with the running of the ship, Sarana walked over to where the barbarian sat in sullen silence.

"I am sorry for your friend, Zarum," she said simply. "Were many of your men killed?"

"All of them," Zarum replied grimly. "Nikagi was the only one whose body I did not find. The others I found butchered on the rocks upon the mountain, some of their bodies were thrown upon the wreckage of my ship. They tried to reach the ship, but something caught up with them. Whatever it was, it left little enough of them in one piece."

"So where do we go now?" Sarana asked softly.

"Argos."

Sarana shuddered at the thought of having to return to the seraglio of the king of Argos. She knew if she entered the city, there could be but only that result for her—after a suitable punishment for her escape, which she might not even live through.

Zarum sensed the fear in the girl and motioned her to his side. Once she was close by, he pulled her closer and held her in his arms and brought her even closer.

"No need for you to worry, girl," he told her with a meaningful grin. "I'll not let that fat dog of an Argos king get his grubby hands on you ever again."

Sarana gave a half smile as Zarum wrapped his powerful arms around her. He held her close, but with a gentleness she would not have thought possible. She felt safe in his arms.

"Argos will be only a short stopover, to sell this ship. I've had it with the sea life. It's the lush fields and meadows of Kush where I shall be headed next. Who knows, girl, if you want to follow me, you might even persuade me to pass by your home village. Would you like to go there?"

Sarana smiled joyfully and wrapped her arms around Zarum's neck. She then put her lips to his. They kissed for a long moment and then he picked up the laughing girl and made his way down a companionway to the captain's cabin below.

"Whatever do you have in mind, my barbarian from the North?"

"You shall see, girl," Zarum replied with a lusty wink. "You shall see."

Sarana giggled lightly, "Well, then, let us get on with it!"

THE MUMMY OF QUELANG

Sweat dripped steadily down the ragged furrows of Balta's face, while his nerves grew taut with fear and apprehension at the vast riches he and his confederate would unearth tonight from the ancient tomb of trice-damned Kwa-Thath.

Carefully, Ramool the burly Shamar desert man, watched the moon overhead. It was bright and at its zenith, yet seemed full of what looked like a dark and foreboding mysteriousness. It sent a bleak chill through both men. Ramool's keen eyes darted about though he could see naught to sound an alarm. For now, all seemed quiet and peacefully lonely.

"My Lord," Ramool whispered, as he gave his scraggily black beard a nervous twitching pull, "all is in readiness."

Balta shot a quick glance above to the illuminating moon and then his sharp eyes scanned the area around him. Satisfied that they were alone and all was safe, he smiled a deep grin of insatiable greed as he carefully reached into the silken folds of his robe.

Slowly the master withdrew his clenched fist and then opened that fist to reveal what lay within.

"By the Gods of the Red Rimmed Desert!" Ramool whispered in shocked wonder, his eyes wide in disbelief. For what he saw in Balta's hand lay a shimmering blood-red gem that rolled about like the element named for the god Mercurius, and yet did not appear to be made of any liquid silver at all, but of freshly spilled blood!

"My lord, that is it? The Blood Stone? The fabled Blood Stone of Kwa-Thath… I thought it safely hidden away in a monastery in far off Kanasul."

"So the legend says," Balta replied with an almost sensuous rubbing of the gem with the tips of his long well manicured fingers. "But a young thief, from far off Gilfiere, has stolen it from its sacred hiding place, and now I own it. The man was a fool, selling it to me for a mere pittance. He must not have realized what it was. The vast power of it."

"Or, he saw to be rid of it as soon as possible, for a quick payment?"

The master nodded sagely, "Yes, perhaps. In any case, I have it now!"

With a sneer of delight and contempt, Balta walked towards the huge door that for three hundred years had effectively sealed the crypt of the sorcerer Kwa-Thath. For in all that time no thief had ever managed entrance through that magical portal, and the villagers of the region hoped that such would continue, for these simple folk feared terribly the legends of that being which rested within.

With nervous fingers, Balta stood before the door and carefully lifted the pulsating stone and held it out before him with unsteady hands to be used as a focus for his wizardly powers.

With terrible strain showing on his face and shaking form, Balta concentrated the power on the portal, and soon to the desert man's surprise the great doorway to the antiquated tomb opened upon creaky hinges with a mighty scream of the ages. Immediately, both men were assailed by the fierce stench of decay and corruption which spewed forth from the portal, while inside was all soon grew quiet, dark, and sinisterly foreboding.

After an appropriate time, Ramool followed Balta with his drawn sword in one hand and empty sacks in the other. Sacks that both men hoped would soon be filled to the brim with gold, gems and the ever valuable olden tomes which contained all the dark laws of Quelang's ancient magic's.

As they entered the portal they found themselves in a long corridor that gently sloped downward. With each step Balta took he noticed the Blood Stone of Kwa-Thath pulse and glow with an unholy red aura while it was getting noticeably warmer to the touch. A shadow of fear touched the face of the wizard and his fingers and hands soon began to burn from the now fiery gem. Soon it had become so hot and painful that the wizard was afraid the gem might eat right through the flesh of his hand. He tried to put the talisman away in his pocket pouch but he saw that here too it would soon burn through the heavy leather, so he had no choice but to put it down upon the stone floor by the entrance, and no recourse but to pick it up later, on his way out of the tomb.

Julane, a warrior from the fortress city of Gilfiere, grinned in amazement at the little scene being enacted below. That crafty wizard thought Julane to be such a fool, but in truth it was the other way around. For, though young, Julane knew only a great and powerful magic could ever hope to open that mighty sepulcher of aged darkness. So Julane sold the wizard the gem at a decent price, and now watched with a wry grin as the portal was being opened *for him.*

Soon Julane would come out from concealment claim what he desired from within. He smiled now, it was a good idea and he was full of anticipation, yet he remained ever watchful below to see that all was proceeding according to plan.

It was truly an ancient tomb and weirdly designed, with strange bas-reliefs of pre-human animals fighting in mysterious tropical swamps. Nervously he ran his fingers through his long dark hair as he cautiously looked within. Far off he could see the flames from the torches the wizard and his companion held, receding into the inner darkness.

Suddenly his eyes darted to where the blood-red gem lay, and Julane noticed the strange warmth it produced in his hand. Soon the gem was getting warmer, and then ever hotter to the touch, so that Julane could not hold it any longer. He was just about to put it down when he heard an ear-piercing shriek coming from deeper within the tomb and almost simultaneously the blood-red gem darkened and grew hard and cold.

"What's the meaning of this?" Julane whispered to himself eyeing the strange cold gem. Then he realized the truth, "All the power has left this gem—but gone where?"

For answer Julane heard a pair of hideous screams from Balta and Ramool and knew that the fools had somehow awakened something which was now feeding and drawing away the power of the gem to give it pseudo-life. Quickly Julane put the gem in his pouch and carefully walked deeper into the stygian darkness of the eerie crypt.

To Julane it seemed as though he was walking into the very bowels of Hell itself, for in the semi-darkness he could just barely make out the cold slabs of the stone walls with an unnatural greenish glow in the stifling corridor. The putrid smell of death and corruption assailed his nostrils, while his eyes wide with terror beheld the aged stone walls covered with obscene paintings and glyphs of grotesque beasts and humans engaged in horrid actions that drove one to the farthest limits of sanity.

For one moment the wily thief covered his eyes, reeled drunkenly, and then collected his stunned senses, to proceed with his hand wrapped in a tight hold on his sword hilt. So tightly that his knuckles shone almost chalk white.

Julane walked deeper into the ancient mausoleum. Soon he heard another ear-piercing shriek. He knew that it was Balta and Ramool, and that there was deadly trouble ahead if the wizard's powers could not be of any use. As he quit the passageway and neared the opening of the dimly lit chamber, he saw a scene that sent his bones cold, his blood congealing in his veins.

There, huddled on the floor in a corner, with terror etched into every line of his face was the wizard, Balta. He held a sack, full to the brim with gems and gold while he mumbled incoherently—his mind shattered by what he had seen. Next to him lay a scattered pile of old books and parchments from long lost Quelang. While in the forefront stood the giant desert man, Ramool, his sword drawn in a vain effort to protect himself and his master from the horror which now advanced upon them.

For it was indeed a terror from the dim and distant past of immortally evil Quelang that now confronted the two men. There, advancing toward the terrified desert man was the mummy of Kwa-Thath, alive and glaring through blood-red eyes of unknowable cruelty and hate. The most fearful thing about the creature was that it did not appear human at all, but looked to be the remains of some large bird-like creature with a long sharp beak and extensive bony claws. It was certainly something from some alien plane of existence unknown to man.

Julane looked with fear at the seething corruption of this creature of walking death. Parts of rags and shrouds blew in the unnatural breeze created by its passing, while from holes within it, gnawing worms writhed as if the whole body was in convulsive agony, causing it to move unnaturally. Ramool stood frozen in deathly terror. Balta finally panicked, dropping his burden to race blindly away until he collided with, and fully knocked over Julane in his haste to leave that damned place. Julane grabbed the ashen-faced wizard by his silken garments and held him fast.

"Look well at what you have conjured, wizard!" he growled at Balta, who was now shaking with terror. Finally Balta recognized Julane as the young thief who had first sold him the gem. It all seemed ages ago now.

"Release me! It will kill us all, fool! It is not of this world!" the wizard barked madly. "Release me!"

Julane held him even more firmly, "What manner of beast is this, wizard? And how can it be killed!"

"It is the living corpse of Kwa-Thath come alive to avenge itself upon us for desecrating his tomb," Balta screamed in terror as he struggled to escape, but to no avail. "Please. I beg of you to let me go."

"How can I kill this thing?" Julane demanded for his eyes had spotted the sack of gems and gold, and if there was a way to beat this terror Julane would find it, and be sure to profit in the process!

"We can do nothing. We are doomed!" Balta cried tragically. "I need the gem, the one you sold me, and I do not have it!"

"How do you use this gem?"

"Crush it under the heel of your boot," the wizard cried, his eyes pleading to be let go. "Please!"

—

Ever so slowly the mummy neared Ramool, who stood as one mesmerized, too terrified to even move. Ever so slowly, icy, long dead finger-like claws reached out for the warm throat of the desert man.

...advancing toward the terrified desert man...

Quickly those white bony claws tightened until Ramool, perhaps now finally awakening, looked full into the eyes of the mummy, and seeing the doom that was upon him futilely tried to put up resistance. With both sword and dagger he stabbed the monster repeatedly, but it was all to no avail and his actions had no effect upon the creature. For how do you kill that which is already dead? That which has been dead for centuries! That which is not even of this world!

Ramool's voice was cut down from a loud scream to a whispered gurgle as the mummy's grip tightened.

Meanwhile Julane dragged the cowering wizard forward.

Julane retrieved an ancient bejeweled sword that was formerly a part of the wizard's booty.

"Here!" and Julane shoved the hilt into the wizard's hand. "Now, come and help me save your friend."

Balta would not move so Julane finally had to give him a very prudent kick in the backside which sent the wizard sprawling forward, screaming in terror.

Ramool was dying, and though Julane tried to break the iron grip the monster had upon the desert man's throat, he soon found that it was a useless effort and that there could be but one result. As he attacked the creature—some kind of giant bird-like fiendish mummy—Julane was thrown down to the floor by its powerful claws. He lay stunned in a corner, his body slumped up against the wall and his hair matted with his own wet blood. He never heard the final terrible death-scream of the desert man as the monster crushed the life out of him. Ramool was no more.

Alone now, and terrified beyond measure, Balta had seen the mummy bash the desert man's head repeatedly upon the stone flags. Be-spattered in his companion's blood, Balta screamed as that tattered and enshrouded walking death now turned its hollow gaze in his direction. Its long beak of a face, those empty hollow eyes that shone blood red, that looked upon him with doom. Slowly the mummy began to come for the wizard.

Regaining some of his nerve, Balta vainly tried some of his spells and incantations to fight off the advancing creature. To his horror, nothing he did worked, as the deathless horror was soon upon him. In bare moments it was all over as the mummy grabbed the neck of the unfortunate wizard and quickly snapped it clean. Then throwing the lifeless hulk aside, the mummy turned his gaze upon the motionless form of Julane of Gilfiere.

Slowly Kwa-Thath's corpse advanced with bloody hand-like claws outstretched and dark murder coming from its hellish red eyes. With a Herculean effort, Julane stood up and quickly fought off the weakness and dizziness that clouded his mind. With an arm he wiped the caked blood from his face and stood watching the monster as it lumbered down upon him. This was no mummy of a man, but some otherworldly creature in human shape and while it terrified Julane, he would not allow it to best him.

——

He was dismayed that he did not have his sword. It lay across the room where he had dropped it in his defense of the desert man, so Julane drew his dagger and was determined to fight for his life as dearly as possible. He was still numb when he remembered the gem he had secreted in his pocket pouch and the words of Balta regarding that gem and the mummy. He could not comprehend what it might all mean, but it did not matter. It was some form of magic and it was certainly worth a chance!

"Curse Balta, and this damnable stone for what he has unleashed!" Julane cried in rage, as he drew the gem forth in a bold action. Quickly he threw the stone to the floor and then smashed it into dust with the sole of his iron-shod boot.

The stone broke like glass into a black smoky dust, and no more than a second later, the mummy—as though all strength and power had left its mighty limbs—dropped down to become a lifeless pile of dust upon the cold stone floor of the tomb.

Julane's expression now changed from horror to utter surprise, and soon to mirth as he collected his senses and realized what had happened. With the tip of his boot he stirred the black dust that was all that was left of the mummy of Kwa-thath. Even now the breeze entering the chamber from the outside was disturbing the small mound of ash, dislocating it and moving each little particle until soon there would be nothing of it left at all.

Julane of Gilfeire nodded with satisfaction. He quickly picked up the sack of treasure that Balta had so thoughtfully provided for him, and then regaining his sword, the master thief strode out of that chamber of horrors into the warm light of early morning.

With haste he rode away from that dead place to soon come to a town where he could enjoy the fruits of his labors. And maybe, he thought, smiling, he would find a young lass or two to share it with?

THE LAST CITY

This is a story of the last days of Earth when man is reduced to living in a single mighty city. It is called Gilfeire, and it exists upon the huge land mass called Xanduris, the last vestige of ground upon the Earth. All else in the world is wild barren ocean, all of it estranged to humanity. Only on Xanduris does the once prolific seed of man persistently hold a slight toehold onto existence, and it is only in that last great city of Gilfeire. This is all that is left after the Great Cataclysm of centuries before that had brought the world of man to its knees. Gilfeire, the last refuge of man—and even now it is under attack!

"It was the last city of man upon the Earth, and its days are numbered"
—Lord Krosis, Governor of Segunda

It was a dark night, for there were no stars visible through the constant haze, and the moon that rumor said had once shone so brightly overhead ages ago, was no longer in the heavens. It was gone. No one knows where.

Julane of Gilfeire walked down deserted streets. He could feel the fear that drifted through the city, much as the way the morning mist curled at his feet, slow and persistent, but with an enveloping obscurity that blinded vision and the senses.

It was damnable dark, and his mind drifted to what he remembered said about there once having been a moon in the night sky, a moon large enough to brighten the heavens. It was no longer so. He shrugged, for he doubted there had ever been such a huge thing hanging in the sky, though the sages spoke of it as being described in ancient books. How could such a huge thing hold itself up in the sky? Sooner or later it would have to fall.

Julane allowed a wry smile, remembering what his old teacher Alturia had said regarding the Great Cataclysm. Perhaps this thing called a moon did exist once, and perhaps man at one time in the dim past, was master of this world—and not confined to one small corner of it. Many sad things were written in the ancient texts, though few could read them in these later days. Mostly, the old books meant nothing, for their words spoke of long dead glories that the last men would never know, much less understand.

Julane noticed that the streets were unusually quiet as he walked to the Eastern Gate. The gate was one of the only two exits from the city. The other exit was the Blue Gate, which opened to Torgais, the Dark Fortress that guarded the pass through the great mountains which formed a natural shield for the city. The Eastern Gate led into the great fortress of Sequnda on the other side of the land upon which stood Gilfeire. It was these two forts, Torgais and Segunda, that guarded the passes, and protected Gilfeire from the attacks of the half-men and other monstrous creatures that constantly made war upon mankind and its last city.

Julane continued his walk down the dreary streets and saw no one about. The houses and shops were all boarded up tighter than the gates to Lord Krosis' pleasure garden. Of course most of the able bodied men and women were already stationed upon the city walls, or posted to either of the two forts. Nevertheless, there should have been some of the city dwellers around; their absence was very odd.

All around the darkness of the night blended into the darkness of doorways and alleys, as he passed. It was an eerie feeling, like walking through an already dead city, or a city of the dead. Maybe, he thought, a city could tell when it was going to die? If so, the people of Gilfeire seemed certain of that fact. He tried to put these morbid thoughts from his mind, for he knew he must be on his guard in this section of the city. This was a good place to get yourself knifed by a thief, or a Hydran agent.

Julane walked on quickly, all the time his hand resting upon the hilt of his short sword. The weapon gave him some feeling, however small, of being master of his own fate. It was a deluded feeling, he knew. Finally he turned a corner onto the Avenue Of Kings, which led straight to his destination, the Segunda Fortress.

Suddenly Julane stopped dead in his tracks. He heard a strange sound, known as The Sound. It was a low shuffling noise that came from behind him. He had heard it before and knew that such a sound could not be made by anything human.

Julane quickly ducked into an alcove and drew his sword. He could see the creature clearly now. It was a Kaith, one of the huge flying reptiles that were the servants of the wicked Hydrans.

The creature moved slowly, and Julane realized that it was looking for a certain building. It finally stopped at a doorway across the street from where Julane was concealed. A man opened the door of a large house. The flying monster landed, folded its wings, and then bent down low as it entered the house. It had apparently been invited inside.

Julane stood by in shock. He had heard stories of men who were collaborating with the Hydrans, but he could not accept the fact. It had never been proven. It was only talked about in whispers, for no human could believe that another of his kind would wantonly ally themselves with such alien monsters. Now Julane had to believe it, for he had seen it with his own eyes, and even more—he had to do something about it!

With drawn sword the young warrior moved closer to the house of Aron Miklis. Once there, he looked through a crack in the shudder, but saw nothing in the empty large room. The conspirators must be in one of the rooms on the upper floors.

Julane's heart raced as he thought of what they were planning—the delivery of the city into the hands of the Hydrans and their allies, no doubt. It would mean the torture, debasement, and death of thousands of people—all human beings, like Julane—by creatures that were man's realization of his most terrible nightmares.

As quietly as was possible Julane forced open the door to Miklis' house. He was astonished at how any human could deal with the Hydrans, the sworn enemies of humanity. It was their goal to exterminate the human race, which they had boasted many times. Julane wondered what they could possible offer Miklis for his aid in their murderous scheme?

Julane understood only too well why the Hydrans were bent on the extermination of all humans. It was because of some kind of massive religious difference between the two races of beings. The Hydrans were fanatics, who, after trying to convert the neo-Christian humans without success, decided they were a blasphemous cancer that had to be wiped out. The choice given humanity was simple—debase themselves and join the Hydrans, or die. Since humans would not forsake their own God for the Hydran belief, and they inwardly hated and feared the reptilian Hydrans, they selected to stay behind the walls of their great city in strict isolationism. The Hydrans would not accept this, and soon their leaders declared—Shre-dath—or holy war against all of humanity.

As Julane entered the dark room, he noticed that it was empty, but he could hear whispered voices coming from the upper level of the building. He strained his ears to hear the words that were being said.

"My Lord Kre-da bids me tell you to make all preparations. Already the hosts have gathered from all parts of Xan-duris. The Solom Ones from Cedan, the Rikes and the Kaith, the Jungle Peoples, Shum-nof-arous (those who live under the earth), and all the Clans and Torgs of the sea dwellers. They are all ready for war. The Kaith shall fly on the winds and rain death from above, as the legions of the Hydrans march into Gilfeire. We will destroy everything. Nothing of the unbelievers shall remain. The Shre-dath shall be won. You will have all in readiness."

"As my Lord bids, it shall be done," a voice replied that Julane recognized as belonging to Miklis the traitor. "My followers and I wish only to serve Great Kre-da. It is our one and only desire."

"It is my one and only desire," the Kaith said repeating the formal phrase. "I will go now to alert the host. You do what must be done."

Julane had heard enough. He ran up the stairs and burst into the room. Its only occupants were Miklis and the winged Kaith. Quickly, before the traitor could draw his sword, Julane knocked him unconscious with the pommel of his blade. Then he rushed forward to meet the charge of the giant Kaith. Before he could get a cut at it, the monstrous reptile hit him with a great blow that sent him flying into the wall at the other end of the room. Stunned and barely conscious, Julane watched as the big Kaith hopped to an open window sill. Within seconds he was in the air and gone.

Atlan and Lord Seth came out of the room and walked over to Julane. Their faces looked full of fear born out of hopelessness.

"Aron Miklis will not talk," Atlan said practically spitting out the words, "And we tried all forms of persuasion."

"He will not tell us who his followers are, or what it is that they plan to do," Lord Seth added. "Oh, there can not be many of them, but they can do much to cause trouble in our city. A few people in key places betraying us, and we may even lose the city."

"We must place extra guards," Atlan answered, "The forts, Sequnda and Torgais must be strengthened…and the city patrol…"

"Where do we get the men, Atlan?" Lord Seth replied in a tired voice. "Every man and woman who can use a sword is already in service. Even Yamina, the daughter of Lord Krosis, is now at station in Fort Torgais."

"The enemy can strike at any time. We must be ready," Atlan answered as if by rote.

"We are as ready as we ever will be, there is nothing else we can do without more information, and Aron Miklis will not provide it. He always was an obstinate fellow," Lord Seth replied. His face showed the fear and hopelessness that had overtaken him now. He did not know what to do, nor was there much of anything that he could do. They were trapped, under siege in the last city of mankind and at any time the enemy might decide to break the siege and invade.

"What of Balistry?" Julane asked with a glimmer of hope, "they helped us once against the Hydrans."

"Aye, when it was to their advantage, but they'll not enter the war this time, the sides are too uneven. If what you heard is true, and I don't doubt it for a moment, the Hydrans have the mightiest army in history ready to crush us. Balistry has ignored all our pleas. I cannot say that I blame them."

"We are not defeated yet!" Julane snapped back, he did not like the hopelessness with which things were being spoken. He asked Seth to give him permission to try once more with the strange inhabitants of Balistry. At least let me try!"

"No! It is too late for that now. We need every man here when the trouble comes," Atlan snapped, a nervous order.

Lord Seth was quiet and then he nodded his head. "I suppose you must try again? If so, then do it, but be back in Gilfeire before tomorrow eve."

Julane nodded and bowed, "It will be done, My Lord."

Then he left the chamber. When the young warrior was gone, the two older men spoke up.

"He's a fool," Atlan grumbled in anger.

Lord Seth ignored the harsh words. "Come, I want to inspect the defenses at Segunda again. I have a feeling that something is not right there."

<hr>

"In war it is always best to be on the winning side."
—Lord Tantuvall, Commander, Torgais Fortress

Yamina saw the defeated looks in the eyes of the defenders of Torgais as they stood upon the parapets and looked out at the mountainous crags that loomed before the great fortress. As far as the eye could see there stretched the fires and tents of the Hydran host. There were more than ten of the enemy for every man and woman in the city. Meanwhile there were hundreds of Kaiths flying overhead. They hurled insults and zhaths, the small steel, razor-sharp disks that held a deadly poison. Already dozens of the defenders were dead, and the battle hadn't even begun.

All day zhaths were rained down upon the defenders with their deadly poison. Yamina saw many of the men struck down around her. Once hit, the poison acted quickly. She herself was almost hit by one of the whirling blades, but luck was with her and she unknowingly moved out of its path just in time. The young man behind her was not so lucky; the blade embedded itself into his chest while he screamed in agony. Already the poison was beginning to act upon him, so that when Yamina and a young warrior named Talis had brought the wounded man down off the parapet and into the medical room, he was already quite dead.

"He's a fool," Atlan grumbled in anger.

"If we only had an antidote to the Kaith poison," Talis said in a tired tone. He and Yamina began their walk back to their positions upon the wall.

"But we do not. There are only a few hundred Kaiths now, but when the attack begins…, the sky will be full of them," Yamina replied trying to calm her useless anger. Better to save it all for the fight to come. She was the kind of person who became stronger in the face of hardships, and rather than become fearful at the hopelessness of their situation; her rage and anger only grew and gave her strength. If anything, it made her a more formidable and furious fighter, so she would take many of the enemy with her before her time came to die.

"I have given up all hope, we shall all die," Talis said gloomily. "I only pray that it is in battle, and not in what will come afterwards. The slaughter."

"Yes, I know," Yamina replied resigned to their fate. "I keep thinking of the children. We are the lucky ones; we get to die in battle. As heroes, for all that it matters. They will die on the butcher block and the rack. And if not, they will be mercifully killed by their own parents, so as not to fall into the hands of the Hydrans. Their's is not a promising future."

"Nor is ours," Talis added with a grim laugh.

They were up on the wall now and they could see a great commotion in the Hydran camp.

"It must be Kre-da and the rest of his lords," Yamina said to Talis.

He nodded silently, wondering what thoughts were in the Hydran leader's mind.

"It won't be long now, I think," Talis said as he watched the milling horde swarming in the enemy's vast camp. His concentration interrupted by the sound of a warrior yelling Yamina's name.

"Lady Yamina! Lady Yamina!" he yelled as he ran along the wall.

"Over here!" Talis yelled back, as the man took notice and immediately came over. He saluted Talis and bowed towards Yamina.

"Lady Yamina, I have been sent by Lord Tantuvaal. He requests your presence in his office immediately," the messenger told her.

It was with the greatest reluctance that Lady Yamina followed the young man to the quarters of the fort's commander.

Lord Krosis, commander of Fortress Segunda looked with distaste upon the two visitors that had entered his office.

"Lord Seth, and Minister Atlan! I had not thought to see the two of you here again," Krosis said as he noticed the tired look in Seth's eyes, while Atlan just looked on in moody depression.

"We have come, Lord Krosis, to see that all is in readiness. We have reports from Fort Trogais that they are already under attack, and it seems strange to us that there has been no action around your fortress."

"It will come, My Lord," he said with a surety. "It will come."

"That we know, Lord Seth stated.

"What I want to know is…" Atlan stopped sort, looked around at the sound of something strange. "What is that? What is going on…"

The door to the commander's office at that moment was broken down, and standing in the portal were now a dozen monstrous Kaiths. Before the three men could draw their weapons, a dozen whirling zhaths were thrown into the chamber. It only took three clean neck shots, and all three of the men were instantly decapitated. They never knew what hit them.

Within the hour Fortress Segunda had fallen. It had been a fool-proof plan, the underground people, Shum-nof-arov, had tunneled into the fortress allowing thousands of Kaiths and Rikes to enter the fort. Once inside, and on equal terms with the defenders, the battle changed to become a massacre. Gilfeire was now completely open to attack and the mutants from outside ran to the city to kill the last of the Truhumans.

"Lady Yamina," Tantuvaal said watching the young girl enter his office. "It is good that you have come. I am afraid that I have bad news. I have received word that Fortress Sequnda has fallen."

"My father?"

"All the defenders were put to the sword," Tantuvaal replied trying to show a sorrow that he did not really feel. His large jowls shook as he spoke and he wiped the sweat from his face. "It is obvious to me, as it must be to you, that our defense here is useless."

Yamina was visibly shaken, her breasts were rising and falling with each labored breath, nevertheless she struggled to reply, "What else is there for us to do? Withdraw to Gilfeire?"

"I think not. The city will eventually fall; we both know that it is only a matter of time, and not much time at that. Soon everyone will be put to the sword, but it does not have to be that way. In war it is always best to be on the winning side."

Yamina said nothing, but looked at the fort commander carefully as Tantuvaal continued. His eyes flowed over her body wantonly.

"You are a very beautiful woman, Yamina. It would be a shame for you to die here. It will be all for nothing. Come with me, I can get us out of here with safe passage through the Hydran lines."

"How can you do that?"

"I have my ways."

"You filthy traitor! You are in league with the Hydrans!"

"And why not? I will not die here for a dead cause. I will be one of those to escape and live, but you can come with me."

Yamina's eyes burned with an intensity that Tantuvaal had only seen in the eyes of warriors deep in the fighting lust. He saw something other than hatred there in those delicate blue eyes. With a snarl she drew her sword, and walked towards the commander.

"Do not be a fool, girl!" the commander said angry, then growing nervous. He too now drew his weapon. "This fortress will be passed by the enemy, now that they have taken Fortress Segunda."

"Passed by, through your foul treachery, you fat pig! My father and thousands of other men and women were in Segunda, and you sold them all out. For what? What is it you gained besides your miserable life?"

"Sometimes, young woman, life is enough."

"Then you shall not even have that! Raise your weapon and prepare to die!" Yanina barked in furious rage as she sprang upon the commander like a maddened hell-cat.

As his blubbery bulk tried to escape the maddened girl, he swung wildly, and she ducked his first blow. Then she returned a thrust to his arm, when she withdrew her sword he bled profusely. He then tried to run, but he was fat and slow while Yamina was young and strong. She was a trained fighting woman of Gilfeire, and he could not get away from her in time.

The traitor ran to the door, but she was there waiting for him. Sweat was dripping from his forehead as blood poured from his arm. The commander slowly walked back, but he was out maneuvered again by the quick girl. She let go with another vicious cut to the head that severed the man's ear in a clean, swift stroke.

Tantuvaal screamed full of pain, the blood pouring from his severed ear and flowing into his eyes. He was having trouble seeing and keeping his balance, and the pain was unbearable. He cried for mercy and ran desperately for his life while the girl cut him off at every turn.

Finally he reached the door, but the girl was waiting there for him. She let go with a monumental stroke that clunked deeply into his neck and cut his throat from ear to ear. The cut neck opened a bloody smile spraying crimson all over the room in uneven spurts.

Lady Yamina took her blade and wiped it on the dead man's silken blouse;

she would not let his foul blood linger on her sword a moment more than necessary.

As she left the office she ran into Talis. The youth showed signs of battle himself, minor wounds and a bloodied sword gave evidence that he had not been idle.

"I was just going to get Lord Tantuvaal. The enemy have ended their attack on us. They are all moving eastward," Talis said trying to catch his breath. As his eyes looked at Yamina he saw a strange look in her eyes. Her clothes were soiled and spotted with blood, and he knew that something was wrong.

"We have been betrayed," Yamina said angrily. The blood-lust had not yet left her; it grew more furious every time that she thought of Tantuvaal. "I have just killed the traitor—it was fort commander Tantuvaal!"

"What? How did this happen?" Talis asked incredulously.

"It is all true. I will tell you later," Yamina said hastily. "For now, we must get together all the able bodied men and women and march to defend Gilfeire."

"I doubt if we can scrape up more than a few hundred warriors. It will not be enough. And what of the wounded, we can't leave them here?"

"It will have to do, Talis," Yamina replied firmly "Do not concern yourself with the wounded now, they are safe here, the enemy will not return to attack this fort. Such was the price of Tantuvaal's treachery. Now get moving! We must leave immediately!"

***

Julane never made it to the camp of Acredan of Balistry. His lost cause of hope for any aid from that dubious agency was squashed when the fortress at Segunda fell.

Instead he cut out through the isthmus in which Gilfeirie lay—the city now under a mauling rampage by all manner of outsiders and mutants—Rikes and Kaith beasts, underground dwellers and all other Hydran agents and warriors, and even some Truhuman traitors such as the hated turncoat Aron Miklis.

On the road to the Fortress at Torgais, Julane met up with Lady Yamina, Talis, and hundreds of steady swords. He was informed of Tantuvaal's treachery and his punishment, and of the overall situation. He took in this news carefully, thoughtfully.

"We must face the facts," Julane insisted trying to sway the few survivors from a hopeless suicidal attack against the Hydrans, "Gilferie is doomed—the city is dead and there is nothing left for us to do but continue the fight on our own terms and not on those of the Hydrans. That means we escape to the forest to wage a war of subterfuge against them and their allies."

"Then we are the last of the Truhumans?" Talis asked sadly, but with resolve. "Let us take our wounded from Torgais Fortress and hide like vermin in the radiation swamps."

"We will continue to fight," Julane insisted boldly, "but this time we fight on our terms, which will be much more effective against the Hydrans."

Lady Yamina, daughter of the Gilferian leader, Lord Krosis, finally broke the argument by bowing to the logic of Julane's words. "The city is lost to us forever, our past is lost to us forever, but our memories of this day shall live on—forever! The Hydrans shall pay for their deeds this day—as well as Aron Miklis and all other human collaborators with enemies of humanity and the true God of our Fathers."

"Then let us pick up our wounded and be gone from this place now," Julane ordered firmly. "Know that some day we shall turn this rout into victory that shall be the death of all our enemies."

———

Atop the crumbled tower of God, in the once Truhuman city of Gilfeire a grim dark visage looked out over the surrounding world and saw that all was in proper balance and order and that the law of Shre-dath holy-war had been spread to every section of this weary old world.

Lord Kre-da, Lord of creation and the Holy Hydran horde slowly tilted his inhuman head to the huge winged Kaith even now alighting upon the tower rim before him.

"Report," Kre-da intoned as his sharp eyes scanned the horizons far away from him.

"It is as you foresaw, Great Master, the last dregs of the Truhumans are in defeat and even now enter the radiation swamps hoping to escape our flyers."

Kre-da nodded his massive head. And the Kaith could not help but tremble as he saw the Great Master's terrible horns glinting with warm red wet blood in the sunlight.

"Shall I instruct my flyers to pursue and destroy?" the giant Kaith asked.

For a moment there was no answer, and then the great monster shook his head and laughed in terrible dark voice, "No. Let them escape, but only into swamps where they belong. There useless Truhumans shall find more horror than they ever thought possible. Have your flyers wall in the swamp, the Rikes and Solom ones as well, and employ the talents of the underground Sum-Nof-Arov to be sure that these last vestiges of Truhuman kind shall never escape!"

"It shall be done," the Kaith responded crisply and then flew off to do his master's bidding.

And then Lord Kre-da, master of life and death of the entire world now watched with great pleasure knowing that the terrible creatures of the radiation swamps would make quick work of their newest inhabitants.

"And that, my dismal Truhumans, shall surely be the end of you all!"

THE TOWER AT THE EDGE OF THE WORLD

The wizard of Tramadore gazed intently into a huge globe of pure silver. It was a large and mysterious instrument which shone with an eerie dull sheen. As the wizard concentrated deeply upon that for which he was seeking, a cloudy, milky-white mist pervaded the area of the globe. Within moments it was no longer a globe of solid, glowing silver, but had become a mistily enshrouded thing which now slowly began to show feature and form. It was clearing rapidly, and before the eyes of Tracis of Tramadore a strange and deadly image was taking shape.

Tracis looked intently into the area of the all-seeing sphere for he recognized the features that were forming there as those of his long dead rival, Zorano of Kanasul. Visible now was the dark and deadly green-skinned form of the arch-mage lying motionless upon the marble slab deep in his burial chamber, far away in the mountains of Gamorath. All appeared quiet, but in the distance Tracis spied something that should not have been in that grim, aged chamber of the long lost dead. There was a torch, and holding it was a man—a man who neared the long dead body of Zorano. He appeared to be of the Hilaki tribe, and behind him followed other men. All these others looked to be of this same tribe also, except there was one sinister-looking man of greater years. Tracis was sure that he had never seen this man before, but he was certain that he must be an aged Hilaki juju man.

The look upon the face of the wizard of Tremadore was not a happy one at this news. He did not know what these men were doing in the thrice-damned tomb of Zorano, but they should not have been there. They could be simple grave robbers —- a usual occupation of the Hilaki people —- yet how had they broken through the powerful magical incantatory and the mighty conjurations which guarded this tomb from the entrance of intruders? Tracis knew that whatever these men were doing there, it could bode no good, for the fools were meddling in something that they could not possibly understand. Tracis hoped that they were only simple robbers, but as he closely watched the motions of the old Jujuman, Tracis' fear was fully realized. For he soon saw the ancient body of Zorano rise, with foul and corrupt features, and maggot-strewn eyes that glared out into the deathly void of nothingness.

Tracis did not know who this old man was who could raise the ancient dead, nor by what manner be accomplished his feat, but as the body of his arch-enemy began to move, Tracis felt a familiar old presence in the room with him. He stared into the globe and was shocked to see the face of Zorano peering at him in mockery and hate, and then the clouded globe of silver cracked and exploded in a terrible roar. Tracis fell forward gripping his bloody face in screaming agony. Within moments he lay dead, his body quickly consumed by a noxious black fire.

In lands far to the north, under the cruel subjugation of the Stone Gods, and the Capuril, their strange and sinister worshipers—a lone rider rode upon a charging steed. He was a young man, who wore the black livery of Castle Mordusfane. Ahead of him the plains stretched out interminably to the red capped horizon. Barely visible in the far stretches ahead, clouded by the eerie redness of the setting sun, was a tall dark spire. It loomed ominously in the distance like some dread pillar of death that drew the young warrior so speedily towards it.

As the rider from Castle Mordusfane neared the gloomy tower, he noted the once lush plains were rapidly becoming parched and spectral. There was a capricious wind now that blew stinging sand into the man's eyes—even in a land that had hardly ever known the feel of natural wild winds. The rider sought to compose himself, to conserve his waning strength and calm his nerves. He rode on and saw many forms of grotesque creatures, and there were other beasts as well that seemed to hint of some unnatural design and origin. Some of these looked longingly at the rider as he flashed by, as fast as his frenzied mount would carry him. It seemed that even his horse felt the horror and danger that loomed so heavily in this shunned land. Blood-red eyes and blood-dripping fangs watched the rider as he passed, moans of hunger escaped foaming lips, tongues lashed out vainly for a form of sustenance that was neither physical nor natural. Whispering hisses, loud barks, raged screams were all heard beckoning the man and his mount closer.

The warrior rode away swiftly, nor did he need to urge his mount to any greater speed, for the beast was racing through the domain of these creatures as though all the inhabitants of the pit of Porthaus were upon its tail.

And perhaps they were!

In good time they traversed that hellish country, and many were the thanks of the warrior to his many gods that he lived to escape from that cursed land. His destination, the great tower, was easily discernible now, and he could see that it was indeed enormous. It was called, 'The Tower at the Edge of the

World' by all the world's peoples and he could easily see why. One could not pick a more desolate and eerie landscape than this location. The warrior eyed the massive structure closely and winced as a feeling of fear ran over him in a great surging wave. Sweat dripped down his face, and his mount jumped nervously. He had reached his destination now, for good or ill.

Carefully the warrior edged his weary mount closer to that strange turret, it was enormous and reached a height into the heavens that all but obliterated its higher reaches from searching eyes. It was a brick-built edifice that encompassed an area greater than the whole of Castle Mordusfane He looked at it in disbelief and awe. Never had he imagined that such a mammoth structure could exist. He nervously rode nearer.

At the base of the tower was an enormous metal door. It too appeared to have withstood the ravages of time—as did the tower itself—which gave the impression of timeworn eternity. It had always been here—it would remain here. Forever.

Carefully the warrior approached the great door and tried its gigantic handle. It opened with barely a touch, as though there were no need of locks or bars here at all. For surely none would willingly enter such a place. Nevertheless, the warrior entered, leading his horse behind him through a portal of such width it could easily have passed four horses abreast.

Now he found himself in an enormous, dark chamber that seemed completely devoid of any furnishings. Before him, as if appearing from nowhere, stood a dark shadowy figure. Slowly and in complete silence it approached, in its hand a large candelabrum. For tense seconds the warrior stood with drawn sword as the figure came ever nearer. When it was no more than ten feet away, it produced a flame from somewhere and in an unknown manner lit the five candles—producing an eerie light that was diffused and obscure in the vast enormity of that seemingly infinite hall.

Each man now looked upon the other in silence. What the warrior saw was an ordinary enough man of medium height and build, but upon closer observation he noticed that the eyes were of a peculiar and particularly disturbing appearance.

That the man's eyes were large was no exaggeration—the pupils alone were the size of a normal man's eye—as if this one's entire existence had been lived in the subterranean darkness of this gloom enshrouded cavern. As if to lend evidence to these thoughts, the warrior also noticed the particularly yellow pallor of the man's skin, along with a dusty dryness and leathery appearance. To be sure, this was a man who had never seen light of the sun, nor felt the chill winds of winter, or even nature.

The man was also looking over the newcomer, but whatever thoughts were

...the man's eyes were large...

moving through his mind he kept secret, for he never spoke other than a few terse words of command. In mechanical words of strange and foreign accent he said, 'It is good that you have come. My master awaits."

With these words he began to walk away, the warrior followed with a strong, but none too firm hand upon his sword hilt. Silently they walked on until the servant brought the warrior into an even larger hall—the end of which had a massive fireplace where a man sat in a throne-like chair.

"Ah, bring him closer, Atumi," the seated man ordered, eyeing the warrior intently. "It is not every day that we have a visit from the son of Tramadore's greatest mage. So tell me youth, how is your father, Tracis?"

The youth stared at the seated man for a long frozen moment.

"Lost your tongue, youth?"

"Until now, I had not thought it possible. I thought the words were mere fables and myths, but they are true? You are really Zorano of Kanasul? Returned from the grave?"

"And you have found that which you seek?" Zorano laughed bitterly, "And in finding me—just what do you propose to do now?"

"Kill you. Send you back to the grave where you belong!"

"I see. And have you not noticed that it is you who are my prisoner? It is you who are in my tower, under my guards—not the other way around."

Then as if for emphasis, the chamber suddenly filled with scores of wild Hilaki warriors—their weapons trained and ready on this lone man who stood so boldly before their master. At a word they would cut him to ribbons, and each eyed their master with much eagerness, waiting and ready, for any type of a sign to begin their deadly work.

"You are a murderer! My father is dead because of you."

"Not directly, I assure you. He should have kept his nose out of my business." Zorano allowed a smile for some bit as if savoring fond memories of old bygone days. "A long time ago we were enemies. It began with our quest for the Fire Gem of Tais, and continued with the *Rose of Exumanites*. Both of which Tracis had the good fortune to find. Then once the existence became known of The Tower at the Edge of The World—a tower where time has indeed stopped!—I found it and Tracis killed me so that he could possess it! For you see, in this ancient manse the age process stops. In here, you can live forever—in here, a wizard may study his art for all eternity and eventually he may know all that time itself knows!'

The young warrior, the son of the greatest mage of Tramadore, steeled his nerves, for he knew Zorano lied about his father. Boldly he said so, calling Zorano a liar and a murderer.

"He is the murderer, not I! He killed me years ago!" Zorano replied, then lifting up his velvet jerkin he uncovered a large scar. "See here. The weapon mark where your own father thrust his sword into me!"

"It is not true! That is but a wound and could have been made by anyone and in any manner."

Zorano grew angry and looked at the youth with fire in his eyes. Slowly the coals died down, and then Zorano said, "I have no wish to harm you, lad. You had best leave. My Hilaki will escort you to the border—from there you are on your own."

In answer, the youth drew his sword and took a bold step forward, "I am not leaving."

"Then you are a fool!" Zorano barked angry now. "Get out while you can. I've no wish to kill you—but one signal to my Hilaki guards..."

The youth took another step closer to where Zorano sat—this time the undead wizard was alert and intense—his hand upon the pommel of his own dagger, though more for comfort than protection—for he had no need of mere physical protection as his magic was powerful and world-renown.

"Leave now!" Zorano hissed in dire warning, "While you can."

The youth moved one step closer.

"You fool!"

"Aye, I'm a fool, Zorano, but know this—you are not the only mage gifted with eternal life. There are even a few of us who know the secret of eternal youth as well!"

"You? So then if that is true, then you are Tracis?"

"Yes. I am he, as I was when a young man. I am Tracis!"

"But how?" Zorano stammered his confusion spread to the faces of all the Hilaki in that chamber. "This can not be!"

"With the Gem of Taris and a pedal from the *Rose of Exumanities* —- all things may be possible. Eternal life, eternal youth—you can not kill me, Zorano!"

Zorano stared mystified. He had noted the resemblance of this youth to his ancient enemy of so long ago, but never in a million years had he guessed the truth, that this youth was actually his arch enemy—now alive and here before him. Suddenly Zorano rose from his seat and barked to his Hilaki guards, "Leave us. I wish to be alone with this man from Tramadore."

Within seconds the huge chamber was cleared.

Both men were now alone and eyed each other with the hatred of hungry wolves. Eyes blazing, they stood a few dozen feet apart, slowly moving around each other like planets in orbit about a sun.

"So Tracis, so you have returned," Zorano whispered. "I thought it impossible after I caused your death with the exploding globe."

"Yes, a neat trick, but one that could only kill my physical self—not the other."

"I shall be more certain of your death the next time!"

"There will be no next time!" Tracis barked defiantly. The two men stood scant yards apart and the air between them seemed supercharged with the force of their wills. "It is all over for you now, Zorano."

Then Zorano suddenly spouted a time-worn incantation and moved aside as a huge green-mottled monster armed with all variety of weapons suddenly appeared from nowhere—apparently out of thin air. "My inner self, Tracis, the ego monster I have liberated to do battle against you!"

"I see!" Tracis said watching the demon-thing intently, the fear welling up inside him at the terrible thing which soon would be set loose upon him. He had never seen a more grotesque apparition—a huge lumbering green monster—its head, arms, and shoulders full of bone spikes—while its large eyes were blood red and full of furious hate. Its mouth dripped a viscous and foul fluid that almost caused the youth to vomit in disgust, while the monster smiled invitingly with a thin-lipped mouth of large black pointed teeth.

Surely this inner Zorano was no worse than the real being—both of which now stood before Tracis.

"Destroy him!" Zorano ordered the green goliath, though that huge killing machine surely needed no urgings, for it was obvious that it was a creature whose sole purpose for existence was to kill.

"A pretty beast, Zorano, and one I'd expect to spring from your foul and rotten soul," Tracis said. Then smiling he added, "And now prepare to meet my magic—you son of a stinking Hilaki mongrel!"

Then Tracis drew his sword and the green monster was upon him. The two fought a furious duel, the likes of which has not been seen by any mortal man since the ancient serpent men of Atlantis were banished from the world in lost eons of prehistory.

The green thing was immensely strong—large muscles bulged like mountains under its skin—yet Tracis was faster and so agile that it became clear to all that if the youth could keep up his endurance the beast might never catch him.

As the fight raged, Zorano screamed insults and tried to use different magical incantations to alter the outcome, but with no result. Tracis watched the older man and countered his every move magically, even as he countered every sword stroke of the green behemoth he was fighting.

Eventually the creature of Zorano's inner self began to show signs of fatigue. Whether this was because it was actually tiring, or that Zorano himself was tired from the constant strain of keeping this other self alive and fighting,

Tracis did not know, nor care. The results were what he had hoped for, the results were what mattered.

Soon afterward Tracis saw his opening and with a vicious sword stroke put the point of his weapon deeply into the area between the green monster's huge blood-red eyes.

There was a squeal of pain and rage and then instantly and suddenly the beast simply disappeared—while before the fireplace Zorano fell to the floor—a wide gash dug deeply into the forehead between his eyes!

"So you kill me again, Tracis! Well, I shall come back for you!" he whispered as he collapsed and died.

"Not this time, Zorano! This time you die the death of all mortals—a far cry from your mottled green monster. With your inner self dead, your outer self shall now die the death of all mortals, from which there can be no return. Die, Zorano, and know that it is I who have the Fire Gem, The Rose, and now the Tower to live in forever—to be forever young! Goodbye, Zorano, your time has come—and gone."

And then Zorano let out his last death breath, as Tracis called to him all the Hilaki chiefs and they prepared to take obedience to their new master—one no better, nor no worse, than the previous master. Such are the tangled ways of magic!

THE JUSTICE OF RED VENUS

The girl crawled from beneath the massive wreckage of the great temple of Ornepapas, The Delightful One. She struggled with difficulty to her feet and surveyed the vast destruction and carnage that lay all around her. Everything was in smoking ruins and the stench of death drifted upon the wind to bring that horrible flavor to her senses.

"Sisters!" She yelled out, hoping to see at least some of the motionless female forms around her begin movement to her urgent plea. Yet all was motionless and the silence of death held sway in whatever direction she gazed.

"What have they done?" She cried tears of awful rage. "They have destroyed everything! They have killed us all!"

Red Venus, last Warrior-Daughter of The Delightful One, late high priestess of the temple of Ornepapas, staggered out of the ruins and without looking back began her weary trek upon the southwesterly road. She walked as one in a daze, full of conflicting thoughts, hates, and violent passions. She would go to the city—the city where the she-bitch Narfeti and all her jackals ruled, and would suffer by her hand! For she was sure warriors under the command of Narfeti had done this evil deed.

So she walked onward. Her soles burned to blisters on the harsh brown clay of the road, the sun's rays pelting her short dark mane with heat. Red Venus had been upon the road for many days before nearing the massive gates of the great city of Tharma where Narfeti ruled.

With a light sturdy rapier slung over her shoulder and ever at the ready, she approached the main city gate. A light wind blew through her thin silks causing them to sway about her supple youthful body as though she were caught in an almost invisible vortex of violent emotions.

The guards did not notice her until she was right before them—and then were a bit startled by her sudden appearance and beauty.

"Who are you and what is your business within Tharma?" one guard asked eyeing her hungrily. And Red Venus was a feast for the male eye—but strangely, the guards did not seek to overly familiarize themselves with this woman as they did with so many other women of the city. No, for there was the smell of deadly danger around this girl, and the guards decided to handle her most carefully.

Red Venus smiled at both warriors with a toothy grin that unnerved them both. She knew that they were scared of her, and the thought made her even stronger and bolder.

154

"I am the priestess, Red Venus—I seek your mistress for a redress of grievances I have against her."

"What are these grievances?"

"Narfeti and her jackals looted the temple of Ornepapas and killed all but myself.

I want her life in return!"

The guards laughed, then they looked more curiously at this young woman before them. Was she mad to admit such plans before Narfeti's own soldiery?

"You are one bold bitch!" the leader stated, and then as though on cue both warriors drew their lean-bladed rapiers—but as fast as they were—Red Venus was faster. She had anticipated their actions so that her boot heel was already being withdrawn from the folded form of one man's stomach, while her rapier was out and already had disarmed the other warrior. She smiled as the sweat ran down his face—his eyes transfixed on the point of her blade, which she held snuggly pressed against his rapidly beating heart.

"Please," he cried in a whisper. "I am just a guard—I do not..."

"Call your companion off then—or I'll run you through!" Red Venus ordered as she pricked him lightly with her blade and drew forth a precious drop of blood, just to offer encouragement to the man's cooperation. His fear needed no encouragement.

The warrior winced, ordered, "Sasmar! Hold!" Now the man was relieved to see his companion withdrawing his rapier and putting it away in its scabbard.

"Let me pass unheeded. My quarrel is with Narfeti and not with you two—unless you desire it to be!" She drew another drop of blood for emphasis.

"Please," he whispered, his strong voice grown suddenly hoarse, "Pass in peace. We'll not stop you."

The girl smiled, and so Red Venus, last daughter of The Delightful One, passed unheeded into the ancient city of Tharma—the stronghold of the hated she-beast, Narfeti.

⸺

Hidden by their dark robes of concealment, lurked two priests of Dar-El-Son – Beloved Sun – who watched the affair at the gate with intense interest.

"One of them lives! How can it be?" the taller whispered and an icy fear etched his voice. "That is an unforeseen occurrence and a bad omen, especially since it is the violent one, the one known as Red Venus. She is the worst of them all. Our mistress must be told at once."

"Lord, why not call extra guardsmen and have her taken captive for our pleasure later – better still, why not have her killed right now, out here on the street? I can summon the extra guards. She is but one woman after all, and we do know her intentions toward our mistress?"

The taller looked at his young companion and shook his head sadly. "Why do you suppose they call her Red Venus? Do you see her wearing any crimson raiment? And her short tresses – are they a crimson red? No, they are not red, but black. My friend, she is called Red Venus because red is the color of blood, and Venus the star of love. She is the lover who delights in the shedding of the blood of her enemies. I doubt there is anyone who can stop her. She was born and raised to be the sword-mistress of her people and it is said she cannot be bested." The taller man looked at the other after this explanation, "However, if you feel you can stop her – you are most welcome to try."

The other forced a gulp as he remembered how easily the girl had just bested the two trained guardsmen. Slowly he nodded his head in the negative.

The taller smiled, "You are getting wise."

Through the crowded streets of Tharma walked the girl who called herself Red Venus, and many were the citizens who stepped aside to be out of her path.

She strode with strength born from of a single-minded purpose, an obsession to punish those who had done her wrong. It was not long before she reached that area of the city where Narfeti's palace was located.

Warily she trod the two hundred marble steps to the huge portal that was guarded by four well-armed warriors. As she passed the first hundred steps the guards stopped lounging and talking – twenty five steps closer and they watched her warily – twenty five steps closer still, and they nervously asked her identity and business within the palace – and twenty five steps further and four arms drew four steel bladed rapiers. Twenty five steps closer and Red Venus reached the portal and the four guardsmen were at her in an instant, attacking her with drawn swords. It was a big mistake. For them.

It was a furious battle but the girl was in top fighting condition. Lithe and trim, her endurance great and her weight negligible, the four guardsmen could not stand up to her ability and speed – though theirs' was by no means limited. She weaved a web around them with such speed and finesse that the four could not catch her – and rather than aid their battle – their superior numbers served only to slow them down where each of them got into the others' way. Red Venus skirted between each guard, running rings around them, and always her blade thirsted for blood, taking a drink here and there as she saw opportunity. And in her hands, opportunity was rife with a good sword.

It was over almost before it had begun.

Red Venus wiped her blade clean as she opened the great oak doors to Narfeti's lair. Instantly she was set upon by two more guardsmen who she dispatched without preamble and then proceeded to enter deeper and deeper into the home of her greatest enemy.

She encountered more guards along the way, leaving a tell-tale trail of corpses behind her – for by now she was soaked and splattered from hair to ankles in the blood of her foes, but she continued to make her way relentlessly to the huge throne room where Narfeti ruled great Tharma and its environs.

"I am here, She-bitch!" she yelled into the echoing hall, not caring who should hear in her foolish anger. Her voice reverberated throughout that huge edifice as she passed the last doorway to enter the throne room. Through a hundred yards of beautiful marble floor and intricately carved pillars she walked to reach the far end of that room where sat Narfeti, upon a dais of purest white gold.

Narfeti smiled carefully, thoughtfully. Though flanked by a dozen armed guards instantly ready for the order to swoop down and kill this danger to their Queen, she held them back for the moment. Behind these guards, protected, stood the dark-robed ones – those of the cult of Dar-El-Son, The Beloved Sun, who wanted the girl dead at all cost, but were too scared to do the dirty work themselves.

"You owe me, Narfeti!" Red Venus growled in a low defiant tone. She elicited great confidence, and that fact unnerved Narfeti who had never actually thought the girl would get this far.

"Your dogs made the mistake of leaving me alive – me of all the others - -your most dangerous foe!"

"Yes, I see that it was a mistake, but it is one which I shall rectify now," then Narfeti turned to her guard captain and with a simple order said, "Kill the slut!"

With sword metal and hard eyes both agleam, as though in some kind of deadly symbiosis, the guardsmen crept toward Red Venus.

"I will have my revenge, Narfeti," the girl said boldly as she stood ready for their attack unconcerned. "None can stop this last daughter of The Delightful One!"

The guardsmen closed upon her. However to everyone's surprise Red Venus surged forward with a great acrobatic leap far into the air to land upon the dais within a foot of the startled queen.

"I am here," she said simply. "You calling me a slut is just the last in a long line of insults to me and my people – people who you have robbed and murdered. Now it is your turn!"

Then Red Venus skewered the breast of Narfeti, her blade drinking deeply into the queen, while the guardsmen now came at her with a dozen thirsty swords.

But Red Venus was too quick for them, barreling into the two priests of Dar-El-Son, she bounded over the throne and out of a large open window. Swinging ape-like through the maze of carved statues and combing, it was not long before her agility had her upon the roof of the palace and away.

Within, all was turmoil, priests and guards wailing a thousand laments, rages and insults; while a medical man was summoned for the dying queen.

Red Venus heard the cries of rage and lamentations as she disappeared into the night of the city to become a ghost dissolved into the blackness of the dark.

In the palace troubled medical men examined the queen's wound once more. With a nod and a frown they approached the two priests of Dar-El-Son.

"Thank Beloved Sun!" The doctor said quietly, "The damage is bad, but not fatal. The queen shall live."

And from the bed behind the speaker came the hoarse angry words, "But that slut shall not! I will not rest until my soldiery have hunted her down and brought her to me!"

There is a tavern in Tharma, and in as unlikely a place as possible, upon its terraced roof, was a simple praying place. It was here, alone, that Red Venus sat, her gaze upon the full moon overhead, her mind blocking out the riotous oaths and drunken cries from the tavern below, as she recanted the roll call of the dead daughters. They had been sisters all, beloved friends, now lost to her forever because of one woman's baseless greed and violence.

"…Sarde, Toral, Vvana, Zalis," Red Venus whispered each woman's name in that fateful roll call. "The Bitch-Queen has paid for her transgressions, and to beloved Ornepapas, he who is the father of us all, I commend her stagnant life!"

Red Venus then rose slowly and went to examine her weapons. She had been through quite a few bloody fights recently and noticed that her rapier and dagger were both gutted and nicked from many sword strokes. She carefully sharpened these, honing out the blemishes as best as she could, and then cleaned herself with sponge and water to remove all the blood that had now caked dry and browned her skin. She had bought a new wardrobe from a clothier across from the tavern – this time her garments were of leather and wool, with a light mail shirt and high cuffed boots – the uniform of a warrior and not a high priestess of Ornepapas.

Those old days were behind her now, and Red Venus would not dwell upon them. Instead she shifted her gaze to the future, and the whole wide world that lay before her, and now, her place in that world. What would it be? Her inner self told her only one answer; her's would be the life of a mistress-of-arms – a warrior woman!

Red Venus was little concerned with the citizenry of Tharma, nor with the death of its queen – who she thought now must surely lay in death's cold bosom. However, what she did not know was that Narfeti was still alive, and in her palace on the other side of the city, she was now coming back to consciousness from death's door. Her first thoughts upon entering the world of life again were of the girl who had tried so hard to take that life away from Queen Narfeti. Immediately she was demanding of her generals and ministers the freshly-hewn head of the upstart wench who had brazenly entered the palace and by a slim hair of fate missed taking her precious life.

"I want her brought to me! Alive!" the queen coughed, as a frantic medical man tried to steady her, "then I shall cut that lovely head form those shoulders with my very own sword!"

So, unawares to Red Venus, the call went throughout the city of Tharma to soldiers and citizenry alike. Where was the outlander woman? A thousand golden coins to the giver of this important information! And then the eyes of the city came forth, the rogues, the bounty hunters, the street harlots, the quite merchants, and all those who lived in the shadows of the great city – those from the underground and the underworld. And they all were very eager to tell Narfeti's jackals where and when they had seen the girl – and the jackals put two and two together, and soon gathered before a small tavern on the Street of Lonely Complacency.

Red Venus heard the commotion that was building up from below her and knew that as it came closer it could mean just one thing – enemies – enemies who were after her with cold steel and blood in their hearts.

Quickly the girl offered a short prayer to Ornepapas and all her dead sisters and then disappeared over the wall of the tavern roof to become lost in the night's all-concealing blackness.

Meanwhile in the tavern below, Captain Shartre of the Queen's household guard was busy questioning old Alban the tavern owner. He did this by severely depressing his right thumb down into Alban's left eye until a soft sucking sound was heard and a small round object fell from the old man's face to dangle back and forth along his cheek like a whore's ear bangle. The bloody orb was precariously held by a few strands of flesh, and amid a gusto of splattered blood, Captain Shartre began to ask his first question of the terrified man.

...disappeared over...the tavern roof...

"The girl?" he said very simply, and there was no need for any other explanation for a man has but only two eyes. He would not risk his remaining eye.

The old man, crying full of pain and fear shouted, "Atop the roof, in the praying place!"

Then the herd of soldiery ascended the steps and came upon the empty roof. And though Red Venus had fled, the pack could all see the signs of her past presence – the old discarded cloths, so full of their Queen's dried brown blood, the towels she had used to clean herself of the muck of battle, and the empty bowl and flagons which attested to the health and hearty appetite of this very dangerous mistress-of-arms.

"She has eluded us," one of Shartre's dogs growled full of anger and vaunted bloodlust.

"Then we shall comb every inch of this city until we find her. And when we do…" And there Captain Shartre was forced to halt his words for his eyes caught sight of a sinister movement on the wall behind him. It was a slight shadow, but it was enough to warn him and cause him to turn around and see a sight he had never expected to see. There, standing boldly before him and all his soldiers with drawn rapier and dirk was Red Venus, come back to dole out a new flavor in her repertoire of bloody mayhem and violence.

Captain Shartre smiled full of assurance. He had her now! And why not, when it is the lamb that has walked into the den of hungry wolves? Shartre muttered, "By Beloved Sun, so the bold fool would have at all of us, would she? Then take her, lads!"

And then Red Venus silently launched herself from that high wall straight down onto the form of Captain Shartre himself, and her eyes burned with fire and hatred into the startled expression of the man as both rolled around that rooftop – each one trying desperately to slice the other with dirk or sword.

By then all Shartre's command had circled the two fighters, and a couple of stalwart men came forward to grab the girl from behind and lift her off their commander. Both received much more than they bargained for when they were found by Red Venus's dirk blade, but others kept trying to aid their commander, so that soon a dozen hands were upon the girl and she was almost helpless – her last act of fight and defiance – to plunge her dirk into the left eye of Captain Shartre. Then she was hauled off of her enemy, beaten unconscious, tied, and finally taken downstairs and thrown into a cart to be hauled away to Narfeti's terrible dungeons.

There was no passage of time in the sink hole of a hell where Red Venus was imprisoned. Days, nights, moments, weeks, they all seemed the same. She had been stripped naked and then chained to a wall ring and now sat alone and quiet in a tiny cell in the lowest depths of the dungeon catacombs. Across her feet ran various hungry rodents, while overhead silent huge spiders busily wove furious webs to ensnare the roaches and other vermin that were her only companions in this dark, dank universe.

Many days passed and in all that time the guards, who only occasionally brought her food, told Red Venus that Queen Narfeti still lived and that once she had recovered her strength from a certain wound, would personally take care of her in a very special way. Red Venus allowed a grim smile; she was neither frightened nor impressed by these words, only a bit chagrined for a job not properly completed.

So she passed the days on and on in quiet solitude until finally an escort of palace praetorians arrived to bring Red Venus before the recovered queen. Carefully, these elite of all Narfeti's dogs, unlocked their prisoner's shackles and then with swords at the ready, they led her upward and upward through winding corridors, from that lowest of earthly dungeons into the upper stratospheres of the palace – and finally into the presence of Queen Narfeti herself.

"So you have returned?" Narfeti said with an evil leer, as she looked over her prisoner most carefully. Was it truly this slip of a girl that had almost killed her? She did not look like so much now, but she had bested many of Narfeti's own vaulted praetorians. What kind of woman was this who called herself Red Venus and proved it each time she held a rapier in her hands? Narfeti noticed that weeks within her dungeons had not done the warrior woman any good. She was dirty and hungry, and smelled badly, and yet her hard gaze retained a fire of spirit that all in that chamber could feel, fear and respect.

"And I might say the same for you," the girl answered firmly. "You have returned also, but from hell – where my sword should have sent you weeks ago!"

Queen Narfeti was shocked by the words, but she regained her composure rapidly and actually sneered and said, "The sword is held in another's hand this time, my girl, and I intend to use it as no other has ever done before. Upon you!"

Red Venus stood mute for the moment, her mind looking for any avenue of escape but at present finding nothing and having to await the inevitable with the stoic resignation of her people. She was the last bold daughter of The Delightful One, the rich old mage known as Ornepapas, who with his dozen wives had years past spawned a race of woman warriors and mystic spiritualists who would someday control the world. Or so he had planned. Not any longer – for that dream of a divine matriarchy had died weeks ago with all her sisters – and now only Red Venus survived.

"Do you know why I sent my troops to burn and loot your temple? To kill all your so-called 'sisters'?" Queen Narfeti boasted as she strode back and forth before the helpless girl.

"Your lust for gold and gems, your greed, it is well known throughout the Eastern Prelate!" Red Venus spat with vigor.

Narfeti laughed it off and then actually smiled. It was like a serpent's jaw dripping venom before it struck. "Yes, that is true, but that is not the real reason why I gave orders for the death of all at your temple – and that was always my main goal – the fire and looting was secondary in importance. After all soldiers must have their fun and make some monetary recompense from my orders or they would not be so eager to serve and obey me the next time."

"So it was upon your order that all my sisters were slain!" Red Venus demanded knowing full well the answer but assured now to hear it fully from Narfeti's own lips.

"Yes, I wanted you and all your kind dead. Your kind, who think they are always better than everyone else, never doing as you are told, never doing what you are supposed to do. You were too dangerous to my own plans, for your damnable sisterhood would seek intermarriage with the kings and princes of the north and east. Within a ten year span you would have members in a dozen royal families, within a twenty-year span you would have had control of that dozen and had entered yet a dozen more families. No dynasty will be founded in Tharma, or anyplace else, that I do not control! And now, you are the last one – the one who escaped all the carnage – but you shall not escape it this time!"

Then Queen Narfeti drew a large saber from one of her praetorian officers and measuring and balancing the blade ever so carefully said, "Now, bring her to me!"

Red Venus was unchained and herded forward, forced to bow down with her head out and low so as to expose her neck to the downward blow that she knew was to come at any moment.

Now Queen Narfeti had that polished sword raised on high and ready for one massive downward stroke, when suddenly from behind her a voice cried out, "Hold! I beg thee, hold your majesty's hand."

Narfeti turned livid at the interruption, so much like an injured lioness that all in the chamber took a nervous step backwards. The Queen's angered gaze looked out over her court and retainers to see who would be so bold as to interfere with her desires. When her eyes alighted upon the speaker she became quiet and only starred at the robed figure slowly dissipating her rage. Finally after tense moments Narfeti said, "So what can Dar-El-Son's preacher have to say about this matter?"

"Majesty," the old robed figure slowly moved forward with outstretched hands," I think I have a more entertaining manner to rid ourselves of this wench."

Narfeti stayed her hand as the man moved closer. His face was totally covered by a large black cowl, but that wasn't important, because no one in that huge chamber wished to see the face of Darkon, the High Lord of Beloved Sun. "I beseech thee, majesty, to slay this wild bitch here will but make a martyr of her and shroud her demise in palace intrigue – I have recourse to a better method – if your majesty would like to hear of such a plan?"

Narfeti appeared to be thinking the suggestion over and finally said, "If the High Lord has a proposal, I am sure it would be of interest, and I shall certainly want to hear it."

"My lady," Darkon smiled wickedly while pointing a thin finger toward Red Venus. "This upstart wench is the last remainder of a dangerous cult of warrior women and sorceresses – they would seek to undermine your power in the Eastern Prelate, and eventually infringe upon the worshiping of Old Sun himself. It is sacrilege! This cannot be allowed! Our Beloved Sun screams out for a fit punishment, for a public punishment, one which will convince the populace that the ways of heresy and blasphemy shall be treated quickly and without the slightest mercy. I suggest that this witch, who calls herself Red Venus, be burned alive at the stake until her singed husk is but a pile of blackened ashes to be blown away upon the wind."

"Well said, Darkon," Narfeti agreed with a delighted laugh, "and any others out there who harbor feelings of independence or disobedience to my rule shall learn by this example. Guards, place the prisoner in her cell until the fires are good and hot!"

There was general laughter in the hall as Red Venus was taken back to that dark dungeon cell once more. This time however, the stay was a short one, though any respite from Narfeti's sword blade was a welcome boon. It was the next day, at mid-morning that they came for her once again.

"The fires are waiting, girl," one of the soldiers laughed with a nudge in the ribs to one of his companions. "Though it seems a waste of prime woman flesh to burn her before she's been properly used. Eh, Grusis?"

"Lay off that now, Satro!" the other guard replied carefully, "this one is a wild she-beast, a killer. You do not fool around with a woman such as her. After this turn I'll take you into the Maze where Sultana can cure your itch. I say leave this girl be if you know what is good for you."

Satro laughed at the older soldier's temperate words and slowly began to grope and grind his way closer with the bound girl.

Red Venus smiled, and with a sneer said, "Is that all you can do?"

"More," Satro said as he grabbed her roughly and pulled her closer. As he did Red Venus tucked her hand around his harness and grabbed the hilt of his dagger.

"We'll have none of that now!" Grusis, the older guard growled seeing what the girl was planning and hitting her hand away with a loud smack of the blunt end of his saber. Red Venus withdrew her hand, which now had a nasty cut along the third set of knuckles.

"You see!" Grusis barked at his companion, "Your glands will be the death of you one day, Satro! Now bind her and let us dump her into Narfeti's lap, and then we go to see Sultana."

Satro pushed the girl away, so that she fell down upon the floor of the cell nursing her bruised hand. "Bitch, you would stab me in my own jail! You'd think a girl in your situation would want to show me the proper attention – after all, this will be the last pleasure you'll receive before the fires fry your soul to ashes."

Both Satro and Grusis laughed, and as Red Venus was dragged to her feet, she defiantly spit upon both men, and received two terrible fists for her favors. All in all she considered the lumps worth it. Then she was quickly dragged up long winding corridors and finally out into an immense courtyard. At one end she could see a large pavilion where sat Narfeti and all her jackals. She noticed Darkon among the crowd, alone, mysterious, and on the other side she saw Captain Shartre – a grim visage with a black patch over the space where his eye had once been scant weeks before. Red Venus approved of the new look, it made Shartre appear as the treacherous dog that he was in reality.

Red Venus was also surprised to see that the royal courtyard had been open to the public – and the people had come in throngs to watch the burning of some poor unfortunate, who for once, was actually in a worse position than they were in life. The starving and the maimed, the diseased and the broken, all strained their eyes to get a view of the unfolding spectacle. Red Venus knew the crowd had to number in the tens of thousands, all manner of revelers, sightseers, hawkers, and even common folk with picnic blankets spread with wine and various foods. There was a holiday atmosphere in the air and it affected the spirits of all but Red Venus. For her, there was nothing to be happy about. At least not yet!

The prisoner was brought onto the sward and instantly the crowd cheered knowing the show was about to commence. Red Venus was then marched in chains before the Queen's pavilion – where Narfeti laughed and spit down at the warrior woman and then flung a fired torch to the earth before the girl's chained feet. An officer in Narfeti's guard bent to retrieve the fire stick, but as he picked it up Red Venus booted him forward so hard that he fell into the torch flame which caused his shirt to catch fire. Instantly all was pandemonium as the man screamed and jumped upon the sword trying to put the fire out – which only grew until the men of his command frantically covered the fire with dirt to eventually stop the blaze.

The crowd absolutely loved the unexpected turn of events, and doubly so because neither Narfeti nor her soldiery were popular in Tharma. As this was taking place, Red Venus was elsewhere, attacking others of her captor's by using body hits and vicious kicks to cause more mayhem among the soldiers' ranks. Finally a detachment of palace praetorians marched onto the field to take charge of things. A hush stilled the crowd as they watched the hated black-armored warriors approaching, you could feel the tension and anger throughout the crowd. Once the praetorians reached the scene, they savagely cuffed Red Venus and then held her down at sword point. Five weapons pricked the skin of the girl and all who held those weapons wanted to run the girl through and be rid of her right then and there. However, like well-trained dogs, the praetorians looked toward Narfeti for commands as the burned officer was being taken off the field in a stretcher. And then the crowd came to life, and they jeered him resoundingly while his companions-in-arms shouted back obscenities and threats at the rowdy mob of dirty citizens.

"We should kill the bitch this moment!" Darsus, the new praetorian commander sneered, "but that will go against the wishes of that damned High Priest."

"Aye, and of the mob too," another warrior replied as he began to notice more and more the cheers and rage of the populace that surrounded them all. "What is wrong with these people? They have no appreciation of a good show."

Finally a messenger from the royal pavilion filtered upon the field. He was a small self-important man, but he spoke the Queen's words and that made him someone to fear and listen to.

"So what's the Queen's message, Kasmir?" Darsus asked the little rodent, but fearful to call him such to his face.

"Hold on killing this woman. Narfeti wants her to taste the fire. Bring her to the stake and set her ablaze so that the Queen may see her go up in a cloud of smoke. Perhaps our Queen will even decide to warm her hands over the flames brought on by this girl's demise."

"Good for her, I say. Alright wench, you heard it. Let's go!" Darsus so ordered, he and his men now escorted the helpless girl down the field to where a tall stake stood upon a high mound of dried branches and timber. "And should you try any more of your games, know that my sword point is poised an inch from your vitals and that it would give me great pleasure to run you through. Shartre is my brother, and it was you who took his eye."

"So what's the Queen's message, Kasmir?"

"And I would take yours, as well, if I only had a good sword in these hands to fight with!"

"You'll not be getting that chance, Bitch!" Darsus growled and pushed her forward so that she fell headlong upon the dusty ground. Her lips tasted the dry dirt and she struggled to regain her feet as her chains were roughly jerked forward.

As they reached the stake the crowd roared with wild anticipation. Cries went up all around the area from thrill seekers and the jaded who wanted to see action. "Burn her!" They yelled as the words grew into a low chant, "Hurry now, get the torches! Set the witch ablaze!"

"You're a popular little minx," one of the soldiers said as he dragged Red Venus closer to the charred stake. Now that her legs had been unchained the girl was able to give the man a defiant kick to the groin that caused him to double over in a flurry of angry curses. The crowd cheered this attraction once more, until the voices went up loud and clear that Red Venus should go free and that Narfeti and all her guards should be the ones cooked this day.

Darsus didn't like that kind of talk and he angrily motioned the crowd to be silent—but of course this only further egged them on – and furthermore, they now began to use him as a focus for all their anger and frustration with the rule of Narfeti. It wasn't long before curses were mixed with angry jeers against the captain and all his warriors.

"I tell you, be silent, or I shall send soldiers to teach you silence!" Darsus barked at the unruly mob. His words were answered by a stream of wild curses and oaths from the assembled throng, and a few moments later it was augmented by a barrage of thrown bottles, fruits, and garbage that littered the field and stunned one of Darsus' men into unconsciousness. And then it was that the arrow came! It was a slim shaft, swift and sure, shot from some unknown location to lodge itself deeply into the neck of a praetorian standing to the right of Red Venus. A moment later another followed, and them another, until dozens of slim shafts flew over the field to lodge their barbed points into Darsus' men. With terrible cries of surprise and rage the guards began to go down to their deaths one at a time, and then with increasing frequency.

"You there!" Darsus shouted to gain the attention of one of his men, "Go to the pavilion and see to it that the commander sets out the praetorians to sweep the rabble away – have them use sword blades and points – not flat edges. Find those damn archers! They are killing my men!"

And the warrior was instantly off. And so was the assemblage, which had now turned into a mob that was pouring from the seats and behind barbicans in such numbers that Narfeti's troops could no longer hold them back.

"All Hell's broken loose here!" one of Darsus' officers shouted in warning to his commander. "We'll need the army here before this day is over."

And then it was that Red Venus saw her chance in all the confusion, she quickly grabbed a dirk from one of the fallen soldiers, and instantly plunged it into both of her guards. They went down among the bloody carnage all around them and in the general pandemonium Red Venus was able to secure the key to her shackles and set herself free.

"What is this?" Darsus yelled, he had turned, as if on instinct, to see his former prisoner a few yards away arming herself with a bloody sword. At that point Darsus saw only fire, he forgot about the defense of the field, he forgot about the mob growing even bolder, he forgot about the mysterious archers, and he even ignored the pleas from his troops. With a bloodlust oath Darsus flung himself at Red Venus full of vengeance and animal hatred.

The sword strokes clanged and shattered the air and the rapid motions of dodge and faint wove an almost ballet like dance that was followed by a thousand pairs of wild eyes.

The fight went on with lunges and parry's, feints and twists but always the slim girl had the advantage of mobility and a terrible momentum to keep her a tiny bit ahead of each adversary.

It wasn't long before Darsus made an error in his defense and the girl stood her ground patient and ready. In a few swift strokes it was all over as she deftly carved her initials upon the liver of the former Captain Darsus. He went down dead, his face twisted in a mocking grin of surprise and utter disbelief.

Red Venus now surveyed the area around her. Everywhere there was battle, noise, and violent confusion. Making sense of it all was a bit difficult for much of what was occurring made no sane sort of sense. General fighting between Narfeti's troops and the populace had broken out all over the courtyard, as well as numerous fights between smaller factions of the citizenry themselves. What had begun as a holiday picnic to watch a burning had gradually turned into a riot, and now threatened to turn into full scale revolution – and Red Venus seeing all this decided that she was just the girl needed to help fan the flames.

With bold confidence Red Venus strode upon the pile of wood and branches that bare moments ago would have been her funeral pyre, and surveyed the confrontation going on around her with an interested and mischievous twinkle in her eyes. Already Darsus' small band of praetorians had been wiped out by the thousands that were still pouring down from the stands; elsewhere, Narfeti's soldiers were in route probably retreating into the safety of the palace. Already general riot and revolution was spilling out into the streets and nearby precincts of the city with first one building and then another quickly set ablaze.

Red Venus knew that all this would end once the army was mobilized, then this spontaneous revolution would be put down quickly and with such force and brutality to make sure such a thing could never happen again. She also realized that she had to move fast, and the first thing to do was to take control of the mob and give it a purpose and direction – and she knew just what that would be – toward the palace and Narfeti!

So atop the heap of wood, Red Venus yelled out to the vast crowd and finally gained the attention of those in her vicinity, shouting, "We must march on the palace, before the army has a chance to arrive! March on the palace with me and we'll drag out Narfeti and all her nest of jackals! Come on now, to the palace! Everyone, to the palace and Narfeti!"

Well those that could hear her followed, for a mob is a creature without a head nor direction save what the strongest will in it decrees. And all the others would follow the rest before them, and at the head of that huge mass of angry humanity was a lithe tigerish warrior woman by the name of Red Venus.

"We are coming to get you, Narfeti!" Red Venus cried in a furious voice that traveled over the heads of the crowd, and then to the mob she waved her rapier and ordered in her loudest voice, "To the palace! To Narfeti!"

And soon the cries went up all around her as citizens picked up discarded weapons or made their own cudgels from convenient branches or broken furnishings, rocks, statuary, and the hardened and angry fists of oppression.

"To the palace!" All now took up the chant, "Down with Narfeti and her jackals!"

Red Venus allowed herself a tiny smile as her mob now approached the closed and guarded door to the palace – while within the throne room, poised at a window, Queen Narfeti and her high lord Darkon surveyed the disorder below with ever increasing nervousness.

"I should have killed that bitch when I had the chance!" Narfeti growled with a vicious look to Darkon, then to one of her generals she barked, "Where the hell is the army? They should be here by now!"

"They have gone to the courtyards and outer environs where the rioters are looting shops and homes," the general replied self-consciously, "I imagine they are waiting to see just how serious a threat this riot is to your rule."

Well that caused Narfeti to explode into a volcano of anger. "To shops and homes! And they leave their Queen alone with a few hundred praetorians and useless old men – deserters! They shall pay for this – all of you shall pay!" Then in an instant movement, Narfeti drew her own slim ornamental dagger and in an act that took all present there by complete surprise, sunk the weapon into the breast of her own general. "Dog! Traitor! Anyone else?"

The room was deathly quiet after that, only the last gasps of a dying man to drift upon the winds to mix with the increasingly dangerous sounds from the mob outside.

"You! Tycara! Come here!" Narfeti demanded of a trim young officer who instantly came forward and bowed before his Queen. "You are now the supreme commander of the army – a post you have seemingly coveted for many years. Well now it is yours, with the proviso that you reach General Lan and have him protect the palace and your queen from those rioters at all cost."

"I understand, majesty," Tycara said with a humble bow that in him seemed a bit flippant, and then he was gone from the room to escape the palace through a secret passage he used on numerous occasions to reach the bedchambers of his Queen.

"I am surrounded by fools and traitors!" Narfeti shouted to those around her in a tone of rage and tightly checked panic. "Where is my commander of Praetorians? Where is Darsus?"

A black robed figure slowly stepped forward in answer, but a one-eyed officer intercepted him and said, "My brother is dead, Majesty, killed by that she-fiend as the riot began."

Narfeti looked closely at the one-eyed man, he had been a favorite of hers before his disfigurement, now she noticed him once again, but this time what came to her mind was his ability as a warrior and a leader of warriors. "Ah, yes, Shartre, and was it not this Red Venus who took your eye months ago even as she just now took your brother's life?"

"Yes, majesty." Shartre muttered.

"Then you have good reason to hate her, Shartre?"

"With all my heart, Noble Queen."

"That is good, Shartre," Narfeti said with a thin smile, "then you shall take half of my palace praetorians, one hundred men, and go into the lower halls. There you shall lay a trap for this conniving bitch and bring me her head! Once she is dead this rabble will all fall apart and the army can dispose of them."

"Yes, majesty, I leave at once." Shartre bowed graciously and then called two nearby officers, "Dalon, Bora, assemble one hundred praetorians immediately. We're going to set a trap for a she-wolf!"

The rioters had long since swelled their ranks, for as word went throughout the city that there was a revolt against Narfeti's rule, the populace rushed to join in the action of rebellion and looting.

Narfeti and her crew of carrion shivered, temporarily safe behind the high walls and locked doors of the palace, for they were now the focus of the attack, and Red Venus had raised the mob to a murderous frenzy with her urgent pleas and chants directed at the queen.

The few praetorians still at their posts soon scattered in fear. Others were swept aside and quickly killed or trampled by the mob as it surged over the walls and broke down huge metal doors to enter the hallowed halls of the palace.

The mob was in the lower environs of the palace now, a mysterious maze of long twisting passageways and countless interconnected rooms and suites. Laying in wait stood Shartre the one-eyed, as he was called now, along with his one hundred praetorians – waiting with bloody anticipation for the warrior woman called Red Venus to approach just a little bit closer.

Shartre saw the girl at the head of the mob and his lips dripped saliva at the luscious spectacle she presented to the male eye as she led that horrible force of rabble. Then he watched her lead them in a charge, Red Venus waving a bloody sword and shouting to all behind her, "Follow me! Follow Me! To Narfeti!"

And the mob cheered and screamed bloody murder and followed the slim girl who led them.

"They come closer now," Shartre whispered to his officers, "Just a little closer is all we need. Remember, tell your men to ignore the rabble, it is that bitch called Red Venus who we want. One thousand gold Tarns to the fellow who can bring me her head!"

And then all was a bedlam of pandemonium as one hundred armed and highly trained warriors flew out from hidden places of concealment and made their way through the riotous crowd—hacking down any and all in their path – so as to reach the lone girl who was leading the mob. It turned into a bloody charnel house as the mob and praetorians found themselves locked in a battle for their very lives.

Red Venus could see the way things were going and she recognized Shartre immediately knowing that this last desperate act of vengeance had to be Narfeti's doing as well. Well so be it, the girl thought as she joined the fray with dripping blade, soon Narfeti would be but a memory in ancient Tharma.

"Kill the bitch!" Shartre shouted to his men. "A thousand gold coin for her pretty head!"

"Kill them all!" Red Venus countered, urging her mob onward with words and gestures that weren't necessary. Many were already fighting tooth and nail with the praetorians, "Kill the praetorians and then we'll take care of Narfeti!"

Well by now all the lower environs of the palace were bedlam, fighting was everywhere and though Shartre's troops only numbered a hundred – they were well-trained and well-armed – and yet, they were no match for the hundreds and thousands who just kept coming at them like the inhabitants of some never-ending anthill.

"We can not stop them!" Dalon shouted to Shartre over the clang of steel and the wailing cries of battle. "There are too many – our ranks are too thin and will break at any moment."

Shartre slapped the youth, "No one quits until that slut is dead!"

However, by then it was too late, the praetorian center had folded and then disappeared altogether as a surge of rioters rolled right over it. It wasn't long thereafter that the last of the praetorians was dead – Shartre and Dalon included – and those few who had thought to escape by flight were being hunted down by small mobs of citizens throughout the lower precincts of the palace and throughout the city.

"The day is ours!" Red Venus cried to her followers. "And now we go after the biggest prize of all, Narfeti herself! Follow me!"

It was almost ten thousand hoarse voices that roared in answer to her words and each member of that mob followed that nimble girl up winding stairs and arching ramps to reach the huge barred doors of the very audience chamber where Red Venus had been displayed in ropes and chains such a short time ago.

"Break the doors down!" Red Venus shouted to the mob who now pressed in upon the huge doors in ever increasing numbers. It wasn't long before the doors came off their hinges with a wild squeak and then suddenly fell inwards, crashing down like two enormous overturned tombstones.

Back at the other end of the mammoth chamber, huddled together in fear and helplessness, were Narfeti, Darkon, and some dozens of rich courtiers, ministers, and officers of the bloody praetorians.

"I am here for you, Narfeti!" Red Venus shouted with a cold smile as she boldly entered the chamber. She was slowly followed by the mob, which had for the instant grown quiet, overawed by the grandeur of these massive palace chambers and ornaments.

"You Hell-bitch!" Narfeti screamed in rage, and it was a terrible thing to see; an anger and hatred cloaked in an even more terrible fear of what was to come. Instantly she pointed to some of her palace officers, "You Portus, Kill that vixen! I said kill her!"

Portus however did not move a muscle, for he saw the hungry thousands following Red Venus into the chamber, saw their eyes full of the blood-lust and anger from many years of abuse, and knew that any fight in this case was a lost cause.

Red Venus smiled a cold grin, her eyes boring down upon the Queen, "Advance, Narfeti, and prepare to die for all your baseless crimes and greed – for the murder of all my sisters, and the destruction of the Golden Temple – and for your countless thousands of other crimes perpetrated against your own people! Come to me, Narfeti, it is your time to pay, and I am your collector!"

"Darkon!" Narfeti shouted on the point of hysteria, "Do something! Do something!"

Then the mighty Darkon, the High Lord of Dar-El-Son, Beloved Sun, surprised everyone in that huge chamber by coming forward and saying, "You may take the Queen if it fits you bloody plans woman, but leave me and these innocent people to go in peace. We are not involved in your personal feud. Was it not I in fact I who stayed Narfeti's eager hand from immediately slaying you, thereby gaining you a few precious hours of life? Which it seems that you have used quite well to your advantage."

Well Narfeti just looked at Darkon in total uncomprehending disbelief, for her expression showed that it would take her a moment to digest what she had heard. Then in a scream of horrible rage, Narfeti shouted, "You filthy lying jackal! You would sell out your own Queen as long as you can save your rotting hide. You, Darkon, and all you other vermin are so very wise, ruling through me, reaping the benefits of my rule, and yet always keeping your hands clean and away from the responsibility of ruling!"

"Sadly, Narfeti Darkon said with a light smile, "That is the way of the world. You cannot be a ruler and fail to understand that simple premise."

"What premise...?" Narfeti shouted in rage with a curious hint in her tone in spite of her anger.

And then it was Red Venus who strode forward before Narfeti and said firmly, "The premise, that in even the most despotic of nations no ruler may rule without the consent of the governed. Once that consent is withdrawn, or refused, a ruler stands alone and must pay for all crimes as a ruler. Now Narfeti, it is your time to pay!"

Then Red Venus approached Narfeti and withdrawing her rapier quickly impaled it hilt deep into the Queen's heaving breast. With a stilled cry Narfeti slowly fell to the floor and then Red Venus withdrew her blade to wipe the bloodied steel upon the dead Queen's own gown.

There was a lonely silence in the hall, courtiers and officers all looking at their dead sovereign, some of the masks of anger and fear had fallen away to become faces of almost joyful realization as eyes finally beheld the death of Narfeti and her foul practices. Others were not so happy, but tried not to show it as they could see very well which way the political winds were blowing that day. And the mob behind Red Venus, the thousands she had brought with her into the palace, were now straining to get a view of the proceedings in that huge chamber.

"They're just as guilty. Murderers! Traitors! You should all die!" It was a chant taken up by the crowd as it slowly advanced upon Darkon and his small group. They were led by an old man who held a quiver of slim arrows. Red Venus saw that it was Alban from the tavern, the owner who Shartre had gouged out one eye. Now she understood why the arrows that found their marks and freed her from her captives flew so accurately. Shartre had made a grievous error, the old man had but *one* good eye, Shartre had taken the *bad* eye. He unknowingly left the old man with his useful eye – to devastating effect. Alban had been a keen archer his entire life, his arrows easily freed Red Venus and began the riot and rebellion. Darkon and his group did not know this of course.

"No! Stay back!" Darkon shouted to the mob, and for a brief second the harsh intensity of his voice actually had them all motionless, "You cannot do this! We are innocent!"

No sooner had he finished that sentence than a rotten fruit whizzed by his head, and then a slim arrow suddenly found his vitals. Alban's work, once again! There was a terrible surprise growing upon Darkon's face as the reality of the assault dawned upon him, and that it had not been done with rotting vegetation, but with a deadly arrow.

"No! It cannot be!" Darkon cried, as he sunk down to kiss the cold stone flags of the chamber's floor. "Red Venus, you must help us. Call them off! We are innocent!"

———

The girl who called herself Red Venus, the last Daughter of The Delightful One, had accomplished what she had set out to do so long ago. Soon she was gone from that chamber of death; leaving all the troubles of the city-state of Tharma behind her, as unconcerned as the day she had entered the city scant weeks ago.

On the way down the palace steps, a crowd of late rioters and looters ran passed her and one of the more talkative of the lot called out, "Missy, you're headed in the wrong direction. The throne room is up this way, and I hear tell it's full to the brim with gold and silver and all manner of riches – as well as a lot of dead fat nobles and courtier bodies to take these prime pickings off of."

Red Venus smiled but ignored the man and his entourage and continued out of the palace and the city, to find herself afoot and alone out on the road – a road that led out into the desert and to the Golden Temple of Ornepapas The Delightful One, a place that is no longer in this world – upon a road that now leads to nothing, and nowhere, for the girl known as Red Venus.

THE OASIS

Alsivard knew all the rumors about the land. It was barren, parched, the result of some long-departed blight that had swept down upon it and ravished it. Today, it was empty, void of all manner of life.

The bleak land stretched far between the horizons, a place of firmly entrenched death and desolation. Nothing could grow or live here — not man, beast, nor the lowliest insect or plant. Or so it seemed.

Even so, there was one small area, miniscule by comparison to its stark surroundings — a grain of sand upon the beach — that was lush and supportive of life.

It was the Oasis. The Oasis was called many names by the thankful travelers who stopped here. And many of those names showed true reverence for such a blessed sanctuary of life, obviously put here by the very gods themselves, to offset the surrounding sea of absolute desolation and death.

As Alsivard approached the Oasis, he remembered all the wondrous stories he had heard of the place. Nevertheless, he looked the area over carefully before abandoning the safety of his lonely hilltop dune to enter the area proper. It seemed like a place tailor-made for ambush, or some type of trap, and he was surely wily enough to take care as he approached it.

"By the Great God's Whiskers!" he thought curiously amazed, "there are trees here, and plants! And water! Water in abundance!"

Even now he thought he could hear the water as it bubbled up from some wells or springs that brought the life-giving fluid up from the deepest recesses of this parched ground.

With a great sigh of relief, Alsivard rejoiced that the legend he had heard of the oasis was actually true, and that now he would soon get the water he so desperately needed and not die of thirst in this dark barren land.

Alsivard walked calmly toward the lush green area of the oasis with renewed hope now, urging his weary muscles onward with the last bit of energy he possessed. He moved forward, then stopped, curious.

"Halt there, boy!" a voice now called to him from behind trees and shrubs of the oasis, and soon a burly man appeared. He was attired in warrior harness and robe, and armed with a variety of evil-looking weapons. Upon his head was a metal helmet topped by gaily-colored plumes, while upon his chest he wore a finely-linked, chain-mail silver shirt. He was a warrior for certain, and he looked formidable.

Alsivard stopped, watching the man carefully as he approached. In his hand the warrior held a wicked-looking sword, that by its dark staining and the deep gouges in the bright metal, indicated it had seen considerable use.

Alsivard gulped thoughtfully, too weak to run, not wanting to fight this formidable warrior, but not wanting to die of thirst, he stood his ground bravely and hoped against hope for the best.

"It is well you stopped when you did, boy," the warrior advised the youth with a wide grin of menace. "Another few steps and you would have defiled Holy Ground. I have the honor and strict orders to take the head of any blasphemer or desecrator. As you can see by the sharpness of my blade, I mean business."

"I am neither blasphemer, nor desecrator, nor defiler of any type. I am merely a lone traveler seeking nothing but drink and rest before I continue on my journey," Alsivard replied truthfully, walking toward the oasis.

"Halt, I say!" The warrior growled, and Alsivard stepped back as the man lifted his massive sword in an unmistakable gesture of warning.

"What say you?"

"I say, I shall part that unwise head from those youthful shoulders if you step closer. This is Holy Ground, not to be set foot upon by any man — for any reason."

"I see that you are a man, and you are there."

"Aye, I'll not argue with you about that. However, I am a special case, a chosen warrior, and defender of the Holy Places. The High Lord himself grants me and my men special dispensation to set foot upon this Holy Ground."

"Well, perhaps this High Lord will kindly allow me to take water and shelter here for the night?" the youth said, looking around for any other men and seeing none.

"Perhaps, but you must ask the High Lord first," the warrior said sternly.

"Fine, then bring him to me, so that we may talk," Alsivard asked curiously. He was beginning to lose his patience with all this foolishness and the weakness was setting in on him again now. He must have water soon or he would surely die.

"The High Lord lives in that temple yonder," and the warrior pointed far off to a large and ornate building surrounded by the lush trees of the oasis. "The High Lord is in seclusion however, he never leaves his temple. You must go to speak with him there."

"Very well," Alsivard replied in evident relief and moved forward. "Then I will go to see him then."

"Halt! Move not one step further, lad, or I promise you it will be your last step upon this earthly plane. How many times must I tell you, you are not permitted to set foot on this Holy Ground upon pain of death!"

Alsivard stopped cold in his tracks. Until this moment he had not realized the extent of circumlocution in this warrior's warped logic. It was a twisted logic, which if allowed to continue, might soon be the cause of Alsivard's rapid and undesired departure from this vale of tears and earthly existence. He would not have it!

Alsivard looked carefully at the warrior who was blocking his path into the oasis. "Let me see if I understand you, sir. You tell me I may not enter the oasis, even though I will surely die unless I have the water that is there. If I try to enter the oasis, you are ordered to kill me. The only way you will let me pass is if this High Lord of yours allows me to enter, and yet, he never leaves his temple, and I am prohibited to go to his temple to speak with him."

"Such is the simple truth of the matter," the warrior shrugged rather matter-of-factly, but he still blocked Alsivard's path.

"Simple! It is you and your High Lord who are simple! Or simpletons! I tell you I am in dire need of water. I will pay for what I want. What can be fairer than that?"

"This is Holy Ground and I have my orders!" The warrior said with grim determination.

"Orders to murder is what they are, for I shall die without water, and I will be as dead as though you ran me through with your very own sword."

The warrior made no reply but stood as firm and unyielding as ever.

Alsivard decided to try something different. He collected his thoughts and said, "I have heard tales of this oasis, of how it is a veritable Garden of Delight in all this land of bleak desolation. Here is the only water for as far as the eye can see in all directions."

"That is true," the warrior responded. "Because of its uniqueness, because it is a speck of beauty and life in this ocean of barren desolation — the only refuge within all this morass of dread — it follows that it must be a blessed and holy place."

Alsivard made no reply as the warrior continued.

"It is said that long ago a group of Priest kings — one from each of the Seven Cities—while trapped in these wastes, came upon this oasis. These Holy Men were so struck by the beauty and uncompromising fertility here that they naturally blessed it as a Holy Land. The job of guarding it from defilers and rogues such as yourself fell to the High Lord, and to me, his most loyal of vassals."

"Surely a little water..."

"Never!" The warrior threatened. "In olden times rumors abounded about this place, and one group after another reveled in the wealth of food and water that was found here. Thus saving their miserable lives on the long passage through the bleak desert. Men from all corners of the known world drank the sacred water that brings life to this land, and ate ravenously of the lush fruits and vegetables that grow with such abundance from the many trees, bushes and vines within. Even their animals were nourished upon the lush grasses of this land. They were all defilers!"

Alsivard was shocked by the man's words. They were full of a vile and twisted religiosity that would calmly allow him to die rather than offer even one mouthful of the life-giving water that he so desperately needed for his survival, and it was all the more frustrating since he was so close to the water now.

"You fool!" Alsivard yelled in frustration. "If this oasis is sacred as you claim, and blessed by whatever creator you want to name, it exists for the very reason of nourishing and comforting weary travelers such as I. You, and your High Lord have perverted that blessed bounty so that it has become the death of the very ones it was meant to save. Can you not see how wrong this all is? How many have you turned away to starve and die of thirst in the everlasting bleakness of this desert?"

The warrior did not reply. He stood steadfast in his faith. Finally he muttered, "This is sacred land and I dare not let you pass."

"If our roles were reversed, I would let you pass," Alsivard countered hopefully.

"Fortunately for me they are not reversed," the warrior added, "but enough of this talk. Leave here, I say. Go back to where you came from. I am a peaceful man and do not wish to shed your blood."

Alsivard tried to speak but was unable to get the words out. He looked to the heavens, then gasping, fell to the ground before the warrior. He lay completely motionless upon the hot sand. Finally, he felt large hands upon his body lifting him upward. His ruse had worked! Quickly he got a grip on the warrior, and before the man was able to draw his dirk, Alsivard knocked off the man's helmet and had his hands around his throat. The warrior was so surprised by the youth's unexpected action that Alsivard was able to render the man unconscious with a couple of well-placed blows to his unprotected head.

Swiftly and silently, Alsivard stripped the man of his harness, robe, arms, and mail shirt. He donned these and then dressed the warrior in his own clothes, after which he dragged him out into the desert behind one of the larger dunes.

━━

Alsivard now carefully re-entered the oasis, on constant look-out for any other guards who might be about and perhaps able to see through his flimsy disguise.

For some time he concealed himself lest there be other guards lurking about, however after some time, he saw no one, and began to think that perhaps the warrior had been lying to him — that in fact, there were no other inhabitants of the oasis at all. It all seemed very strange.

Alsivard walked on without encountering man nor beast, but he did notice something else that piqued his interest. He noticed that of all the trees or bushes he passed, all had one simple but terrifying thing in common — nothing at all grew upon them. They were completely devoid of fruits, nuts, or anything else edible at all. A horrible thought struck Alsivard then. Perhaps there was no food here at all? If so, did that mean there was no water either?

Soon Alsivard came upon the temple, and still he had not encountered any guards, nor any sign of human habitation. It seemed most strange.

The temple was much smaller than it had looked from the periphery of the oasis. It was also completely overgrown with weeds, and obviously now that he was up close and able to view it properly, in a terrible state of ruin. In fact, the temple, like the rest of the oasis, appeared to be completely in ruins and deserted.

Alsivard knew that, if in fact, some ancient High Lord had ever lived in that temple, it must have been many years ago, for this building showed no sign of any habitation for a very long time. It was most strange.

However, Alsivard was much too hungry and thirsty to dwell upon this eerie turn of events. He now began a desperate hunt for water. He knew there had to be a well or spring somewhere in this huge mass of trees and grasses — had he not heard the water moments before?

So the youth investigated the area, but he was unable to find even one drop of water anywhere. Had he imagined the sound? The thought sent him running in panic, desperate now, deluded and dizzy with exhaustion and fear.

Then Alsivard heard the sound again. It came from a little way off, and it did sound like the trickle of water. Perhaps it was a falls? Or even a lake? Now wouldn't that be nice! He let his mind run away with the fantasy as he ran furiously throughout the trees in the direction of the sound.

He soon reached a large rocky depression. Here he heard the sound again, closer this time, fuller, but there was no water to be seen in any direction that he looked. It seemed incomprehensible. Finally horror gripped him as a realization dawned upon him, the sound he'd heard was merely the rising desert wind passing through the rock wall around him and echoing in the small make-shift canyon. He had been tricked, and he now cried out in rage and frustration at the terrible unkindness that fate had dealt him.

Alsivard had just about given up hope when he saw the water. It was a shiny wetness upon a section of pitted rock that formed one of the canyon walls.

nothing at all grew upon them

Cautiously, he rubbed his hand upon the porous rock face. It was water, alright, but awful little of the life-giving fluid. It seeped slowly out of the pitted rock, much as sweat pours from the skin of a running man in the heat of summer.

Alsivard quickly put his face to the rock, lapping up the water like the thirsty dog he was. It was warm and brackish but not salty, and he was so thankful to find it that he did not care about the tastes of it as he drank all that was available.

He realized that this small amount of water could never satisfy his craving thirst and knew that he needed more water than this small amount to survive. He carefully examined the strange rocks around him. All were huge and of that same strange porous rock that he had never seen before. Perhaps, Alsivard thought, these rocks somehow absorb moisture from the air? If so, they might be full of the life-giving liquid.

Alsivard drew the sword he had taken from the warrior and with a hearty slash struck the strange rock. His blade made a loud whack as it hit, and when he withdrew the weapon he noticed a tiny amount of water had gathered in the slight depression his blade had created.

Alsivard hit the rock again, harder this time, and soon was rewarded by a small gushing of water. He smiled now. This was more like it. Next he took the sword and drove it deep into the rough rock. It was a monumental lunge. A moment later as he withdrew the weapon he heard a thunderous, throaty roar. It came from all around him. Above him. Beneath him. It was so loud in intensity that it knocked him down on his back.

Alsivard rose with some difficulty, and noted with panic that all the rocks — the entire landscape around him — was now shaking and trembling violently. In fact, the entire oasis seemed to be in the throws of some massive eruption, as if he was in the middle of some terrible earthquake. Everywhere, the land beneath his feet was roiling with titanic movement and shifting destabilization. Trees were falling all around Alsivard, and he was hard pressed to get out of their way and still keep his footing on the trembling earth beneath his feet. He was shocked when an entire section of rock suddenly shot up and out of the grass and bushes before him like a wall. Most of the rock had vegetation still clinging to it, as though it too was fearfully holding on for dear life during the cataclysm.

And still the violence of the quake grew. At this rate it would not be long before the entire oasis was completely leveled. Even the old temple had not been spared, though it surely had been a sturdy structure. It came down in a resounding crash of pillars and marble slabs as the building was totally demolished.

Alsivard meanwhile was knocked about like a leaf upon the wind, the huge rocks that lay beneath his feet jutting upward with incredible and sudden fury. The violence of the quake was so sudden and intense, the youth was surprised he was still in one piece.

And still the quake showed no sign of abatement, while Alsivard's mind raced in near panic. He'd never experienced anything like this before. Escape was impossible since he could barely stand in one place long enough to take a step in any direction. He knew he'd just have to wait it out, but he began to wonder just how long he could remain alive in this trembling inferno.

Then all of a sudden Alsivard was hurled upward and onto a small rocky hillock that shot a hundred feet skyward like a great tower overlooking everything from horizon to horizon. Nervous fingers held on in sheer terror to a small protrusion that stuck out from the hillock. Below him, a hundred feet away, Alsivard could see the completely destroyed oasis, and in its place a meandering growth of crashing rocks. Yet to Alsivard's astonishment it all seemed to form some kind of curious pattern.

Horrified, the truth finally dawned upon Alsivard, and now as if to validate his suspicions he saw a large section of rock near his face move, as the soil of centuries was shaken loose. Then the rock slid upward, to reveal a gigantic eye that was looking straight at him!

Alsivard shouted. The eye was almost two feet in diameter, a great glassy black ball that stared at him blankly. Then all at once, and without great effort, the gigantic head of the beast shook wildly, and Alsivard, losing his precarious handhold, plummeted down to the hard sand of the desert below.

The fall was not so bad, but the landing was traumatic.

Alsivard was battered and torn, with ripped flesh and broken bones he now lay near death. He felt the warmth of his blood as it flowed over his body, dripping down, down, down, into the hungry desert sand beneath him. He watched as the desert absorbed his life's blood with such a voracious thirst, and he thought, even the desert must drink. His blood disappeared almost as soon as the precious red drops hit the desert sand.

Alsivard thought it was all over for him then, he drifted off into unconsciousness, but then he heard the voice.

"You are a damn fool lad! A *young* damn fool!" It was the warrior who spoke to him now. He stood over the youth, looking down at him shaking his head sadly. "Now you have ruined things for both of us."

Alsivard tried to get his bearings. He looked to where the oasis had been bare moments before and saw only utter desolation and destruction. Farther on he saw the outline of a huge lumbering beast and knew it to be one of the fearsome dragons that myth said had once lived in the world before the ascent of man.

"It's been sleeping peacefully since the dawn of human time. Until you awakened it."

"I only wanted some water," Alsivard said lamely. He looked up at the warrior, "If you knew about this, why did you not tell me? Why the lie?"

"Tell you? Lad, you'd not have believed me! The heat stored in the rocks during the day was released at night and sweated some scant drops of water out of that beast's tough hide. There's your oasis, lad. The only problem is that there was only water enough for one!

"I was exiled here to die in this desert many years ago, by the very High Lord I mentioned to you. By luck I found this "Blessed Land" as the priests call it in their legends." He spit contemptuously into the dry sand at his feet.

Alsivard noticed that the warrior was once again wearing his own clothing and armor. He saw that the man's helmet was badly dented.

The warrior continued, "I could not let you pass, you see, there was barely enough water here for me. I did not want to kill you though; you remind me of myself, as I had been many years ago, when I was young and foolish and came here to hide away, after I had killed that dog of a priest, Ari Strovis."

Alsivard coughed harshly, some blood dripped from his mouth. He tried hopelessly to utter a few words but his strength flowed out of him and he dropped down to the ground moments later.

The warrior rose, and helped the weak youth get up to his feet. "You are not as bad off as you look. You can still walk if I help you. Some food and water and you will soon be good as new. Come with me now, lad, and we will see what we can find to eat and drink."

Alsivard nodded, "Why not!"

The two men walked on, looking toward the distant horizon where they could still see the massive lumbering hulk of the great dragon that was moving toward it. The youth shook his head thoughtfully, turned around, and began walking in the opposite direction of the dragon. The warrior nodded approvingly. Alsivard made a wager with himself on just how far they would get across the wastes before death might claim him and the warrior.

The lad lost that bet. By sheer luck and indomitable perseverance, Alsivard and his warrior companion trudged the great distance to the very gate of The City of Golden Tears. Once there, they found an inn where they drank a silent toast to a mythical dragon that indeed did exist, and an enchanted oasis that did not and they wished had only been a bad dream — but mostly to their success at living through it all with their hides intact.

THE TREASURE OF SHEOR KHOT

The Afghan sun was slowly sinking into the darkening horizon, casting a rapidly advancing gloom over this area of sandy desert away from the mountains which make up so much of this bleak land. Aboul Yazerd drank deeply from his water skin. He could afford to do so now, for soon he would be at his destination, the fabled oasis city of Sheor Khot.

The temperature was cooling with the setting of the sun, thankfully, and Yazerd's sharp nomad eyes could easily scan the vast desert in all directions far to the distant horizon. Something caught his eye, and as he looked more closely he noticed a gleaming light, a reflection of the sun's diminishing rays off some type of metal. That meant there had to be something, or someone, out there.

Yazerd closed his water skin and replaced it on the saddle. This figure would bare investigation. If it was a man, then he might have articles of value upon him, articles that would no longer be of any use to a dead man – or to one who would soon be dead.

He rode closer and was finally able to make out the form of a man lying still in the burning sands. It was not long before the wily Afghani reached the man. He saw that he was a white man, and by the looks of him, one of the English who were the new lords of the vast southern lands that had been combined under the name of India.

Yazerd dismounted and approached the body. The man was most definitely dead, his flesh having been burned off from the heat or eaten away by vultures and the desert insects so that his baggy trousers and shirt were draped over him like a shroud.

Yazerd did not like the look of this, and his superstitious nomad sense told him that something was very wrong. Perhaps, it was best to leave the Infidel's goods where they lay and to quickly move on? But Yazerd's need for booty would not allow him to leave without first examining the man's possessions for something of value. Why not? A corpse had no need of anything, any more.

With nimble but nervous fingers, the nomad roamed through the man's pockets. He found a variety of interesting goods. There was a chain containing half a dozen keys, a gold watch, a compass, a handful of gold and silver coins, and a folded piece of paper. This last intrigued him. Yazerd stuffed the goods into his pouch and then unfolded the paper.

It was a map, and by the looks of it a map of the nearby city of Sheor Khot. Upon closer observation the Afghani realized that it must be some kind of treasure map, for there was an area with a big red "X" written beside it. Yazerd smiled. It had to be treasure! Whatever the treasure might be, it was not indicated, nor was that important at the moment. Possessing the treasure was. Whatever it might be. So Yazerd decided while he was to visit Sheor Khot, he would find that treasure.

Yazerd's nervous hands quickly stuffed the map into his pouch with the other goods. All in all finding this dead man had been a most worthwhile endeavor. The English were a strange people, he thought. Here this man treks hundreds of miles to reach Sheor Khot and then dies a few miles before reaching the city. Perhaps it was Allah's will after all that Yazerd discover the map and possess the treasure. It seemed to be so.

"These English," Yazerd murmured aloud, shaking his head. Then he looked down at the man's boots. They were black leather and although worn form the desert, were still valuable. "You'll not need those either, my friend. At least, your boots shall reach Sheor Khot, though I am afraid you will not be in them."

—

It was late when Aboul Yazerd entered the city of Sheor Khot. It was quiet, the city having bedded down for the night. Only the ever-present city guards betrayed the wide-awake vigilance of any habitation.

"Yazerd? Yazerd!"

The nomad heard his name called and turned to see his old friend, Dijuli of the Zwerda nomads.

"How are you, my friend?" Yazerd asked as he bowed and made the formal signs of greetings and friendship to the other. Dijuli returned the signs and then let Yazerd have a loud whack on the back.

"You old desert dog!" Dijuli laughed in full comradeship. "It is good to see you after so long. But tell me, what are you doing here in our city? You are up to something, I can smell it. Your eyes have the wily look of a tavern wench!"

Yazerd took his old friend over to the side and whispered softly, "Riches, Dijuli. Riches for us both—if you like? That is what I am up to. Look at this paper," then Yazerd brought out the map and he and Dijuli gazed at it carefully.

Finally Dijuli smiled, "Riches? Perhaps gold? Perhaps ivory? Mayhap essences from far Cathay?" Dijuli mumbled, dreaming of all the riches that might be realized.

"Yes, it is a genuine treasure map, or so it must be," Yazerd said boldly. Then he smiled at his friend and asked him that which he had planned, since he had first seen him. "If you come in on this adventure with me, Dijuli what say we split whatever we find? There should be enough for both of us, regardless of what those dogs have said about me, I am not a greedy man, and I may need another able sword on this adventure. Equal shares. Is that not a good deal? Two rogues are better than one when you enter the seraglio of Kafira the Mendicant. He is said to be the greatest liar in the land, a master of lies."

"Kafira? I have heard of him, of course, and nothing good…!" Dijuli whistled carefully. "Is that his house marked upon the map?"

"None other, my friend. And next to the mark is a big red 'X' for the treasure. What we seek lies somewhere within his house."

"Then let us be off, my palms already itch for this treasure!"

"Good enough, but be sure that your sword arm has lost none of its strength or accuracy. I feel that our weapons will get much use this night."

"So be it," Dijuli smiled, thinking of amazing riches. "So be it!"

"So this is the lair of Kafira," Dijuli whispered as the two men roamed through the dark and desolate halls of the huge mansion. "This is an enormous place. He has come by all this wealth from the trade in slaves and hashish?"

"Among other things," Yazerd replied. "Some of which I have heard are even more repellant ways to earn gold."

Yazerd led his nomad companion into a dimly lit courtyard. "The apartments that we seek are those of Latasha. I knew her once years ago, she came from my village in the hills. If anyone here knows the gossip concerning this treasure, and the truth about it, rest assured it will be that girl."

Latasha lay in the seclusion and luxury of her private bath, enjoying the chilled water as it awakened her body, two female slaves gently rubbing her back with sweet smelling salves and unguents.

As the two nomads entered, Latasha drew up startled – then with a harsh word she sent her two slave girls away. "And remember," she added firmly before they had left her chamber, "should fat Noguntu hear of my visitors – neither of you shall see another morning!"

"Yes, mistress," both were heard to mumble as they quickly left the chamber.

Latasha stood boldly nude before the two desert men now.

"Ahhh…" Dijuli said with a sly wink to Yazerd, "Is she not a sight for a hungry man? A vision of loveliness? A true gem of great price, eh, my friend?"

"One which neither of you two rogues can afford," Latasha said tartly, though of course it was the truth. "So tell me, what is of so great an importance that the two of you risk your private parts by entering the seraglio of Kafira?"

Yazerd gulped nervously at the taunt, for it was not an idle threat," A great treasure, lovely Latasha. A treasure beyond all value." Then he carefully took out the map and showed it to the curious girl. "I took it off a dead Infidel. The "X" shows where the treasure is. Imagine, Little One, it is somewhere in this house. But this house is vast. Dijuli and I want your cooperation. In return we split whatever we find three ways."

"And what if we find nothing?" Latasha asked acidly. "Then I must leave my easy life here as Kafira's toy – to make my way alone in a hostile world where every man's hand is turned against a sweet and lovely girl of pure innocence."

"Ha! Sweet and lovely you be, I'll gladly grant you, Little One, but innocent? Even years ago in the village of our birth you were anything but innocent," Yazerd responded, and he could not help but laugh as he fondly remembered his first encounter with a younger version of the magnificent woman who now stood before him.

Latasha smiled and laughed also. "So be it then. We must take a risk if we dare seek great rewards. Still, I will miss my easy life here – but it will be wise to get away from that long and vengeful arm of Kafira if I do this thing that shall desecrate his house."

"The rewards will be worth it, Little One," Dijuli added.

"I hope you are right, nomad," she said, then she looked over to Yazerd and asked, "By the way, what manner of treasure are we looking for?"

Yazerd smiled, "Direct us to where the "X" is marked in this vast house and we will all find out soon enough."

Latasha nodded, "Then follow me, but be very quiet for we are going into the secret catacombs that run below this huge old house. Some say they were built eons ago by a pre-human civilization that was destroyed by the wrath of the Old Gods. Before Allah, may his eternal mercy be shed down upon us. You know, the ones the Nasarany, and even the followers of the True Prophet, may Allah bless him, are loath to mention."

"Sslasaloth and Gemnorgoth!" one of the men muttered fearfully.

"Those and others even more terrible," the girl replied. "Now be quiet and follow me."

Latasha led the men down twisting stairways into deep corridors and passageways, which had not known the disturbance of human feet for a very long time. There was an ill feeling of dampness and decay that only increased the deeper they went, until it appeared that they would be going on forever. Then abruptly the girl stopped in front of a large wooden door. Painted upon the massive boards, in old peeling characters, was a design of such strange appearance that both nomads muttered a silent prayer to Allah.

"It is some ancient sigil. It means that within lurks a danger from beyond the earthly realm of men!" Latasha whispered in a sinister tone.

Dijulia and Yazerd looked at each other nervously, each loathe to enter the portal. Yet after a few moments the mental vision of all that treasure within, just waiting to be discovered, finally won out over their fear.

"Are you sure this is the right place, girl?" Dijuli added, just to be on the safe side. He thought it wise not to enter here unless absolutely necessary.

Yazerd agreed.

Latasha smiled, "Are you scared, nomad? Aye, so am I, but truly, this is the place. There can be no other."

"Then let us enter and take our riches," Yazerd said impatiently, the nervousness in his voice showing all too easily now. "For the faster we get in, the faster may we get out."

"Then warriors," Latasha said, "if you truly want to enter, withdraw your blades and break down the doorway."

With swords of cold tempered iron, the two hacked away and in a few minutes of strenuous work had the door cracked, splintered, and finally opened. Then Dijuli and Yazerd entered while Latasha quietly followed a few paces behind.

The room that they found themselves in was large and dark and full of the damp mustiness of timeworn decay. Yazerd lit a torch he had brought from another room, and Dijuli and Latasha used its fire to light their own. Now with the considerable illumination from all three torches the chamber was open to the inquiring vision of the three intruders.

What they saw in that huge room caused their faces to fall and their anger to grow, for to their astonishment the room appeared to be completely empty. Though the three rogues looked about carefully, there was nothing but the cold damp bricks of walls and floor to stare at.

"So where is the treasure?" Latasha asked, cold sarcasm creeping into her voice now, a fitting companion to the anger she felt also quickly growing within her.

"Is this the right place?" one of the men asked. "The place indicated on the map?"

"Yes, it is the right place!" the girl replied with a deep scowl.

Neither man could say a word, but as if to heap coals upon a raging fire, the girl boldly walked into the empty room and with hands outstretched mocked the two men, crying out, "Well? Fools! I have defied Kafira's house for... What? A big empty room!"

Latasha walked on inside, glum, her anger increasing. The two men watched her and could only shrug, there was nothing for them to do. There was nothing that either of them could say. They had made a play for vast riches and it had been unsuccessful. Such is the chance you take. Yazerd was about to say as much to Latasha when, there was a loud scream that filled the chamber, and he saw her suddenly tip over.

It looked as though she had tripped upon something – but there was nothing to trip over in that large empty room. Or was there? Yazerd and Dijuli now heard the distinct sound of tinkling coins. Then Dijuli pointed to where Latasha had fallen – for he noticed that she had not hit the floor at all – instead her prone body lay suspended a foot in the air. *With nothing at all apparently holding her up!* However, something was very obviously underneath her. Something was holding her up!

"The treasure!" finally Dijuli shouted in amazement. "It must be – invisible!"

Well, the three intruders ran into the room banging into things and falling over things, all of which they could not see – and perhaps it was because of that fact that the amount and value of the riches grew in each of the hunter's minds. With cries of joy, and much clattering of falling objects, and the sound of coins being scattered around the floor, the three now hugged each other in triumph as each mentally planned how to spend their share of the loot.

"Invisible treasure!" Latasha said and the sweet taste of greed rolled around her lips as she said the words. "Who would have thought of such a thing?"

"It must be a vast amount of wealth," Dijuli added his excitement growing, "but how do we make it visible? For it must be visible to be useful to us. Surely having a million golden Dinars, or ten millions is a fine thing – but if no one can see them – how then can they be spent?"

"An interesting problem," Yazerd replied, trying to work out a method when their attention was caught by a sound at the far end of the room. The treasure hunters startled as they saw a large portion of the wall rise and then slowly lower and close again. Though they had not seen anyone enter, all three had the uncanny feeling of some malevolent presence now among them.

It was Yazerd who guessed the truth, and the realization sent cold shivers down his spine. "An invisible treasure?" Quickly he tugged his friend's back towards the door. "What better guardian for such wealth—than one that is also invisible?"

Dijuli startled, "But can such a thing be possible?" He shivered now and drew his sword, as he and Latasha followed Yazerd back to the doorway.

Dijuli was heard to mutter an ancient nomad prayer, while Yazerd heard, all too clearly, Latasha's invocation to one of the Old Dark Gods which people have worshiped since a time before the True Prophet graced the world with his teachings.

The three finally made it to the doorway when they felt a cold presence and

"For it must be visible to be useful to us."

the fetid breath of their unknown and unseen attacker. Latasha was the first to scream as invisible claws attempted to rake her soft golden skin, leaving her with one blood red cut. Soon she was on the floor kicking and screaming; vainly trying to put up some sort of resistance as the creature continued to attack her. Eventually she got away and ran to the doorway and her two companions, who stood their guard with sword ready, wondering what they were to fight and how it would come at them.

Yazerd and Dijuli were aghast at the rapidity and ferociousness of the attack against them. It was unlike anything they had ever witnessed in all their years of vicious warfare. With drawn swords, the two men fought back whatever it was that was trying to kill them.

By now, Latasha was hiding in the hall by the doorway, where she saw a vase upon a table. In her anger and frustration she picked up the vase and threw it at the invisible monster, the vase shattering upon the creature. It had been a useless gesture, for it did not stop whatever was fighting the two men, but it did spray the thing with a covering of dark red liquid. Perhaps wine. Now the three treasure hunters shouted as they could see a terrible image outlined in blood red crimson, a horror not of this Earth and born out of the imagination of nightmare.

Lastasha flung another vase of wine that further outlined the image and made it clearer to their vision.

"By the Gods!" Dijuli cursed, seeing the full form of the monster for the first time. "Now that we can see it, what is it? How can we kill such a thing?"

"I do not know, but we must try," Yazerd replied, earnestly doing all he could to protect Latasha as the thing advanced upon her.

Both men now clearly saw the outline of the creature as it moved towards the terrified form of the girl as they came at it again with their swords. The monster was tall and ponderous, and looked somewhat like the forbidden statues of the demon-god, Sslasaloth. It was a muscular, giant humanoid being full of horns and claws and long red teeth that dripped from a frothy mouth which screamed with rage and perpetual hunger. Yazerd and Dijuli froze with fear – both would have run away if they had not been too scared to do so.

"May the gods bless us!" Dijuli cried in a lament, which each man took as a final farewell to the other. Then the monster, now visible in stark outline, its red halo of the wine, or whatever it was, came at the two nomads with deadly fury.

While both men fought valiantly, they felt they were doomed and they knew it. Vainly Yazerd mumbled a small prayer to the True Prophet – though not a believer in anything except cold cash, he reasoned with stark practicality that any help, from whatever source, would be very much appreciated at this dire moment. Yazerd never managed to finish that prayer however, for giant talons sliced at his flesh, and soon he fell with a painful wound.

Not so his partner, Dijuli, for as the wily nomad tried to run – the creature gave chase and pursued him through the long corridors. It was almost as if the monster was playing with the nomad, tearing and slashing from behind – a piece of flash here, a piece of flesh there – until finally Dijuli was almost totally dismembered. Simpering with pain that few of us could ever imagine, yet somehow still alive, Dijuli tried to run away with every ounce of energy he possessed. Full of fear that could shatter a lesser mind; he struggled forward, only to freeze when he came upon a dead-end corridor. Here the monster quickly fell upon him. Giant jaws with huge blood-red teeth drew closer to Dijuli, until with one quick lunge the head of the nomad was deftly plucked from his shoulders, much like a bird would swoop down upon a berry or small fruit and pluck it into his hungry maw. Then the creature shut its massive jaws with a terrible crunch. Dijuli the nomad was no more.

⸻

Back in the treasure room, Latasha was terrified, alone, and in some pain. She could not believe that she was still alive and that the monster had not come to finish her off yet. She had heard the faint cries of Dijuli and knew that one of her companions was no more. She seemed so alone now. She could expect help from no one, and she knew that soon the monster would be back to finish her off.

Latasha dried her tears, blocked off her pain. She had no choice but to gather herself together and try to get away from this terrible place. She moved over to the opening where the monster had first entered the treasure room. She moved steady, increasing her speed, once she heard sounds from the corridor outside the room. She knew that it was the monster returning for her and that fear gave her added energy.

Terrified beyond comprehension, the wily girl crawled into the doorway from whence the monster had come, quickly recessing the panel but a crack so that she could now observe the chamber from this new place of concealment and temporary safety.

Latasha had done so none too soon, for immediately the creature entered the chamber. She shuddered as she saw the creature's outline painted in the red liquid, probably mixed with some of the blood of her two companions. Carefully, with rapt fascination she watched as the monster neared her hiding place. Now she could make out a head and what appeared to be an eye in its center. Quickly she withdrew the long ornate ceremonial dagger all the harem women carried. She was determined to sell her life dearly. As the creature neared the opening, Latasha suddenly leaped out at it with a speed and bravery she did not know she possessed. The monster, not able to move away in time, screamed with rage as Latasha sunk her dagger hilt deep into the creature's huge single eye. Her blade went in deep, squishy, wet, and bloody.

The sounds of indescribable pain were terrible to hear and Latasha held on for dear life as she could feel the softness behind the huge eye now giving way as her entire hand and arm pushed the dagger deeper into the very brain of the monster.

Then with a hellish scream the Guardian twisted, shuddered, and fell over dead. To the girl's astonishment the monster's body then immediately disappeared, and Latasha found that she was now safe and alone.

It was only then that the contents of the chamber became visible to her eyes.

Latasha gasped deeply and cried out with joy and triumph. Everywhere in the room were massive chests, boxes, and vases all full or overflowing with small shinny coins and all manner of silver and gold.

"I am rich! I am fabulously rich!" Latasha cried, moving her weary body to pick up handfuls of the shiny coins, throwing them around the room in a joyous expression of greed and victory.

She looked at all that treasure and laughed wildly, "Why, there must be millions of coins here! A fortune in gold!"

Then Latasha looked more closely at the coins. Suddenly anger surged into her features. For now she saw that the coins were actually newly minted and that they shone not with the soft yellow of gold, but with the reddish yellow of newly struck *copper!* The city of Sheor Khot used no copper coinage. She examined these strange coins more closely and moaned angrily.

"What is this!" she cried.

"So you have found my secret, Little One?" a sudden voice spoke out now. Startled, Latasha turned around to see the fat form of her master, Kafira the Mendicant, framed in the doorway.

"Master!" she was astonished to see him and watched with mounting fear as Kafira entered the chamber. His gross weight waddled into the room belying the terrible menace that sprang from his cold cruel eyes.

"I had hoped to keep my ambitions secret for a little longer, at least until the Board of Regents decided to choose a new leader for the city," Kafira said, smiled, picked up a coin and tossed it to the girl. "Yes, they are copper, Little One, and though newly minted medallions, they are quite worthless."

Latasha investigated the medal closely. Upon one side was an embossed bust of Kafira looking suitably heroic and mighty – a younger pose with more muscle than fat. Upon the other side of the medal, in cursive Demballah script was the legend: "One Free Meal payable To Bearer. Give Your Vote to Kafira for City Leader."

"A damn election medal?" now Latasha was full of rage, shaking with anger.

Kafira laughed, "Just so, my Little Princess."

"What of this map?" Latasha demanded, showing her master the map Yazerd had taken off the dead Anglo a short time ago in the desert.

Kafira laughed, "The Anglo was my accountant, a man named Wilson of dubious intent and little honor or honesty, who stole the map from my house. It was merely a directional map for the deliverymen from the mint at Delhi so that they would know where to store the medals in my house. I wrote in the 'X' for that reason. Little did I believe the chain of events which would begin with Wilson's finding the map in my papers, believing it held the key to real treasure, and stealing it."

Latasha grew furious at what she was hearing.

Kafira smiled and continued, "Ah, Little One, today we live in modern times, all my wealth is safely secured in the bank at Delhi. As a personal affectation I regarded these medals as the treasure by which I could buy the affection – and votes – of the people of Sheor Khot." Kafira laughed loudly, and then added, "The treasure of Sheor Khot, indeed!"

"Then it was all for nothing?" Latasha asked, incredulous, "Wilson, Dijuli, and Yazerd, all dead for nothing?"

Kafira smiled, "Not to mention my own invisible guardian."

Latasha had forgotten that. Something did not add up, and where was Yazerd?

Kafira added, "It seems my secret is no longer safe."

Latasha tensed, "It is safe with me, Master."

Kafira smiled once more. Latasha never liked his smiles; they always would bode ill for the recipient. He now told her, "Such a good and devoted girl you are, Latasha. Of course I know my secret is safe with you, and so it shall always be. You see, you have inadvertently stumbled upon my true secret—the magic and invisibility which the forbidden teachings of Sslasaloth and Gemnorgoth give to but a chosen few."

"I will never tell, Lord," Latasha cried nervously and meant it.

"I know my darling, but just to make it a bit more easy for you…" Kafira showed teeth stained by too many poppy leaves as he drew forth a long revolver from beneath his voluminous robes. He quickly fired off two shots, Latasha screamed. The bullets went wild, for suddenly there was a long ornate dagger that protruded from Kafira's back.

Latasha stood by in shock. Kafira lay dead upon the floor. Then she saw Yazerd standing in the doorway with a grim smile. He was known to be good with a knife and he had proven so with a deadly throw. He was alive, and she was shocked and joyous to see him—and then she noticed something else...

With Kafira dead...

Now the copper medallions suddenly shimmered and shown to become truly gold Dinars!

Latasha was awed, astounded, she ran over to Yazerd to hug him.

"Yazerd! You came back for me?" Latasha cried, deftly moving aside the corpse of the fat Kafira, reaching down to hold the nomad in her arms.

"The treasure? What of the treasure?" Yazerd demanded.

"Oh, Yazerd, it is glorious, it is everything – every thing you ever dreamed of! I do not understand it, but we are rich, you and I! Rich! Rich together, Yazerd! But you are wounded!"

Yazerd smiled, "Nothing serious. We are rich, girl—rich!" and then he smiled as he held her tightly in his arms.

"Yazerd!" Latasha shouted, still holding him dearly in her arms. She pretended to pout, saying, "All you think about is that treasure! Well, what about me? Us? Maybe you should have died from your wound at that! You have no manners at all – never have, never will. I do not know why I waste so much time and affection on you – all you care about is that damn treasure."

"That is right, girl," Yazerd said, as his eyes sharpened and his voice grew in power. With a great effort he grabbed up Latasha in his arms, his lips to her ears whispering, "But you are all the treasure I will be wanting, girl. You are the real treasure of Sheor Khot, and damned if I will loose you now!"

Latasha looked at Yazerd closely, smiling with that knowing smile of hers' that always set men hearts afire. She kissed him lightly, saying, "Why Yazerd, you know, I believe that for once in your life, you may be right."

AN INTERVIEW WITH CROM

The dry Texas wind of Cross Plains blew through the open window of the small bedroom where pulp writer Robert E. Howard was busy pounding away on his old 1924 Underwood #5 typewriter.

He was typing the final draft of an article on the gods of ancient myth. It was not soon afterwards that his mind began to wander, finally fixing itself onto his greatest creation, Conan the Barbarian, and the mythical realm of his Hyborian Age. He thought of Conan, and his grim grey god, Crom. The huge towering form of this moody and most powerful force of primitive and ancient men, his stern demeanor and grim outlook, came into his mind as well, through the life and actions of his wild children of the frozen Cimmerian north. Mighty Crom! He wondered what he was like?

Howard typed wildly, pounding the keys like he was Conan himself, writing and loudly voicing the narration and dialog of his story as if he was being chased by the wizardly minions of the evil snake-god Set. He smiled, grimly, just as would have Conan, relieved that he had now finished this latest Conan tale. Earlier that day he had received by the morning post his contributor copies of the May and June 1935 issues of *Weird Tales* containing his newest Conan story, "Beyond the Black River." Wright had sent him copies, but as so often, he neglected to include his check to the author's disappointment—late payment just part of the pulp writing game during these dark days of The Great Depression. Now that he had finished his story he was exhausted and sleep soon took him. His head gently nodding down upon his desk, his hands lying motionless upon the keys of his old Underwood.

How long he slept, he did not know, but it seemed some hours had passed. He was surprised to notice that things did not seem quite right in his small bedroom office. Something mysterious was happening.

He looked around him in consternation and wonder, and rubbed his bleary eyes at what he was seeing. Surely he had not been asleep that long, but he awoke to find something very strange. All around him there was this great grey mist, which he knew could not be real, and must be some kind of a dream. Or nightmare? His writer friend, H.P. Lovecraft, surely would have understood this all much better than he, but H.P. was not here.

Bob Howard was alone and now he saw ethereal forms and images that seemed to spring full blown from his mind and dreams. They slowly formed before him, walking out of wild swirls of grey and cream clouds to show a being that can only be described—as a god!

Howard knew instinctively that this was mighty Crom himself, the war god of his fierce Cimmerian hero. It was indeed Crom, and he looked just as Howard had imaged him to look, and just as he had described the war god in his Conan stories for *Weird Tales*. It was truly the war god of the fierce Northlands! Mighty Crom, the patron of the greatest warrior ever to hold a sword—Conan the Barbarian!

Crom looked like some ponderous Viking warrior from some Asgard-like realm. His massive body of thick muscles, barrel chest, long grey shoulder-length black hair, and a beard that put Eric The Red to shame. His jet black mane flowed down to rest upon his chest to lie upon his leather jerkin. He stood tall—at least twenty feet—or so it seemed to Howard who could not figure how it could be in his small bedroom. He wore two furry boots made of the skins of monstrous sabre-tooth tigers—the heads of the beasts were still on the skins displayed upon the massive boots with the tiger's faces starring straight out at him.

Suddenly, a great booming voice spoke the words, "All right, little man, I am here! What are your questions?"

Robert E. Howard's mind swirled with a myriad of mixed emotions and wild imaginings, but paramount among them all was the call of the professional pulp magazine author. The man who wrote sword and sorcery stories for *Weird Tales* and other pulp magazines. The man who, years later, would be acknowledged as the creator of the genre of Sword & Sorcery and Heroic Fantasy fiction.

Howard gulped nervously, "Where does one begin when interviewing a god?"

"Hah, that is easy! At the beginning of course," the powerful voice boomed with a tightly withheld impatience. Howard knew he had to make this good.

After a few seconds, he began, "well, what was it like to be a god in the Hyborean Age?"

Mighty Crom shrugged his massive shoulders, gently boomed out, "Why, no different than being a god in your own time, I suspect. Many of my brothers, such a vile Set, suspicious Erlik, and mischievous Mitra had much more interest and influence in human affairs than I did—or your own gods today. Perhaps only Bori and I most loath contact with humanity. A weak and cowardly species. For we are stern warrior gods, and there are few men who have the prowess to earn our notice—much less respect."

"Was one of those youth's named Conan?" Howard asked boldly, knowing that had to be true, for had he not written many stories telling the tales of his hero in Crom's world?

"Conan? Aye, yes I remember Conan. I took notice of him occasionally—

aided him once, in fact. He was a warrior that I could be proud of, and I knew that if he lived long enough he would go far in accomplishing those things you puny humans consider important.

"Eventually he became the King of Aquilonia. That was the mightiest of all the human kingdoms during the Hyborean Age."

Crom allowed a smile with a fond remembrance of things past. Then he said, "What care I for Aquilonia and human empires when I have my own godly empire! We have a place here for the greatest of warriors. My war maidens bring them to me at the moment of their death, and they sit to my right in the great council of the gods. Yes, little man, Conan is here, along with some others."

Now it was Howard's turn to smile at that realization that he had been correct in the telling of his tales of Conan. Then he changed the subject, for if there is anything that irks a god, it surely is being asked questions about someone else—and since that someone was Conan and a mortal—well he just decided to keep to the subject.

Howard looked carefully at great Crom, standing there before him like he owned all of creation. He was a stern and foreboding character, terrifying, but not cruel or heartless—not for its own sake. Not like, say Set, or Erlik. Howard wondered what the real being that stood before him was like. Finally he asked, "Why do you remain aloof from your worshipers?"

Crom sighed mightily for a moment, and then with head held high he began, " I need, nor want any worshipers as such. For I am not vile Set! I require no such worshipers! I am merely here, I exist as I have always been, and will continue to be. I am a symbol. The Cimmerians recognized my presence and respect it for its power. Power and prowess represent much to these humans, and I admire their admiration of me. It is a relationship born out of mutual respect—and perhaps mutual need. I have been accused by soft city people of being a grim and stern god—well so be it! I am the god of war and I am proud of it! A man needs a strong back and powerful sinews to live in the barren and frigid hills of bleak Cimmeria. There they worship the sword, which is a more practical means towards salvation and long life, than your soft city gods with their temples, priests, and their numerous foul rites."

"So you worship the sword?"

"Hah! If a god may indeed be capable of worship, then yes, I worship the sword, and occasionally those few bold warriors skilled enough to use it well."

"What are your thoughts about the Stygians and the god Set?" Howard asked boldly.

Crom laughed, his ponderous voice filled the limbo where they stood with echoes that seemed to bounce off the cliffs of eternity. "I do not think of the

"Why do you remain aloof ...?"

Stygians—they are a weak and foul people. However, I often times think about my brother god, Set the Snake. At times there are wars here in my realm, such as there are on the surface of your world, except our wars are of such power and violence that they dwarf your mightiest conflicts into insignificance. I have fought Set numerous times. The Snake has an appetite, that one does! The Snake and Mitra are bitter enemies, and sometimes other gods are drawn into their conflicts so as to maintain the equilibrium. Or destroy it. The power of the gods is held in a delicate balance. Set seeks to destroy that balance so that the scales will tip in its favor. Regardless, at times I have found it necessary to take a hand to make sure the balance is maintained. A realm where Set rules would not be a happy place, for men or gods—there would be too much sorcery and a warrior's sword would be useless. A god of war can not allow such a thing to come into being. I will not allow it!"

"I think I understand," Howard replied quietly. His mind raced with all the implications which the war god's offhand disclosures revealed about the nature of the world—and beyond. Finally able to continue, he asked Crom, "Now that the Hyborean Age has slipped away to become a dusty memory, a long-forgotten myth by many—do you miss it?"

Crom looked grim, then allowed a look that was wide and warm. "Ah, yes, it was a good and lusty time and I enjoyed it much, but all things must change. No, I do not miss it. Why should I? There are other realms, and I am known by many different names in these realms. The battles continue as before, and my war maidens are kept forever busy."

"Are all these heroes...human? And do men exist in any of these other realms you mentioned?"

"Some are human, many are not. It matters to me not. Man is scattered like the leaves upon the wind, but he is not the master in all of these differing realms. In some places his arrogance and foolishness have caused him to be wiped out of existence. Then in others, such as upon the Earth, he flourishes— at least for the present."

Howard nodded gravely at Crom's words. Did this grim grey god know something he didn't? Most assuredly. Howard thought it over, and looked upon the image of mighty Crom in awe. After all, he was a god, so he must have knowledge of future events. Howard was going to ask about this when he thought better of it—after all, our future is ours alone to live and know—and by living it, we shall see where it leads us in good time.

"You are right about that, human," Crom said suddenly in a more somber tone, as if reading his very thoughts, looking down carefully upon Howard with a wistfulness that seemed most strange, almost as if he felt some form of celestial sadness.

Howard asked boldly, "So do you have any words to say about *me*?"

Slowly great Crom nodded his head, knowing that young Robert E. Howard's life would end just a year later at thirty years of age by his own hand. How tragic! Had he lived, he would have become one of the greatest storytellers of his age, but it was not to be, so mighty Crom did not worry about such matters. When the time was right, he would lift Howard up to take his rightful place in the Council of Heroes, beside Conan, Kull, Brak Mak Morn, Solomon Kane, and others of his creations. For now, all the grim grey god said to him was, "Howard, you are my vessel, and I fill you with the stories of Conan, the Hyborean Age, and other great heroes—much as I am telling you my own story now. These are tales that need to be told, and you tell them well."

Howard smiled widely at that praise, yet he had always had suspicion that some force was tampering with him and his Conan tales in particular, but he had thought it was the ethereal voice of the great barbarian himself telling him his stories. Now he was not so sure. What was the truth of it all? Who could really say?

It was then that Bob Howard heard a soft whispering voice deep within his mind. The voice softly told him, "*We are done now. You know, of course, that when you awaken, you will have forgotten all that I have told you. You will sleep a dreamless slumber, not remembering any of my words, nor that you have set them down with your very own hand.*"

Suddenly Robert E. Howard awoke, and there in front of his old 1924 Underwood #5 typewriter was a typed manuscript, entitled, "An Interview With Crom", and it had apparently been set down by him as if through some manner of 'automatic writing.'

Howard wondered about that, and what it all might mean as he read the words that he had undoubtedly typed there. How could it be? How had this communication transpired? He recalled none of it. Finally he just shrugged and put it away in a drawer where he kept the fragments of unfinished manuscripts. He would work on it another day. After all, he was just twenty-nine years of age, young and healthy, and he had all the time in the world—an entire lifetime ahead of him to finish his stories.

COVER and INTERIOR ILLUSTRATOR

RON HILL - has been an editorial cartoonist, humorous illustrator, graphic designer, educator, author, armchair theologian and video documentarian (not all at the same time, of course!) for over 40 years. Born in Cleveland, he graduated from the Art Institute of Pittsburgh and immediately returned to Northeast Ohio to begin working in advertising.

In the 1980s–90s, as part of the illustration team of Lombardo & Hill, Ron drew countless interior illustrations for role-playing games published by TSR, West End Games, Iron Crown Enterprises, and Chaosium, many involving licensed from The Lord of the Rings, Dungeons and Dragons, Indiana Jones and Star Wars. An accomplished quick-sketch caricature artist, he has drawn (to date) probably a quarter-million faces at thousands of private and public events from Chicago to New York. His editorial cartoons have appeared in the *Chagrin Valley Times, Solon Times, Geauga Times Courier* and *West Life* since 1999. In 2000 he started illustrating the popular "Armchair Theologian" book series for Westminster John-Knox; these 15 volumes have been translated into German, Japanese, Korean, Portuguese and Italian.

From 2002–2015, he taught an Interactive Media College Tech Prep program at Alliance High School, and has always conducted workshops at area art centers (including the Valley Art Center) since 1990. After co-founding Act 3, a media company and indie publisher in Cleveland in 2016, he has recently embarked (once again) on his solo career as a freelance artist, and is also currently working on a number of personal documentary projects, including"Go-Kart Therapy" and "We Are Doc Savage: A Documentary on Fandom." He has always lived in the Chagrin Valley of Northeast Ohio, and you can learn more at www.RonHillArtist.com. He can be contacted and found here: ArtistRonHill@gmail.com RonHillArtist.com

Also by Gary Lovisi:

The Return of Baron Gruner

In 1902 Sir James Damery enlisted the aid of Sherlock Holmes to prevent the daughter of an old friend from marrying a womanizing Austrian named Adelbert Gruner who was suspected of murdering his first wife. Dr.Watson chronicled the case as "The Adventure of the Illustrious Client." By its conclusion, Gruner's evil intent was exposed to the young lady when Holmes came into possession of an album listing his many amorous conquests. A former prostitute mistress of the Baron's then took her own revenge by throwing acid in his face – permanently disfiguring him.

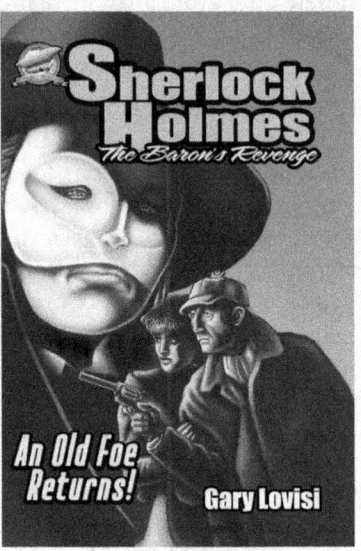

Holmes believed the matter concluded. He is proven wrong when a hideous murder occurs rife with evidence indicating the Baron has returned. Soon the Great Detective will learn he has been targeted for revenge in a cruel and sadistic fashion. Not only does the Baron wish his death but he is obsessed with causing Holmes emotional suffering. He desires nothing less that the complete and utter destruction of the Great Detective in body and soul.

Gary Lovisi spins a fast paced tale of horror and intrigue that is both suspenseful and poignant, all the while remaining true to Arthur Conan Doyle's original stories. "The Baron's Revenge" is a thrilling sequel to a classic Holmes adventure fans will soon be applauding.